Praise for *Crowning*

"Through River's eyes...re   ɪey
through sexual discovery, sc   ⸴nd
the process of awakening...both enlightening and engrossing."

D. Donavan, Senior Reviewer, Midwest Book Review

"This novel is a spectacular read by a very talented author. ... [featuring] a strong female character, a captivating plot, and exquisite prose. It is entertaining, heartbreaking, and mesmerizing from start to finish."

Emma Thompson, USA Book Review

"[Taylor Thompson's novel and] its truths about emotional trauma are universal. They apply to all races and cultures. This could be required reading for any ... college class in American history or American literature or trauma psychology."

Dr. David C. Hall III, Family Psychiatrist

"River is a character readers will quickly learn to love. She is a fighter and I love how she fights to claim her place in the world. An engaging read, indeed. Five Stars."

Ruffina Oserio, Readers' Favorite

To Maniel ~
Enjoy the journey!
Thompson
11-13-2019

Crowning Glory: River's Journey

Crowning Glory: River's Journey

A Novel

Taylor Thompson

Brightblacklight Publishing LLC
Houston

Crowning Glory: River's Journey is a work of fiction. All names, characters, places, and incidents are products of the author's imagination or are used fictitiously. Any resemblance to actual events, locales, persons, living or dead, is coincidental.

Published By Bright Blacklight Publishing LLC

Houston, Texas

Library of Congress Card Number: 2019931563

Taylor Thompson

Crowning Glory: River's Journey / Taylor Thompson. 1st ed. 2019

ISBN 978-0-9822400-4-5

1. Child abuse – Fiction. 2. Domestic abuse – Fiction. 3. Bigotry – Fiction. 4. Interracial relationships – Illinois – Chicago – Fiction. 5. African American families – Texas – Houston – Fiction. 6. Racial relationships – Fiction. 7. Erotica - Fiction.

eBook ISBN 978-0-9822400-5-2

Printed in the United States of America

Dedicted to Michelle, Lynn, and Sierra

Once riding in old Baltimore
heart-filled, head-filled with glee,
I saw a Baltimorean
keep looking straight at me.

Now I was eight and very small,
and he was no whit bigger,
and so I smiled, but he poked out
his tongue, and called me "Nigger."

I saw the whole of Baltimore
from May until December;
of all the things that happened there
that's all that I remember.

"Incident"
Countee Cullen

"There is a tide in the affairs of men,
which, taken at the flood, leads on to fortune;
omitted; all the voyage of their life
is bound in the shallows and in miseries."

"Julius Caesar"
William Shakespeare

Part One

≈Thinking Back≈

R iver leans in hard more to escape the hot pressing-comb her mother drags through her thick hair than to find comfort in her mother's soft breasts. Her eight-year-old legs struggle to reach the first rung of the kitchen chair in the hopes she will be able to push further away from the heat of the pressing-comb and the flame burning on the kitchen stove.

"Be still, River. Keep up all that fidgeting and you'll get burned again!"

Just at that moment, sizzling pomade drops from the hot comb and burns her young scalp. River thinks she should be used to this by now. She's been getting her hair pressed for several months and this is just part of every Saturday's ritual of getting ready for Sunday church.

The stifling heat, expected in mid-summer in Hopewell, Texas, is made even worse by the heat from the burner and hot comb making it hard for little River to breathe. Finally, her toes reach the rung of the chair and she pushes hard into her mother. "Mama, that hurts!"

"I'm almost done, honey. Be still."

Then, a quick breeze, loaded with the scent of gardenia from the bushes her mother planted by the kitchen window, wafts into the room. River breathes in the gardenias' sweetness, settles back into the chair, and tries hard to ignore the stench of Royal Crown Pomade and scorched hair. Today, like many times before, the heat brings tears to River's eyes, but she forces them back, because she understands that her mother is only fixing what is wrong with her hair, making it nice and straight as hair should be. When she finishes, just like always, River will pluck a bloom from the bush outside the kitchen window and rub its sweetness into her hair. Sweet gardenia to make it all better, that, and her father's strong hand that almost covers her face when he gently brushes away any tear that lingers.

Come Sunday morning, the Thomas family makes its way across the stepping stones that her father dug deep into the thick carpet of Saint Augustine grass, the only grass that can endure the scorching summer sun. River climbs into her place between her older sister and brother in the back seat of the shiny 1953 Chevrolet, bought three years old, but kept looking like new by her father. River feels safe in her world, protected by the hills of her parents' shoulders before her and the nearness of her brother and sister beside her. The black asphalt road, made spongey by the Texas sun, tries to hold onto the tires which make a sucking sound as they make their way to church. Her father drives into the church parking lot and looks back at his children.

"Y'all look so nice." The girls' hair, pressed straight, is pulled up and tied with large white bows into two ponytails. Just like many Sundays before, he tells them they should "keep their hair nice," reminding them the Bible says it is their "crowning glory." River smiles. Once inside, from her seat in the row just behind the deacons' bench where her father sits, River gazes up at the larger-than-life-size picture of Jesus painted above the baptismal bay. Jesus with white skin, blue eyes, and long brown hair that is blown from his face by a gust of wind. She looks around the church and, just as before, notices that no one there looks anything like Jesus, except maybe in some ways, her father, due to skin that is just a little darker and eyes that, instead of blue, are gray. With a furrowed brow she tries to see what he'd look like if he would let his wavy hair grow long like Jesus'. Maybe it would blow in the wind, too. She studies the women in church and tells herself that even though their hair looks as straight, the wind would need to be a lot stronger to move it, being as rigid with pomade as her own. By the time the choir, led by her mother's rich soprano voice, sings "At the cross, at the cross, where I first saw the light," River finally works it all out and decides that you are stuck with your skin and eyes. She can't see any way to fix those two problems, but smiles, satisfied there is something that can be done about your hair, even if it doesn't blow in the wind.

Suddenly, the woman in the pew across from River jumps up and starts twirling about. Eyes big, caught up in something she doesn't understand, River watches her jump around and cry out, "Thank you, Jesus!" Several other women join her and thrash about, violently tossing their heads around, shouting words

11

River's never heard, while their hair remains firmly in place. River watches as the men in church catch and hold the women, some who have grown as stiff as their hair. She watches as the men pass something under their noses that brings them back, relaxed and calm, with every hair as it was before. No, she decides, there can be no wind strong enough. Then, she reaches up and smooths her hair and, with the wisdom of an eight-year-old, understands that straight hair is about as close as you can get if you want to be perfect, just like Jesus, whom her parents pray to each Sunday and every evening before dinner. For five years she endures the hot comb and pomade while she stares up at the white Jesus above the baptismal bay and watches the women praise his name, as they shout up and down the church aisles, until the day when everything changes.

~ ~ ~

River takes good care of her hair, washing it and having it pressed straight each Saturday, creating a few curls from rollers made from twisted pieces of brown paper grocery bags, and until a few days after her thirteenth birthday it serves her well. This is the day her sister destroys everything, including her first true love. Elvis is the first man River falls in love with and dreams about making love to. It is not a fantasy, of course, but the best love she can imagine. If ever they meet, she knows Elvis will love her just as much. His pictures, torn from every teen idol magazine she can buy with her small allowance, hang from every available wall space in the bedroom she shares with her sister, Vallie Lynn. Then one day, when her sister needs more wall space for her current fantasy love, River's world shatters.

"River, you need to take down some of these pictures." Quickly, her sister rips down two that are clearly on her side of the room.

"Don't touch them!" River screams. "You have enough room on your side." She runs over to rescue Elvis.

Vallie Lynn, who has had enough of Elvis, runs to the far side of her bed and refuses to hand over the pictures. One, River's favorite, is of Elvis lying in a bed covered with teddy bears, and he is smiling that wonderful sideways smile that she loves, that makes her feel warm inside. Her sister hurriedly crumples the two pages in her hand and throws them to the floor.

"I hate you!" River screams, her eyes filling with tears.

"Really, River. Over a white guy! Why would any black girl want Elvis, or any white guy for that matter? You're black, River!"

River slumps across her bed, tears now falling. "I hate you, Vallie," she whispers, "I really do hate you."

Vallie Lynn holds her ground and hurls her rage at her sister. "Well that's just too bad. I'm sick of this white man's pictures all over this room anyway. He probably hates black people. Probably calls us niggers, and I bet he wouldn't even look at you, or speak to you, if he passed you on the street."

Vallie Lynn's words cut River to the core, taking the wind right out of her. She slides from the bed onto the floor, smoothing the crumpled pages. River knows about racism and has had that word hurled at her more than her fair share of times. Still, she wonders, can Elvis do such a thing? No, not her Elvis. How can he make her feel pretty when he asks her to "love me tender," and warm inside with that smile if he can't like her? She can hardly speak for the hard knot of pain welling up inside her chest, but she simply must fight for Elvis' love.

"You don't know, Vallie Lynn. Maybe all white people don't hate us." River, now huddled in a corner, caresses and smooths the crumpled pages, lovingly, until there is hardly a crease left,

13

and Elvis' sideways smile returns. "He could love me, if he knew me, maybe, you don't know." Her voice fades until it is barely a whisper while she pleads, "He could like me, Vallie. Couldn't he?"

"What do you think, River? Use your head! How many black girls do you see in these jillion pictures you've got of him? Not a single one! And what makes you different, so special? Little Miss *River*!"

River knows, by the way she says *"River,"* that her sister is teasing her about her name. She had hated it when she was younger. Too often she'd been asked, "What river are you?" or "Where are you running to?" But over the years, River has grown to feel her name suits her. Deep inside, River also knows her sister is right about Elvis, and the part that causes the most pain is that she is helpless to do anything more about it. She can't change the color of her eyes or skin. She is already, while holding back tears, enduring that hot straightening comb, pressing her hair straight and burning her scalp, and sometimes the back of her neck, in the process. But she can't escape her sister's words and chokes down the hard truth that straight hair is simply not enough. Slowly, over a couple of weeks, the pictures come down while she gives up the fight against the painful truth she has always known—being black will matter for as long as she lives. And the worst part, she thinks, is that it can matter to the one person you want it not to at all. *And how am I to know?* she wonders. Something tells River contempt, especially her own, for her blackness will always stir something deep in her bones. She will always know it. *Please God,* she prays, *take away the hurt.* She doubts the white Jesus will answer. Teenage love dies slowly, however, so for a little while longer she endures the hot pressing-comb, the scorched hair and burned scalp that have not been enough to win her Elvis' love, even with the sweet scent of gardenia from the blooms she rubs into her hair.

The hurt settles deep inside her, solid, like a rock, until the day she decides she's had enough and angrily takes back her love from Elvis. He doesn't deserve it. The anger feels good as it dulls that rock of pain inside her, smoothing its jagged edges. She feels a little braver with anger as her friend, more able to face a world that doesn't feel quite as safe as those Sunday morning rides to church. Then one evening, prodded by anger, she walks in the door from school and announces to her mother that she doesn't want to have her hair pressed with the hot pressing-comb anymore. She starts to wear her hair in a short afro, just like the one her sister has been wearing for years. Vallie Lynn is proud of her little sister and she tells her so.

~ ~ ~

Now, almost twenty years later, after listening to the message on her phone, River smiles and wonders what it means and why, after so long, he has called. As she pours another glass of wine, she stands in almost total darkness and looks out the floor-to-ceiling windows in the living room of her sky-high Michigan Avenue apartment, unable now to read any more words from a worn and dog-eared copy of writings by Anna J. Cooper. The one in her hand is titled, *What Are We Worth?*

River studies the snow that gathers on the busy street below and looks out at the Sears Tower and wonders again if the building that stands in its shadow has a name other than the one that she gave it. When she first moved to Chicago, it became her favorite building in the nighttime skyline, with its lighted rooftop enclosure that looks like three huge crowns that made her think of her father, so it became the Crowning Glory building. River trembles, takes another sip of the Pommard Burgundy, and pulls her warm, cashmere robe tighter. She glances up at the building and runs her fingers through the soft kinky thickness of her hair, no chemicals, no color, no curling iron, just her natural hair. She feels better. Through the glass walls of her apartment, she feels the city wrap itself around her, girding her safely. She relaxes, nestles down on the floor next to the gardenia-scented candle burning in a brass bowl on the floor. Its flame, barely there, flickers low in the puddled wax. The candle sputters, spewing some of the wax to land on Cooper's writings there on the floor. The candle sizzles out, the scent of gardenia begins to leave the room, and River smiles again when she thinks of how proudly she had worn that afro all through college. River pulls her robe tighter and, even though she knows Chicago is miles away from Houston and Adam, she thinks of him and the ugly and painful time that left her no choice but to escape him and leave Houston. Her smile fades.

≈The Early Years≈

G regory Smith enters River's life at the beginning of her eighteenth summer, before she is to start college on a full scholarship. It was her second day waitressing at her sister's restaurant, Vallie Lynn's Café, in the small Texas town of Alvin Heights. She thinks he has a wonderful smile. Sizing him up, she thinks he is probably the same height and weight as she is and not striking in any way, except for his quick, broad smile of gleaming white teeth. Teeth that look even whiter framed by his dark brown skin. It's that smile that puts her at ease and makes a quick "yes" fly from her mouth when he asks her to go out. She, nor anyone else, would believe he is thirty, a fact he keeps well-hidden, preferring to be "mid-twenties" when anyone asks.

"River, I don't think you need to be getting so serious with Greg. Remember, going to college is what you need to be thinking about." River looks at her sister with surprise.

"You don't like him?"

"He's fine enough, but you're spending way too much time with him. And just where are you two spending all that time anyway?"

River's face burns. Quickly she turns from her sister and

begins folding napkins, wondering how much she knows, if she looks as different as she feels. "Mostly movies, no one place in particular."

"Well, just be careful. Understand? And why is his car parked out front?"

"He wants to take me shopping for clothes for college this evening. I'm picking him up from work." River, who has now regained her composure, turns from her busy work and looks directly at her sister. "He loves me, Vallie Lynn." *Besides,* she thinks, *Greg always uses condoms.* He'd promised. She had never been able to bring herself to look.

Everyone in Alvin Heights swears this is the hottest summer anyone can remember. The small air conditioner in the restaurant is doing a poor job of keeping it cool, and the heat causes River bouts of nausea. A few days after her talk with Vallie Lynn, River returns from the restroom and one of her nausea bouts when a tall, attractive black woman walks into the cafe.

"Are you River?" the woman asks through a smile that, to River's thinking, doesn't look real. Somehow it stays on her bright red lips never traveling up to her eyes, eyes that stare too long without blinking and scare her. Looking at the woman's mixed-up face, River wonders how she knows her name. She's only been in Alvin Heights for three months and hasn't gone any place to meet anyone other than Greg and Evaline, the other summer student who works for her sister.

"Yes? Can I help you?"

"Greg told me to come by and get the car."

"What? Who're you?" River feels her stomach tremble.

"Let's just say I'm a friend of the family."

"Well, why didn't Greg tell me you were coming? He didn't

say anything about this. That I could give you the car. I don't understand." The tremble finds its way into River's voice. "What did you say your name is?"

The woman repeats, without blinking, "Like I said, I'm a friend of the family."

Surely, the woman knows Greg because she knows the black Cadillac parked out front belongs to him, River thinks, *but Greg had told me that his family lives in Austin.* They are planning a trip to meet them before she leaves for school in two weeks. River, unable to still the tremor in her voice, is angry with herself for being afraid and even more for showing it. "Are you from Austin? Do you know his family there?"

The woman leans over the counter and brings her face within inches of River's who, frozen in fear, is unable to step away. She can feel the woman's hot, wet breath when she speaks. It smells like cinnamon and cigarettes when she smirks, "I'm talking about his family right here in Alvin Heights."

River feels her stomach churn when she whispers, "I don't know what you mean." The woman, pleased to see River shrink from her, doesn't pretend to smile anymore and her red lips spread into a wide, scary sneer while she rushes on.

"Well, you need to know. I'm talking about his wife and two children who live right here, less than a mile from where we're standing. Over on Anderson Street."

The floor rises quickly to meet River, but she wills herself to hang on. She will not faint, but she loses the battle with nausea that sends her fleeing to the restroom. When she returns, the woman is gone. The car is still there.

Young, and, in what for her, is true love, River doesn't know what to believe. She refuses to see Greg, but over the phone he pleads he is sorry he didn't tell her he is married, but he and his wife are separated. And that woman who came to the cafe is someone he'd been seeing, and only came by because she is angry he ended the relationship now that he is in love with her. She wants to believe it, but she has her pride, and even better, her anger. Soon, River understands it is more than the Texas heat causing her nausea. Scholarship surely gone, the bus ride back to her small Texas town is as endless as River's self-recrimination. The bus turns off IH-290 on one of its scheduled stops in another small Texas town, kicking up dust and loose gravel as it comes to a stop on the unpaved parking area. River leaves the bus last with the other black riders who are seated in the rear, and once inside the terminal her steps slow when her eyes fasten onto the "Whites Only" sign, painted neatly in big, block letters above the first ladies' restroom she sees. Anger urges her to simply walk into that one, and she wonders what anyone will do if she does. She checks her reflection in the window of that door, picks at her afro with her fingers, lifting it higher, and then walks on past to the smaller, dirtier, ladies' room in the back, the one with the "colored" sign scribbled above it. She pushes the unpainted door open, holds her breath, and walks inside.

In Hopewell, the bus comes to a rough stop, and with her head pressed against the window, River dries her eyes and looks harder to be sure it is Greg's Cadillac she sees parked in the bus station lot. She waits until the last person leaves the bus before she slowly walks down to where Greg is waiting. She walks past him.

"How could you leave like that? Without saying a thing to me! Your sister told me about the baby. How could you not tell me?"

River keeps walking, picking up the pace.

"River, talk to me. I love you, I want to marry you!"

"It looks to me like you already have a wife. How many do you need?"

Greg takes her hand and forces her to stop walking. "I told you. We were already separated. I know you love me. I want to talk to your folks, to tell 'em I want to marry you."

"Believe me Greg, you don't want to talk to my folks, especially my father, not now. And I don't know what I feel. How can I be pregnant? This is all your fault; you promised this couldn't happen, and I believed you!"

"Come on, it's nobody's fault, accidents happen, let's get in the car and talk, then I'll take you home."

"No, my parents told me to call when my bus got in; they're coming to get me. And I'm serious Greg, I don't know what my father would do if he saw you now. He's a kind man, he's never fussed at us or spanked us, even when we probably needed it. My mother has, but not Daddy. Once I saw him slap a man so hard, because of something he did to my sister, the man fell on the ground."

"What?"

"Yes. The only thing that stopped it from being worse was my mother calling Daddy back to the house. So, I don't think you want to talk to my parents. Not right now." She didn't tell him that her father had looked back at the man, trying desperately to get into his car, and said, "Believe me, there's not a poison in the drug store that'll kill you any quicker than I will about my daughters."

~ ~ ~

When Greg meets River's parents one month later, her father fixes his gray eyes on him. "Me and my wife been married for twenty-five years. I never raised my voice or hand to her once. I

21

don't expect no less from you with my daughter, understand?"
Greg's face hints at the pain he feels from Mr. Thomas' crushing handshake when he answers, "Yes sir."

Three months later, River feels her prayers are answered when she marries the newly divorced Greg. Their baby boy comes two months early and dies three days later. It takes River almost a year to want to live again, to find the strength to return to school and rescue her sanity, and in that year her short afro grows taller. She doesn't question why she feels anchored by the large afro, or how it seems to be the one thing that keeps her from simply floating away.

≈School Days≈

River sits at her desk at Alvin Heights Elementary where, with thirty credits from the local community college, she works as a teaching assistant when the pain seizes her, spreading from the pit of her stomach to her back. She hopes it's not what she thinks it is. Just six months ago, seven weeks into her pregnancy, a pain just like this gripped her when she miscarried, but she is almost nine weeks now; she reasons this must be better. She holds her stomach tenderly, and gingerly walks to the teachers' lounge to call Greg.

Worry clouds Greg's face when he holds the car door open for River. "We better head on to the emergency room. Don't you think?"

"No, Greg. I already called Dr. Davis. He said for me to stay off my feet for today and come in tomorrow."

"Oh, okay then. I'll stay home with you the rest of the day."

"That's all right Greg. Your shop is just minutes from here. I'll call if I need you."

Greg, who knows his way around any car, is the assistant manager at one of the larger auto-mechanic shops in Alvin Heights. He's taken on extra hours so that his child support payments don't make too much of a dent in his take home pay. When he walks in the door from work that evening, River doesn't have to tell him there is no more baby. From the bed, where she softly cries, she watches him turn and walk into the bathroom. Through the closed door, River hears him plead to God for forgiveness for his sins—she wonders if she is one of them—and ask him to please let his babies live.

River is waiting for Greg to pick her up after work the next Monday when she is surprised to see her brother pull up in a rental car. He is living in New York where he is an investment banker with Paine Webber.

"Ernest! What are you doing here? I didn't know you were coming."

"Just checking up on my little sister. I'm leaving for Europe tomorrow and wanted to see you and Vallie before I left. I saw Mom and Dad earlier today. How are you?"

"Fine. I'm doing fine."

"Listen River, I've been thinking, and if you and Greg can swing things, without you working, I'd like to pay your tuition at Texas Southern. So, you know, you can go full-time and get this behind you. What do you think?"

River leans in to kiss her brother who smiles and pulls away saying, "I don't do that mushy stuff. You know that."

That night at dinner, Greg doesn't seem quite as happy about River going to school full-time as she, Ernest, and Vallie.

~ ~ ~

River comes alive at school, making friends who are her age. She is still working part-time at the elementary school, and for extra income, has started tutoring Jason Long, the university's star quarterback. And as good as he is at handling a football, he seems just as committed to "handling" as many of his adoring female fans as he can.

"Gotta run, River. Got a date." Jason is ending another

tutoring session early.

"With Vera?"

River has met his girlfriend, Vera, and she likes her a lot. She chides River often about paying so much attention to her hair and seems to never pay any attention to her own, which she wears in a very short afro.

"Not this time, somebody else." His smile is telling.

"Jason, I don't understand why you have to run around on Vera. Don't you love her?"

"For sure! She's my main squeeze, without a doubt! And when I settle down, it's gonna be with Vera. Just not ready to settle yet."

"Oh," is all River says. Then she thinks of Greg and is glad he, at least, is settled. While Greg is praying for River to become pregnant, River is planning what she will do when she finishes school. With Greg's overtime and River's work as teaching assistant, they've moved into a nice house on Bay Area Boulevard in Clear Lake. Greg seems happier since River has been attending the church he's joined and attends a lot more frequently than she does. It's a lot like the church of her youth, where women shouted up and down the aisles, with one big difference for the better; they have a black Jesus painted over the baptismal bay. She is fastening her necklace when Greg calls out again, "Are you ready?"

"What's the problem, Greg? We have plenty of time, it's only ten-thirty. Church doesn't start for thirty minutes."

"No problem. Just don't want to be late."

Just before the preacher adjourns church, River looks around, surprised, when he calls her and Greg to the alter. Greg takes her hand and almost drags her to the front of the church where he kneels and pulls at her, encouraging her to kneel before the alter with him. She tries to, but her knees won't bend. The pastor begins to pray loudly, while church members gather around them with their arms raised in the air, asking God to bless them with a baby.

There is dead silence in the car as they drive home, and Greg eases the car into the driveway. River reaches to open the car door when he stops her.

"Do you think God is punishing me? Do you think that's why you can't have a baby, River?"

"Greg, I don't believe there's someone somewhere deciding if I can or can't get pregnant. I can tell you one thing I know for sure, though. That's the last time I set foot in that church."

"Can I ask you something, River?"

"What is it?"

"You wouldn't be taking those new kinda pills that stop women from having babies, would you? I think if we have a baby, things'll get better for us."

"No, Greg, I'm not."

River walks slowly into the house, finally answering something she's asked herself for the six years she's been married. Would she have married Greg if she had not been pregnant? The answer is no.

≈Paradise Palace≈

With college behind her, River and Greg are finalizing opening night plans for the business they have built. River did not forget the summer work at her sister's place and how much she loved it. Vallie Lynn had been the boss; River had especially liked that. She knows her accounting degree will serve her well in making a success of the grandest nightclub for blacks in Alvin Heights.

River and Greg saved every cent for six years to buy the land for their dream, really River's dream, a restaurant and club built on five wooded acres that back onto a small lake in Alvin Heights. All along, Greg resisted the whole idea, telling River it might be a sin to sell liquor. She told him she'd get the license in her name. He argued they couldn't afford the land. At her brother's suggestion, she searched the real estate ads and found five acres that were being sold for back taxes and, with her brother's help, bought them. When they ran into problems getting a liquor license, her brother gave her the name of his friend, a black attorney, who learned the city was having a blind bidding auction, with the license going to the highest bidder.

Ernest's friend, thinking the bidding might not be all that blind, hired a white attorney who entered the blind bidding and won the license. It has been a long, hard process, and she often felt Greg was more a hindrance than a help, but finally, it is done.

One requirement River had in the design was that the building was to have no hard edges, no corners, and the architect designed a circular building. Their place was to be soft and inviting, a retreat from the sharp edges that often were too much a part of a black person's life. River walks slowly through the building where curved walls, painted in a soft apricot hue, embrace you when you enter the building, and silk bird-of-paradise flowers bloom on every table that circles the parquet dance floor. River named the club "Paradise Palace."

Opening night for Paradise Palace is scheduled for New Year's Eve, 1968, and River sits at the thirty-foot circular mahogany bar; in her hand she holds the signed appearance contract from Jerry Butler's agent. She smiles, finding it hard to believe that Jerry will soon have everyone in the club swaying slowly to "Are You Happy?" or bumping to the beat of "Only the Strong Survive."

And to top it all off, Jason Long, the star quarterback from Texas Southern University, and his girlfriend, Vera, are going to be at the grand opening. River knows some people will be coming just to rub shoulders with the Heisman Trophy winner, rumored to be picked up in the first round of the National Football League draft. Jason and River grew to be friends when she tutored him during college. Evaline, her friend who recently finished X-ray school, and Vallie Lynn have agreed to be waitresses on opening night. River folds the contract and laughs, a loud, happy laugh that bounces off the walls around her.

River and Greg meet with all the town's officials during the planning, licensing, and permitting stages of their club. It is tortuous and doesn't surprise her to learn that there isn't a single black officer on the Alvin Heights police force, and River feels a little of that old familiar anger stir to think Dr. King's struggles haven't made a lot of difference in Alvin Heights. She refuses to hire white officers for security in what will be a predominately black club and, instead, hires two black officers from the Harris County Sheriff's Department.

Paradise Palace becomes the place to be for every black person in the area. The year 1969 starts out as a good year, and there are even a few white patrons coming as the club enters its second year. There are times when River thinks it's just too good to be true. She tries to ignore that feeling of dread, that fear, lurking always close by, that if it's good it won't last, that life is not meant to be good, at least not for her, not without a fight.

≈Chief Manders≈

Paradise Palace is well into its second year, and River has often seen the Alvin Heights police officers patrolling their grounds. She's sitting in her office at the rear of the club, balancing the books, when she hears a car drive around to the rear entrance of the building. She peeps through the small window in the door, and recognizes the Alvin Heights' police chief, Manders. He walks slowly toward the door that River holds open for him.

"How y'all doing ma'am?"

"I'm doing fine, Chief Manders." She steps aside to allow the man to come inside. He stoops his tall, thin body through the door, slowly.

"Yes'um, didn't know if yall'd 'member me."

He speaks as slowly as he moves. Bony hands reach into his shirt pocket and remove a wad of chewing tobacco. He takes a slow bite. River is fixated by his slowness, and thinks she's never seen teeth so brown, almost the same color as the chew of tobacco he pulls into his mouth.

"We got us," he says, "a lil ol' problem." His slowness annoys River and she fights the urge to help him finish his sentences. He drawls on as he creeps around the office, picking up an item and then putting it down, while his hooded eyes crawl around the room as if he's lost something, looking everywhere except at River. Not knowing what to make of him or his visit, River remains silent, mad as hell that he feels he has the right to touch her things.

"I been thanking 'bout it," he yawns, "and I'ma need y'all's help to work this here thang out."

River walks to her desk and picks up the telephone. "Let me call Greg." From the office window, she sees Greg already walking toward the club and puts down the phone.

As he approaches, Greg wonders aloud, "What the hell do the police want?"

"Can I get you something?" River points toward the office refrigerator.

"Yes ma'am," he mumbles. "I'll take a Coca-Cola." He spits his chew into a plastic cup he takes from the trash can, and then wipes his mouth with the back of his hand. River pours the cola into a plastic cup and pushes it in his direction, glad she can just throw the cup away when he is done. Neither of them answers Greg's hello as he walks into the room, but River does glance in his direction, and then quickly returns her attention to Manders.

"Now what's the problem you need our help with?"

"Well, ma'am," he takes a sip of Coke and again wipes at his mouth with the back of his dirty hand, "it's wit all tha traffic coming out ta y'all's place. Mayor Gray bin wondrin jes' what we kin do to cut down on tha dust and dirt tha's bin collectin' in his pool and all over his spankin' new patio furniture. Po man's got ta clean it up pritty near every day. Y'all seen that new pool he don' went and got? It's a beauty, ain't it?" The mayor's house backs onto the unpaved street that leads to the Paradise Palace.

"What'd you have in mind? About cutting down on the dust?"

31

Taylor Thompson

Greg hears the anger in River's voice, and his spirit sinks.
"Maybe he can get a pool cover."
"Tha' jes ain't gon work, ma'am."
"And just why not?"
"Well," Manders stops to take another slow sip from the
paper cup, "cuz most o' y'all's traffic is on tha weeken'. Tha's
when tha mayor likes to be out by tha pool, enjoying it an' all.
Hard thang ta do wit so many cars kickin' up dust. Naw, covered
up jes ain't go work, pritty near sho 'bout that."
Greg speaks, still standing in the corner, having worked his
mind hard to come up with something that he hopes will calm
down River, and both she and Manders turn almost in unison at
the sound of his voice and look at him. River, caught up in her
anger, has almost forgotten he is in the room.
"Why don't we get the road blacktopped? We'd be willing to
help finance it because it would help us too, make it nicer for
folks to get to our place."
Instantly, River wonders if the mayor had paid to have the
road in front of his house paved, and just as quickly, decides,
more than likely, that he had not.
"Well, we thought o' that." Manders answers while
considering the dirt under the fingernails of his free hand. "But
tha town jes ain't got that kinda money. Mayor Gray wuz
thankin," he takes another sip of Coke and River prays he'll
empty the damn cup, "jes maybe, y'all could cut down on ya
hours some. 'Specially on tha weeken's. Mos a y'all's bizness is
late at night, anyhow." He finally swallows the last of the Coke.
"Tha mayor don't use his pool much at night. We wuz thankin
y'all could jes open up later, on tha weeken."
"Well, maybe we can open up a little later, on Friday and
Saturday nights." Greg's eyes plead with River.

32

The sadness she feels for Greg almost makes her forget how much she'd like to rip out Manders' eyes. She wonders just how much and for how long he has suffered before learning to endure almost any indignity. It is a lesson she promises herself never to learn. River turns from Greg, and slowly and firmly says, "We have our largest crowds for dinner on Friday and Saturday nights. There is no way we are changing our weekend hours."

Manders hasn't made eye contact with either of them during the almost hour that he's been there, which keeps River's anger on a low boil. She looks from him to Greg whose fallen face drives her to offer some concession.

"I think that Greg has the best suggestion; pave the road, and we'll be willing to pay for some part of it, a large part."

Manders spits into his empty Coke cup, having replenished his chew. "Tha' jes ain't what tha mayor had in mind. I don't thank he gon' go fa it. Fact, I'm pritty near sho he ain't!"

"Well, it's the best we can do," River shoots back.

"I sho hope y'all know what yer doin," he mumbles, and slouches out the door after missing most of the trash can when he tosses the cup of spittle in its direction. River tells Greg to throw the plastic trash can away as he makes mop water to clean the tobacco juice off the floor.

Shortly after Manders paid River and Greg his visit, groups of white policemen start coming into the club, sometimes as many as four at one time, even though the regular black security officers are there. Often, River thinks the entire Alvin Heights Police Department must be in their place. It has been only two years since Dr. King was murdered. This is South Texas and race relations are not so great that groups of white police officers in a black club don't cause concern. Soon after they show up, walking slowly from table to table, uneasy customers start to leave.

Business starts to slow and Roy, a classmate who had once been a regular at the club, comes by one evening after work just before happy hour.

"River, you won't believe what the police been up to," he rants, finally pausing to order a cognac. He rushes on, pausing every once-in-a-while to listen briefly to Lou Rawls sing about "Dead End Street."

> *But when the odds are all against you,*
> *How can you win?*
> *I'm gonna push my way out of here,*
> *even though I can't say when.*
> *But I'm gonna get off of this dead end street,*
> *And I ain't never gonna come back again...*

"If we hadn't got together to start planning the class reunion, we might not have known just what's been happening. I had thought it was just me."

"Roy, what are you talking about?" River asks while she refills his glass and pours herself one.

"It started, I guess, about six months ago. Just about every time I'd leave this place, a policeman would pull me over and give me a ticket or a warning, more often a ticket, for drinking and driving. I got two DWIs in a little over a month."

"I can't see you driving drunk." She seems to be talking more to herself. "No, I can't see that."

"Well, I started to wonder, first I thought maybe I *was* drinking too much. Didn't really believe it, but I wondered," he smiles. "Then I thought maybe the police had it in for me for some reason. That's why I stopped coming here so often."

"I had wondered about that." River speaks to herself again, her voice little more than a whisper.

"Well, that's why, and I made damned sure the few times when I did come, I didn't have more than a beer or two. Then, I'd wait a long time before I left. Now I've found out it's been happening to a lot of us. Not just me!"

"What lot of us?" This time River's voice is loud and clear, and her eyes bore into Roy.

"River, I found out at class meeting last night that the police have been stopping a lot of people when they leave here. Giving them tickets for driving drunk. You can't afford too many of those bad boys before you lose your license. That's why I hauled my ass to the house. And left it there!" He pushes his empty glass toward River, who, absorbed in her thoughts, pours almost as much Courvoisier on the bar as she does into his glass. "They must have it in for you guys, trying to put y'all out of business or something!" He pauses, looks at the overfilled glass, and after thinking about it, leaves it where it is.

That familiar anger, her friend, stirs. "That's just what it sounds like, Roy, and I know exactly why."

She checks with the attorney her brother referred earlier who tells her the only recourse they have is to file harassment charges. Then quickly adds that they have about as much a chance of winning that case "as a snowball has in hell."

When they leave the attorney's office, River turns to Greg. "We have to go and try and talk to Manders. You know that, don't you?"

Greg is unable to hide his nervousness. "Yeah, you're probably right. But this time, it might be better if I do the talking, you know, so nobody gets upset."

She knows he means her. "Are you sure, Greg?" She thinks of his naturally soft voice and how much she liked it when they first met.

"Don't worry, River, I can handle it."

"Okay, that's fine, Greg." She hopes he has not heard her doubt, and that maybe this time, he will.

The next morning, after they wait for more than an hour, Manders calls them in. They take the seats he waves toward in his cramped office. Manders doesn't look up from the disheveled papers on his desk that he keeps shuffling and reshuffling.

"What kin I do fa y'all?" River remembers her agreement to let Greg do the talking. She waits for his response and hopes that she can keep her mouth shut. She feels hot even though the air conditioner seems to be blowing full blast.

"We need to know why policemen keep coming to our place. It looks like they're in there every night." Greg's forced voice cracks with nervousness. River smiles encouragement in his direction.

"What y'all got 'ginst tha police comin in? Y'all oughta be glad we lookin' in on ya."

"Well, with one or two of them, we would. But why so many of them, all at the same time? The customers think something's wrong, get nervous, and leave."

"Well, *is* anythin' wrong back thar?" Manders continues talking to the papers on his desk. "I bin tol y'all got gamblin back thar. Tha's how y'all wuz able to buy that spankin' new caddy y'all got." River feels a drop of sweat fall from her underarms. "An' y'all always gotta crowd."

"Who could tell you something like that?" Greg seems to be asking the question more of himself than of Manders. "It's nothing but a lie."

River moves to the edge of her seat, an anxious observer. She'd told Greg not to buy that car. Never have given a thought, however, to the message it sent to the white police department, but more concerned that their customers might think they were doing "too well" and find someplace else to spend their money. She'd been angry that he just had to have a new, big, long car to replace the old one he had. She's taking deep breaths, trying to slow her heart while watching her blouse rise and fall with each fast heartbeat. Over and over, she reminds herself to keep quiet.

Just then, for the first time since she met this skinny, drooped shouldered man with brown teeth, he looks up from his desk and fixes his eyes hard on Greg.

"Jes don't lie ta me boy," he spits. "I don't cotton ta bein' lied to. Ya hear me, boy?"

River looks from Manders to Greg, sitting there speechless, for what seems to her an eternity. She hears herself scream to him, "Get up, say something!" But her lips have not moved. Unable to watch Greg for another silent second sitting there looking at his hands folded in his lap, River bolts from her chair, strides toward Manders' desk, and in a voice that Greg has never heard before growls, "He doesn't need to lie to you, understand!" Manders jumps up quickly, not sure if he will have to defend himself, when she slaps her large hand on his desk and gravels, "And just how old does a man have to be for you to stop calling him a boy? Greg's older than you, and he's no boy!" She and Manders lock eyes, and she wishes he'd kept them hidden. They are empty and cold, a milky blue that scares her. As she turns to leave, she looks back at Manders, who still stands motionless behind his desk with his long skinny arms dangling at his sides. "He's a man, understand, a full-grown man!" Greg leaves his chair, follows her from Manders' office, and not knowing what to do with his anger, does nothing. River hears Greg's slowed steps as he follows her to the car, and she has a

37

strong urge to turn and slap him, hard.

"Thanks for sticking up for me like that yesterday, River, but sometimes it's better not to fight, especially if you got a lot to lose, and especially if the fight is one you probably can't win anyway. Sometimes, you know, you just need to wait things out. Not make 'em worse." Greg speaks without looking at River, while he meanders around the office of the club the next morning.

She knows he is probably embarrassed about last night. Their lovemaking, which River could have easily done without but Greg had insisted, had become painful and she, after making him stop, turned on the lamp that was on the bedside table. She stared in disbelief at the long and perpetually hard rubber penis he had strapped to himself.

"What is that, Greg?" she'd heard herself scream. "What the hell is that?" He'd grabbed for the sheet to cover himself but tugged futilely as its corner snagged the footboard, leaving him shamefully exposed. River saw his virility evaporate.

"Greg, please talk to me. Why did you buy that? Why do you feel you need that thing? And what the hell is it called, anyway?" Her anger had been boiling, for many reasons. First, the failed meeting with Manders. Then, how could Greg be so insecure as to think he needed that thing? Then she'd thought, *Maybe he doesn't know how to talk to me about it,* and for a moment felt sorry for him. But the thing that River couldn't get over, the thing about it all that drove her anger, and made her forget about any pity she felt, was that it was pink, with bright red arteries and bluish veins running through it. *Why,* she thought, *didn't he buy a black one? Surely, there had to be black ones!*

"Just leave me alone, River. Just leave me alone." Greg turned away from her and faced the wall. Lessons of survival that Greg learned in the 1940's South taught him to become comfortable with walls. He grew silent, and from another well-learned lesson, would wait for this to pass. River had put on her robe and stormed from the room.

Thinking about last night, River turns to Greg and forces a smile. "I thought you handled the meeting well, Greg." She regrets the lie, returns to her work, and hopes she's made him feel better.

~ ~ ~

With increased visits from the white policemen, business continues to slow, and River, with more free time, and after another failed pregnancy, enrolls in graduate school. She and Greg keep the business going two more years before they are forced to sell rather than lose the club.

December of 1972, River cries as they pack the last of their things before leaving her dream. She hates the police chief and she hates Greg. She would have no problem naming all she hates about Manders. She is less sure of why she hates Greg. When she puts the last box in Greg's new car, she wonders if he needs his long car as much as she needs her big afro. He is a good and decent man, but River needs more from him, needs him to be more like her brother, Ernest. Her brother is the rod by which she measures all men, and to which they all fall short. She doesn't look back as they drive away from Paradise Palace, and she never goes there again. Where she does go, however, is to every black church, to every black establishment in Alvin Heights for the three months leading up to the next city election. She tells and retells how they were forced out of business and stirs every voting black, and many whites, in the area to cast their vote against the mayor. River's impassioned talks lead to increased voter registration in the black community. Mayor

39

Gray is defeated and Chief Manders is replaced.

≈Daryl and Alpha≈

The bills left to be paid when Paradise Palace is sold are staggering, and River turns to Jason Long. Passed over in the NFL draft, he is a coach at Alvin Heights High School, and she knows Jason is friendly with Antoine Bruno, a local restaurateur whom she has met once or twice. Tony, as his friends call him, was a big supporter of Jason and the university's football team, and they remain friends. When, at River's urging, Jason tells Tony she is looking for a job, she eventually is offered a position as a clerk at the corporate headquarters in Houston for Tony's Bistro, Tony's chain of restaurants.

Vera, now teaching math at the elementary school where River once worked as an assistant, stops by to take her to a congratulatory lunch.

"I'm proud of you, River. Getting into Tony's is kind of a big deal!"

"Yeah, with Jason's help!"

"So what? You know you've got the credentials! Don't think for a minute that Tony didn't check you out. He's a business man, River! Stop doubting yourself so much! Jason has that same problem, always wondering if he's good enough, and even if you are, the cards are stacked against you. Always something to prove."

"What? What are you talking about?"

"Oh, he thinks if he'd been playing at University of Houston rather than Texas Southern, he wouldn't have been passed over at the NFL draft. He's pretty pissed off at Sweatt!"

"Sweatt?"

"Yeah. He's the reason Texas founded TSU. They didn't want to admit him to the law school at University of Texas, so they had to establish a school for us black folks. Good old Jim Crow!"

"You know, Vera, I often wonder why they don't just combine the two schools, and have just one, like in Austin. I mean, they're right across the street from each other!"

Vera laughs. "Well, there are two reasons floating around about why that has never happened, and never will! If the schools are combined, they will have to take the name of the first school founded by the state, and that is our dear alma mater, Texas Southern University! Ego or racism stopped that discussion before it got started good. You decide which. Jason thinks racism."

River runs her fingers through her large afro after noticing Vera's hair looks as if it has been freshly cut. "What's going on with you and Jason, anyway? You been wearing that big rock for a long time," she says pointing to the engagement ring on Vera's hand.

"Just taking my time. Want to be sure Jason is ready for this; don't want to make a mistake. I'm no fool, River, I know Jason well. I'm just waiting for him to settle down—if he will." River thinks of Greg and wonders if her hair should be trimmed.

Daryl Johnston is the only accountant at Tony's Bistro, and

when River is first promoted from clerk to accountant, his title changes to office manager. Even with her education and experience, she knows she was hired as a favor to Jason, and it caused her to feel unworthy around both Daryl and Tony in the beginning. Even though she proved herself early on, she often wishes she could stop reminding herself that she is the only black person in the building, and just remember how hard she worked to win every promotion from clerk to senior accountant in her five years at Tony's Bistro. Still, she worries, especially about her hair. The afro she's been wearing since she was thirteen has grown quite large, and once before, after a visit from Vera, River trimmed it short; a price she was willing to pay to feel she belongs. But now, with her last promotion, even the short afro is gone. River chemically straightens her hair with the new permanent relaxers black women are using. Now her hair is nice and straight, without the grease, straightening comb, and the smell of the scorched hair of her past. One less thing to bring attention to her as the only black person in the office, she decides. That nagging discomfort eases a bit, and River is surprised, and happy, that she feels more secure with her straight and slightly turned-under pageboy. With two new restaurant acquisitions, River has hardly been able to keep up with work. Early one morning Daryl walks into her office. She looks up at him and then quickly back at her work. "You're smiling. Does that mean you've got good news? Did Tony agree to hire some help?"

"What do I get if I say yes?" Daryl is attracted to River, and it isn't just about sex. He just likes being around her and that, for him, is troubling. While it is okay for a Southern gentleman to bed a black woman, he knows it is quite another thing for it to be anything more.

"You get an accountant with almost enough time to do her job," River shoots back.

Once, when they'd been working late, Daryl brushed against River's behind, and she wondered if she had felt his hardness. Anger spun her around. "That's enough, Daryl. This office is big enough for both of us to walk around in without bumping into each other."

"What're you talking about?" he'd mumbled, his voice deep with emotion.

"I'm tired of you *accidentally* bumping into me. Just cut it out!"

"So? I like those big butts y'all have. So what?" River had been furious when she knew the "y'all" he meant were black women. She thought of an article from *The Independent*, a periodical she read in one of her Black History classes that had been burned into her memory as if every word had been seared there by a branding iron. The 1904 issue proclaimed the idea of a virtuous Negro woman as "absolutely inconceivable." She nurtured a deep hatred for that writer all these years and wondered if Daryl shared that same view.

"Don't ever touch me again. I don't want to go to Tony, but I will. Buy your wife one of those fake butts I've heard about, then maybe you'd like the whole woman. Just don't ever brush into me again, understand?" She wanted to tell Greg, but then asked herself what would he do? What could he do?

"What if I told you I like the whole River?"

"Then that would make it very hard for both of us to work here, Daryl."

In his mind's eye, he wonders if her tan body is the same color all over, unbroken by bathing suit tanning lines. He had hated it when she straightened her hair; he'd loved her afro. So many times, he'd fantasized about tangling his hands in its thickness. Was it as soft as it looked?

Yes, he wants to tell her how much he wants the whole River, especially that part that makes him curious about how she would be in bed, but instead he says, "Yes, Tony said we can hire somebody. As it turns out, my neighbor's daughter, Alpha, just moved back in with them and needs a job. She and Marla are friends, she's a smart girl." Marla is Daryl's terminally ill daughter.

"That's fine with me, Daryl. I'll just be glad to have someone to help me. She knows accounting?"

"No, but as an assistant, she doesn't need it, and like I said, Alpha's smart. It won't take us long to get her up to speed."

To get in the door I need a graduate degree and a contact; Alpha walks in knowing nothing, River thinks, as she locks the office to leave. Then she pushes away the hint of anger and reminds herself of what a good job she has, regardless of Daryl or Alpha.

The next morning Alpha is waiting outside River's office. She is personable and pretty, except for a hardness about her mouth. Her blonde hair falls long and straight. *Not a very nice figure,* River thinks as she unlocks her office, *a bit heavy with a rather straight body and heavy breasts.* River always wished for nicer breasts.

"Come on in, I'll make coffee." River studies her face and wonders if her blue eyes are tired or sad; they are flat, there is no light in them. "I should tell you, there'll be long hours, especially at first, during your training."

Alpha answers quickly, "Yeah, Daryl already told me. He said I could ride with him until I get a car." She sits in the chair next to River's desk, staring into her coffee cup with her hair hiding most of her face, and pauses before adding, "I don't like taking favors from men. I don't like favors from anybody really, but especially men."

River doesn't understand, and wonders if she is confiding in her, saying she'd rather not ride with Daryl? She studies her face, the part she can see, looking for an answer. "Well, maybe you can ride with me. We'll probably be working the same hours anyway, at least for a while."

River thinks Alpha smiles before she quickly says, "I'd like that. A lot."

"Fine, I'll pick you up Monday at eight o'clock." River wonders why Daryl is so eager to get a job for this woman who appears burdened and seems to have some reservations about him. From what she knows of Daryl, she feels trouble.

"Thanks, I'll be ready."

"Good, I'll see you then." River stands at her door and watches as Alpha, swinging her hair, leaves her office and walks quickly toward the elevator and Daryl, who River imagines has been lurking in the hall waiting for her. She thinks Alpha is very pretty, but her flat behind makes her look sort of like a block. Thinking back on Daryl's earlier comments, River fingers her hair, closes the door to her office, and is happy that she has an assistant, and a nice round butt. She wonders though, if her pageboy hairstyle is flattering.

While Daryl and River make plans for office modifications to make room for Alpha, he makes an exaggerated point of not going near River the remainder of the day. Before she leaves work, River drops the remodel request with the building superintendent, and even though she is glad the week is over, the thought of the walk to the car in Houston's heat and humidity makes her less eager to leave. Friday evening happy hour sounds good to her, so she picks up the telephone and calls the hospital where her friend Evaline works. No question, Evaline will be glad to meet her. They are on, five o'clock at the Side Door Bar.

River locks her office and goes to meet the heat she knows is just outside her door. She hopes the earlier rain shower will have cooled things off. She is wrong. The heat wraps her like a cocoon the minute she steps outside. It seems she can see steam rise from the concrete parking lot. River walks quickly through that natural sauna to her car.

"Houston!" she spits aloud as she cranks up the air. The car cools quickly, and she quietly thanks whoever invented permanent hair-relaxers, or her hair would be one tight, frizzy mess. One quick check at her reflection in the car mirror, as the air conditioning blows her straight pageboy away from her face, and she pulls onto the Gulf Freeway. Evaline's car isn't in the parking lot when she reaches the bar, but she hurries in. A chilled glass of Riesling in the cool darkness will make the wait easy.

≈The Side Door≈

River sits at the bar and watches the Friday evening traffic snake by over the Gulf Freeway and smiles when Evaline's yellow Chevy Z-28 pulls into the parking lot. They've been friends since the summer they both worked at River's sister's restaurant. The summer that River met Greg. There is something about Evaline that, at first glance, might hint she is gay, but that's never mattered to River. She liked her from the start. While she sips her wine, she thinks about the day she overheard customers in the restaurant joking about Evaline's corn-rowed hair, and how it didn't go with her high-yellow complexion. One couple was especially loud, and River was certain they intended for Evaline to hear.

"I'm keeping you away from her. I heard a dyke can take any man's woman," the man laughed, while he pulled the woman's chair closer to him.

Evaline returned from the kitchen and tried to pretend she hadn't heard him while she served their hamburgers. River called over to her loudly, "Ev, how'd you like to go to a movie after work?" River had only heard her speak of her family and some guy named Jim. She didn't think Evaline had many friends.

A smile played around her mouth and Evaline called back, "Sure girl, that'd be great!" Those many years ago, something more than gratitude blossomed in her heart for River.

"Hey girl!" Evaline's happy voice disturbs River's thoughts. "I can't believe I drove through all of that traffic, all the way from Galveston. And just 'cause you had a rough week." She smiles and gives River a quick kiss on the cheek.

"Thanks, Ev. Yeah, it's been one of those weeks. Let's find a table." They make their way to a quiet corner table and call for the waitress. "Greg's making it hard for me. Maybe I am just looking for a reason to leave, just like he says, I don't know. And Daryl, thankfully, is keeping his distance, and I am feeling better about that since we hired an assistant today. That should make things better in the office. Sometimes I think I should just forget about moving out and try and make things work with Greg, but it's all such a lie. There's just nothing between us. And I'm a little concerned about the assistant we hired, well, Daryl hired. Someone from his past, a neighbor's daughter who used to babysit his kids, he said. But there's something more to it, I think."

Evaline throws both her hands in the air. "Hey, hold on. Take a breath. Slo-o-o-ow down." She laughs loudly. "Why not take a couple of breaths, in fact? At this rate you will fall apart. Where's that waitress?" Evaline pushes her chair away from the table and stands, holding a hand in the air, a motion that strikes River as masculine. "Where the heck is that lady with our drinks? You sit here; I'll go and get them and be right back."

River watches as Evaline makes her way to the bar and is glad she hadn't made a big deal out of the night when Evaline had had too much to drink and stayed the night at their house.

Evaline had kissed her good night and missed her cheek, planting an open-mouth kiss on her lips before River turned away. River knew it had been intentional and had said nothing before she turned and walked away. It never happened again. She looks up from her thoughts as Evaline makes her way to the table, leading with her broad shoulders, carrying two glasses and a bottle of chilled Riesling.

"Last night I told Greg that I was getting my own place. We both cried." River's damp eyes hint that tears are close by. "I like being with him, as a friend. It feels safe, you know. He's a great guy. I just don't like making love with him. I feel so cheap, so unfair, saying sexy things, trying to make him hurry and get it over with. And I bet he knows what I'm doing."

"And I'll bet he doesn't care either," Evaline interrupts. "He's probably just glad to be with you. The man loves you, girl! Looks to me like you'd be happy with things the way they are."

"You think?"

"Yeah, I do. Look at your house; it's beautiful, nicest one on the street, and always a new car. You do just like you want. And Greg looks at you with love just dripping. What more could you want?" River thinks Evaline sounds annoyed. "Looks to me like you've got it all."

"Well, I don't know why all doesn't feel like so much."

"You know," Evaline continues, ignoring River's comment, "we black women could learn a lot from white women. Learn how to marry well, and then not to divorce ourselves into poverty. How many white women would be married to those black jocks if they weren't bringing in the big bucks?" She doesn't wait for her friend to answer, but rushes on, "Not many, I can tell you. Why is it so hard for black women to stop trying to take care of everything and let somebody take care of them for a change? And don't give me that 'it's in our DNA' crap!"

River smiles and refills her glass, surprised at her friend's impassioned insight. "And what happens, Ev, if there's nobody out there to take care of us? And anyway, how'd you get so smart about marrying well?"

"Well, it just makes sense to me, and I pay attention. You've got a great thing and you're thinking of ending it because you think the sex could be better. Give me a freaking break! You mean there's nothing about *that* in all those writings by Anna Cooper you're always reading?"

River's smile fades. "It's more than that, and you know it." Her voice is tight.

"I sure hope so. If anybody ought to know better than that sixty-minute black man shit, it ought to be black women. Have you guys tried doing it other ways? You know, maybe he needs to spend a little time before the real deal, you know, maybe do a little oral stuff."

"We almost tried that once. Greg stopped in the middle of it and asked me if I'd had a douche. Kind of killed the mood, you know." Their problem is much bigger than sex. River knows it. "I can't explain it, Ev. It just doesn't feel right anymore." For a minute River thinks about asking her friend how many any-minute men she's known and that's when she decides she's had enough to drink.

"Well River, unless you know exactly why you're leaving, I'd suggest you keep your easy life."

"Sounds pretty pathetic to me. If the only reason I stay is because I can buy things, makes me feel like I'm not a whole lot better than a prostitute."

Evaline is on a roll, eager to continue; she really doesn't want to see River do something that she clearly sees as a mistake.

51

"And you need to lighten up. Quit being so hard on yourself and just enjoy life. Stop this habit you have of analyzing every little thing to death. Always looking for perfection! Good Lord! You know what I think?" Again, she doesn't wait for an answer. "I think everybody prostitutes themselves a little bit, some way or another. We all put up with a little more of something we can do without to get a little more of something we'd rather not do without. That's the Ying and Yang of life. The give and take. It's called living, River."

River suddenly feels heavy, weighted down. "It's getting late, Ev, and you've got a long drive back to Galveston." She stands up and takes money from her purse, but Evaline stops her. Evaline always pays the check. The only way River can repay is to cook dinner for her, which she does often. River wonders if Evaline thinks men always should pay as she kisses her goodbye.

The rest of the weekend River and Greg don't discuss her plans to leave. She thinks a lot about what Evaline said and reads from Anna Cooper's *A Voice from the South by a Black Woman of the South*. When she reads where Cooper admonishes black women, saying, "Woman...your responsibility is one that might make the angels tremble...the regeneration...the retraining of the race...must be the black woman," (p62). She closes the pages and goes for a walk.

≈Adam≈

Monday comes and Alpha is standing on the porch of her parents' home when River turns in to pick her up. After hellos, the ten-minute ride to work is silent, both women sipping their coffee.

A folding table in one corner of River's office serves as Alpha's temporary work area until the office addition is finished. Just when she is about to call and see when the work will begin, the building superintendent taps at her door. River hardly hears a word he says; struck by the tall black man with him who is taking measurements. He is well over six feet, muscle-hard, and he moves with a slow swagger that triggers in her a long-forgotten sexual desire. The muscles in his back flex hard through the thick green cotton of his work shirt when he pushes a bookcase aside. River wants him to turn so she can get a look at his face, and when he does, she stares.

Through brown Elvis Presley lips, he says, "I need to move your desk for a minute." Then he smiles that sideways smile that she thought she had forgotten.

But nothing compares to his eyes; they slant downward at the outer edges, with lashes so long they seem to rest on his cheeks. They are Elvis' eyes, only they aren't blue. They are a brown you can almost see through.

"Mrs. Smith?"

River turns to the superintendent and wonders why he is talking so loudly.

"What? Yes!"

"This is Adam Jones. He'll be doing the work around here. Should be finished in a week or ten days at the most."

River finds her voice and responds, "Oh, that's fine. We can work around the repairs."

Adam finishes his measurements and slow-walks into River's office again. He looks like the Elvis of her youth, the one that hadn't deserved her. Through that same smile he tells her, "I'll open the office early, if you don't mind. I like to get a' early start. Is that alright?"

"Sure, fine," she stammers without looking at him. *This week is getting off to a strange start,* she thinks, and refuses to look in the office annex where he works the remainder of the day.

Adam is busy at work when River and Alpha arrive the next day. Over the next two weeks, Adam's presence fills the office where River and Alpha work, and River tries hard to avoid his eyes. They put her on edge, make her jumpy. The office modifications are just about finished, and the last morning of work rushes by. She is relieved Adam won't be spending so much time in her office after today. Again, Alpha leaves for lunch with Daryl, and as usual, River takes her lunch from the small refrigerator in the office and begins to eat at her desk. She is surprised to see Adam sauntering down the hallway toward her office, carrying a small Styrofoam cooler.

He smiles. "Okay if I eat in here? Kinda hot in my truck." He sits straddling a sawhorse that was left in the annex and starts to open the cooler.

"You know there *is* a lunch room on the first floor."

"Yep, used the microwave to heat this up." Adam glances at the two cellophane bags on River's desk, one holding crackers, the other some apple wedges. He smiles at her when she opens a small plastic container that smells like tuna. "Here, you need some real food." He pushes a partitioned Styrofoam plate at her. There is fried chicken and a mound of mashed potatoes awash in thick, brown gravy. In another section of the plate there looks to be collard greens with bacon and a cornbread muffin.

"You can eat all that, for lunch? And stay awake?" River laughs. "Thanks, but I think I'll pass."

"Suit yourself, but my mama can burn!" And as if to prove it, he attacks the food. River is surprised that he chews as fast as he does, all his other movements are slow and measured.

"Did you just move to Houston?" River spreads tuna from the plastic container on a wheat cracker and puts the whole thing into her mouth.

"Nope. Was in the Marines right outta school. In fact, just got back from Nam. This is home, and I'm staying with my folks over on Carver, just till I get situated." He nods toward her wedding ring. "How long you been hitched? Got kids?"

River is uncomfortable, as if they are talking about something they shouldn't be. "Not hitched, married for thirteen years." The thought of children brings a sudden surge of pain, so she says nothing more.

Silently, she calculates his age. "Enough about me, kind of old for staying with your folks, aren't you?" She notices he isn't wearing a wedding ring but knows that doesn't mean a lot.

"Like I said, till I get some things straightened out. No more than a few months, I hope."

He fixes her in his eyes, forcing her to meet them and when she does, she feels as if he is seeing some part of her that he shouldn't. She feels exposed and quickly looks away. She rebuttons the top button on her blouse that doesn't need it.

"How long were you in Vietnam?"

"Four years too long." He stops chewing and seems to drift to some other place. "A wasted four years if you ask me." He makes a snorting sound, as if he is trying to clear his nostrils, but it's a dry sound. River's calculation tells her that if he joined the Marines right after high school, he should be about twenty-one, ten years younger than she is. "Yes, I imagine even one day was too long."

He doesn't hear her at all and seems to be talking more to himself than to her. "Probably wasn't the best thing, signing up for that. I don't know if I'll ever get over some of the shit I saw over there and some of the things I did. The thing that surprised me more than anything—killing, you know, after the first time, can be the easiest thing in the world to do. Now that's some scary shit." He seems stuck in that other place, alone, vulnerable. The swaggering Adam is gone.

River wants to reach over and touch him, to bring him back from wherever he has drifted and wonders why he is telling her this. Softly, she brushes his arm. "Adam."

He stops talking, looks up from the food he's been staring at, and seems surprised to see River there. "Yeah, what'd you say?"

"I don't mean to pry, but why did you volunteer? You should've known that's where you'd be sent. I mean, that's one place everyone was running away from."

He doesn't answer, but slowly closes the flip-over top of the Styrofoam plate, still loaded with food. "Sometimes some of us don't have a lot of choices. Didn't have much else going for me at the time. I had to get away or me and my old man would'a come to a bad end." He takes a package of Kool cigarettes from

56

his pocket, lights one, and inhales deeply. River thinks of Greg, and the time Chief Manders, who had forced them out of business, called him a boy. She senses something in Adam, something in the set of his mouth, that would never allow anyone to call him a boy.

"What does that mean, Adam, what you said about your father? I don't understand." She studies his face, his eyes now hard and cold.

"Maybe you're just lucky, River. Maybe it's a lot a' stuff out there you wouldn't understand." He stands and heaves his plate of food into the trash bin next to the door. "I better get back to work. Can we finish this after work, maybe over a drink at the Side Door? Celebrate finishing the new office?" He smiles, and before she means to, she says yes. Just as quickly, she regrets it. Something doesn't feel right.

Alpha returns from lunch and hears River on the telephone. "Come on Evaline. It's Friday, and happy hour at the Side Door's always fun."

"I don't know, River. Anyway, why do you need company?"

"It'll be better with a group. I asked Jason and Vera to come, but I'm not sure about them. They don't seem to be getting along so well. Vallie Lynn can't come, and I'm not sure if Greg'll come."

"Glad to hear you asked him. And why wouldn't he? Especially if you mentioned the maintenance man would be there. I'm sure you did, didn't you?"

"I just said I was having drinks with some people from work." Alpha doesn't try and pretend she isn't trying to hear, casting frequent long glances in River's direction. River lowers her voice. "He said we need to be spending more time by ourselves. Trying to work things out."

"Makes perfect sense to me."

"Please, Ev."

"I guess so." Evaline is curious about this guy that River has told her a little about. "What time?"

"I'll be there as soon as I take Alpha home, probably a little after six."

Alpha is standing at River's desk when she hangs up the telephone. "I'm going, too. It sounds like fun. I can get Daryl to come and he'll take me home if you can't. I like going to black clubs—love the music."

The club is cool and dimly lit when River and Alpha walk in. They see Evaline standing by the bar and join her.

"Hi Ev, and thanks for coming. This is Alpha, the clerk we just hired."

Evaline kisses River on the cheek and shakes Alpha's hand. "Glad to meet 'cha."

"Daryl is coming. He'll take Alpha home. She wanted to come," River explains. Just then he walks in the door and River introduces Evaline.

Daryl seems uncomfortable, his eyes darting around. "Okay. We're here, so let's find a table." Just then they see Adam at a table, waving to them. They make their way over, and once again River introduces Evaline. Before they finish the first round of drinks, Greg enters the club with Jason, and after introducing himself and Jason, orders another round for everyone. He moves his chair next to River, between her and Adam. Greg is withdrawn, almost sullen, and is trying hard to make it clear to River that he is not pleased. She hopes he realizes that she is ignoring him. After the second round, Adam's earlier dark mood improves, and he's telling jokes that Greg seems to enjoy. Jason, seeming to enjoy Adam less, and after realizing Vera is not coming, kisses River goodbye and leaves early.

Above the loud music Alpha yells, "Come on Adam, let's dance." She doesn't wait for an answer, but instead leans over, her short, black skirt almost shows her underwear while her breasts strain against her pink blouse, grabs his hand, and pulls him from the table. They sway slowly to Al Green singing, "Let's Stay Together." River thinks the music doesn't require slow dancing or Alpha's frequent flips of her hair. Finally, holding hands, Adam and Alpha make their way back to the group after slow dancing to, "It Ain't No Fun to Me," another fast Al Green tune. River smooths her pageboy and thinks somebody in the place sure does like Al Green. She hasn't noticed Greg's repeated trips to the jukebox.

The evening ends and Adam, really in no shape to drive, leaves his truck locked in the parking lot and accepts Greg's offer to drive him home. He looks surprised when Greg says, "You can ride with me, Adam. River, you follow us. I don't want you driving home this late by yourself." He forgot that Greg and River had come in separate cars.

River follows Greg in her Audi and when they turn off the Gulf Freeway onto Carver Street, she wonders about the crumbling neighborhood. The house at the end of the unpaved street that Greg stops in front of can't be where Adam lives.

The big house, with flood lights shining on it, looks as if it has been added on to in pieces, and none of them really fit. Parts of the house are painted a yellowing white and other parts are varying shades of bare, weathered wood. Four cars, parked askew, litter the yard. She wonders if the several piles of lumber are for another addition to the puzzle. Then she sees the dogs, three of them, tied at various points across the yard, and hates the person responsible for that. They bark as Adam makes his way over a creaky narrow walkway that stretches over a deep, muddy ditch and stumbles inside. River, nestled inside the rich leather of her Audi, falls in behind Greg's truck and follows him back to Bay Area Boulevard. This is the life she knows—neat houses, neat lawns, and lives that appear just as neat.

≈The Big House≈

Adam staggers into the front room of the big, ugly house and drops down heavily on one of the sofas. Angry that he'd had that last drink, he wonders if River thinks he can't hold his liquor, and to make the whole damned thing worse, her husband plays the hero and drives him home. "Shit, I can drive myself," he mutters. "I do it all the damn time." It is after midnight, but the squeak of the opening bedroom door tells him his father is awake.

"Whatcha doing sittin' out here in the dark talkin to yoself, boy? Ya got a problem?" His father clicks on the overhead light. Adam sits in a large room full of clutter. Various tables and chairs, several pieces that look too nice to belong in the room, are placed between three unmatched sofas. Adam is sitting on the good sofa against a wall, that could have once been white, but now is almost beige. On that wall behind the sofa and arranged neatly are several large, framed, sepia-toned family photographs. In the largest photograph, Adam and his father, Harry, both dressed in suits and wearing ties, are seated. His mother, Mary, also wearing a suit, stands behind Harry, and their only daughter is sitting on the floor in front of her father, who has his arm draped around her shoulder. The two younger boys stand behind Adam's chair. Everyone wears smiles that look tight and untrue except the daughter, who has not attempted to smile but seems to be studying something on the floor. Harry's wife keeps the pictures neatly arranged, and the brass frames brightly polished.

"I'm fine, man," Adam slurs. "No problem. You need that light?"

His father shuffles barefoot through the room toward the kitchen. He stops, looks down at Adam, and sneers, "When you go learn? You ain't the man I am. You can't do nothin good as me." Then he laughs an ugly laugh. "Can't hold yo liquor neither, I see. And I mus' need tha damned light. I got it on, don't I?" Still grinning, the large man, wearing droopy boxer shorts and a dingy white undershirt that stretches over his protruding gut, continues his shuffle into the kitchen.

Adam sits there hating his father more than he's ever loved him. He is sure he beats his mother because there are times she doesn't come out of the bedroom for days. He wishes he could catch him hitting her; that he could know for sure, then he'd show him how it feels to be beat. The thing he hates most is that he is so much like him. Sick to his stomach, he heaves himself from the good sofa, but his father's voice stops him.

"Where ya going boy?"

He turns to see his father holding two cups of coffee. "To bed."

"Here, drink this." His father passes the cup of steaming coffee toward him. "You'll feel betta in tha mornin'." Adam plops back down, takes the cup, and thinks how so like his father this is. Just when you can no longer stand the sight of him, he does something nice. Then his evil disappears, just like magic, and love for him wells up in your heart so big it hurts. But no matter how much he loves him at times, he's never loved him enough to forgive the day when he had to leave home and join the Marines.

It was the last week of high school, his junior year, and he and two of his friends skipped school on Friday. The senior class always took off the last Friday before graduation and went to the beach in Galveston. He and his buddies wanted to be a part of it. The school secretary called Adam's house that morning, and his sister, Ruth Ann took the message. She had not wanted to tell her mother because she knew she'd tell their father and then something bad would happen. While she cleaned the kitchen, she had argued out loud to no one as she put the last chipped plate away. "Why does he always have to make Daddy mad?" She wished she had gone to school. Her menstrual cramps had not been that bad and maybe if the both of them hadn't been absent the school wouldn't have called. She dreaded it, but knew she had to tell them. Who could tell what her father would do if he found out she hadn't given them the message? Someone would pay, Harry would see to it, and that someone, she knew, was usually her mother. It was always her mother's fault, no matter what, and then she'd have to spend a day or two hidden away. As bad as what could happen to Adam, the girl knew it would be worse for her mother if she didn't tell him. She wanted to make things better for her mother, no matter what she had to do.

Ruth Ann's father started calling her "Angel" right about the time her breasts appeared and her body started to change. She felt sick from the memory; and like always she tried to swallow back tears when she wondered if her mother knew about her new name, but this time the tears won, broke through and fell into the cup she had just dried. She heard her mother's car pull into the yard and hurried to the front door to meet her. Glad that her father was in the backyard building something, she took the two larger bags from her mother.

"Mama, the school called today to check on me and Adam." The package of dried pinto beans dropped back into the grocery bag Mary was emptying and she sat down hard on one of the kitchen chairs.

Mary was a quiet, pretty woman, with beige skin, large, dark eyes, and shiny, curly hair. Her daughter, lost in her own depressing thoughts, barely heard her mother when she'd muttered, "Where's Harry? I have to tell him."

"Tell Harry what?" he'd asked, after slipping quietly in the back door and taking a sip from the half-empty bottle of gin before he'd put it back into his pants' pocket. His loud voice scared both Ruth Ann and her mother, causing Ruth Ann to drop the egg container. Still, she'd quickly spoken up.

"Nothing, Daddy. It ain't nothing. Is it, Mama?" Her eyes had pleaded with her mother. "I'll tell you later, Daddy." She'd given him the sweetest look she could.

"You be quiet, Angel!" he'd stormed.

"What is it, Mary?" Harry fixed his wife with the look she knew too well. She quickly turned away and stared at the floor. "I ain't gon ask you agin woman. What is it?"

The words tumbled out as her eyes filled with tears. "Adam didn't go to school today." Ruth Ann kept trying to pick up the broken eggs, but they roped through her fingers back onto the floor in a sticky mess where she sat.

Harry looked at the clock. It was already four-thirty. Adam usually got home around that time, and he knew better than to be too late. After thirty minutes, Harry, who after a quick trip to one of the outhouses in the back, had not moved from the kitchen table, stood and hurled the now empty gin bottle into the yard and met Adam gingerly stepping onto the porch. Too much to drink and the hot summer sun from a day at the beach slowed his steps.

"How was school today, boy?"

"Just like always." Adam sensed something bad was going to happen, and just as he turned to leave, the searing pain of the razor strap across his back brought blood and a muffled groan through his clenched teeth.

"When you go learn boy, you ain't smart enough ta lie ta me?"

Again, Harry brought the strap down, this time across Adam's chest since Adam had turned to face his father. Adam drew back his fist and hit him in the face with all his strength, causing Harry to fall backwards. The bedroom door flew open, and Mary ran out. Harry was having trouble getting up when Adam jumped over the porch rail and grabbed his father by his sweaty undershirt. His right fist was in the air, ready to come down on his father again when his mother grabbed it and held on.

"Don't do it son. He's your father. Please!"

"Well, I'm gon have to kill you now," Harry declared, pronouncing each word slowly, as he fought to push himself up from the ground.

"Don't do it man, let it go, let *me* go." Adam stood over his father with his fist still suspended in midair while he backed away from him.

Harry struggled up and still holding the strap over his head, took a stumbling, running leap toward Adam, pushing him back onto the porch, and swung the strap, barely missing Adam's face. Adam wrestled the strap from his father. They were partly on the living room floor now, the weight of the two of them had torn the screen door from its hinges, and it lay on the floor beneath them.

"Please Harry, please." Mary thought she was screaming as she grabbed for her husband, but her voice was little more than a raspy whisper. Ruth Ann, locked in the bathroom, checked the lock on the door again, just to be sure, and clamped her hands harder over her ears.

Mary kept grabbing at her husband the whole time, and each time he simply flicked her away as if she were an irritating insect. Then slowly, he turned to her, and with a calmness that belied his madness said, "If you touch me, jes' one mo time, jes' one mo, I'll go inside, git my gun, and kill every fucking body here."

Mary backed away and mumbled a prayer. "Please God, let it be them, let them hurry. Let them hurry please." Then Harry, having wrestled Adam down and with his fist in midair, froze when the distinct sound of a gun being cocked rescued him from insanity. The policeman's gun gleamed brightly as the bright sun reflected off it. Harry's eyes followed the bright object to the policeman who aimed it cocked and ready at him.

"Get down here! *Right now!* Like I said."

Harry was confused. He hadn't heard the sirens or seen the officers enter his yard. Adam, bruised and bleeding, and without looking at anyone, stepped down from the porch and walked blindly away. Tears streamed down his face as he made his way through the crowd of neighbors who stood silently at the edge of the yard, seeming to respect some invisible fence erected by Harry Jones.

Harry's eyes glinted at Mary when he heard the policemen ask her if she wanted to press any kind of charges. She whispered, "No." Adam's mother's voice had not been much louder when she'd called to her son, pleading with him not to leave. He never looked back. It would be the last time, he vowed, he would ever cry. It was the last time any of them would see him for four years.

Furious, and through eyes he could barely focus, Harry looked at his wife, but Mary was numb to what that look meant. She had lived through its pain many times before, beginning only days after she married him at fifteen. But this was her family, and Mary Jones needed a family; she lived to keep her family together. She had never known her father and had barely known her mother who had been too young to have ten children. Her mother had partied more than she had mothered.

His father brings Adam back from that awful day when he takes the empty cup from his hand and tells him, "Gon' to bed, boy; sleep it off. You'll feel betta in tha mornin'."

Adam sits there for a few minutes more, remembering the letter from Ruth Ann, telling him their mother's right eye had never opened completely again after that day.

Monday can't come soon enough for Adam, anxious for lunch with River as he hurries, with his Styrofoam cooler, along the corridor to her office. He had noticed her jealousy when he danced with Alpha at happy hour and had pulled Alpha extra close when he saw River looking at them. Adam's steps slow when he sees the door to River's office is closed. He pushes the door hard and is surprised to find it locked since he knows River is at work; he saw her car in the parking lot. Then, when he finds her office locked again on Tuesday, he knows for certain she is avoiding him. That evening River sees Adam leaning against her car in the parking lot. "Damn." She knew she would have to talk to him eventually, but hoped it wouldn't be so soon.

"Hey Adam." Her voice is light and airy, sounding as if

nothing is wrong, but she avoids looking at him while busily searching for her car keys.

"What's the deal, River? Is lunchtime over for us?"

"I can't do this, Adam. I've got a marriage to work on. Don't make it hard for me." River keeps fumbling in her purse for her keys and cursing herself for not already having them in her hand. She could have avoided this, or at least shortened it.

"That's just what I mean to do, make it hard as I can. It's something good going on between you and me. And you want me, like I want you, and I know it."

"Adam, move!" She reaches for the lock, but he doesn't budge from blocking the locked car door and fixes her in his eyes. She warms and looks away. They stand in silence for a few minutes, and then he steps aside, smiles, and whispers, "I got time, River, I got all the time it takes." The warmth she feels spreads deeper and she slams the car door hard against it, and vows to avoid him at any cost. The week passes, and she only sees him at a distance a couple of times. Shortly after getting home from work on Friday evening, she can't believe her eyes when she answers the front door and finds Adam standing there.

"W-h-a-a-a-a-a-t?" she is finally able to stammer.

Adam smiles sideways and snorts dryly. "Hey River. Is Greg here?"

"Well yes, but..." She hears Greg coming down the stairs.

"Hey man. Come on in," Greg calls out. River stares at Greg, looking for answers.

"Oh, I forgot to tell you. The other night Adam gave me his number, offered to help me finish the garage. So, I took him up on it. I can sure use the help." When they bought the house, the detached garage had not been drywalled and painted. It was a project Greg kept postponing.

"Oh," was all River said. That evening at dinner, she asks Greg if he called Adam or Adam called him. Greg finishes slow chewing and without looking up mutters, "Why? What difference does it make?"

She whispers, rearranging the food on her plate, "None, I guess."

Adam is there every Saturday for the next several weeks and River finds it easier each weekend to need something from the garage. The friendship that formed between Greg and Adam troubled River. They had so little in common. "Maybe Greg feels I'm safe from Adam if the two of them are friends," she mentions to Evaline and Vallie Lynn. If anything, it makes matters worse, for even though Adam is in the maintenance department at her building, she can always find a way to avoid him. This isn't so easy to do when he stops in to visit with Greg. She wishes Greg had not brought Adam into their home.

≈River's Townhouse≈

Two months after the happy hour gathering at the Side Door Bar, Greg is ordained as a minister at the church with the black Jesus painted above the baptismal bay. One month later, Adam helps Greg move River into her townhouse in Clear Lake. When Greg brings in the last box, he kisses her on the forehead. "I'm better now than when I met you, River. Be happy." Then he throws himself into his religion to help himself deal with their breakup, not as sure as River was that they were right to end their marriage.

She looks around her new home and loves it. The exterior living room walls are formed by windows, except for the brick fireplace wall. River is happiest when there are trees and water around, and here she has both. The houses are arranged around one side of a man-made lake that surrounds a small treed island, just big enough for the gleaming white gazebo built there. The gazebo is only for looking at since the lake is too shallow for boating or serious swimming. A thicket of pine and oak trees are the backdrop for the lake. Mature trees were transplanted between the homes and along the drive leading into the subdivision, buffering it from traffic noise. River looks out at the lake with its inviting gazebo and a calmness settles over her. The lake and gazebo view, through walls of windows, pours into the room, following her from the living room to the dining room, and upstairs to her bedroom.

River has already bought the paint and can hardly wait to see the walls in her new home transform from white to a soft "apricot soufflé." The polished wood floors will remain bare, except for the bedrooms, soon to be covered with "Iced Shrimp" carpeting, warm and cool at the same time. Anxious to see it all come together, she promises herself she will take her time and enjoy creating the first home—all hers. Boxes are scattered everywhere, and she wonders which one holds bed linens since sleep beckons. It has been a long and emotional day. Just as she locates the box labeled bedclothes, the doorbell rings. Looking down from the bedroom window, she isn't surprised to see Adam's truck. He wears that sideways smile when she opens the door.

"Hi, I came back to see if I can help you get settled in." He's been drinking. *It seems*, she thinks, *he is always drinking.*

"No, I'm really too tired. It's getting late. Thanks though."

"I know you need that icemaker hooked up. It won't take long."

He pushes the door open and steps around her, putting down his toolbox. His habit of coming by without calling had become the norm after he and Greg became friendly, and it annoyed River. Her mother had never allowed that when she and her siblings were growing up, especially after they got a telephone.

"Okay, if it won't take too long. Adam, why didn't you tell me you were coming back?" Her words follow his back into the kitchen. She glances at the lightweight jacket he carefully places across the banister and wonders why he is wearing a jacket. It's July and ninety degrees outside.

"I thought we got over that, and anyway, I didn't know if your phone works yet. And besides, I'm here now."

"That's not the point. It's just not the way I want it! It's not the way it's supposed to be. No one should just drop by without calling!" She locks the door and goes into the kitchen to find him already under the sink, lying on his back. The top half of him is hidden while he twists and grunts as he works. He has on tight black jeans and a red knit shirt. River is aroused and embarrassed by the outline of his penis. She immediately wishes he would hurry and leave.

Sexual thoughts naturally mean thoughts of Greg. He was her first and only partner. For the first few years she and Greg were married, she thought what she'd experienced with him was all there was. Magazines, she ultimately read, that told of orgasms some women achieved had caused her to wonder if it was true, and if so, why she never knew that with her husband. Then, accidentally, she brought herself to orgasm one night after Greg, lying in satisfied sleep next to her, had brought her almost there. She'd looked to make sure her movements and soft moans of satisfaction hadn't awakened him.

She watches Adam as he wrestles with the icemaker and wants him like she had never wanted Greg, or any man. Her fantasies take flight, and she wants him to leave so she can do what she's become so good at doing.

"Why do I think of making love to him, just watching him walk?" she'd once asked Vallie Lynn.

"Hand me another pair of pliers outta my toolbox."

River jumps, breaking a glass, and water scatters across the floor. The pliers are lying on the top shelf of the toolbox and when she steadies her hand and gives him the pliers, she is surprised. Adam's hands are only slightly larger than hers; River wonders how she could have imagined the largeness of his hands every time she'd seen him before.

"Why you so skiddish 'round me, River?" Adam laughs, sliding out from under the sink. He helps pick up the broken glass.

"I'm not nervous, Adam. You just surprised me, that's all." River walks quickly from the kitchen.

"Where you going?"

She stands in the foyer waiting to let him out. "It's getting late, Adam. I just want to have a bath and get to bed." Immediately, she wishes she hadn't tried to explain.

"I thought, if your phone is working, maybe we can order pizza to go with this." He makes a big production as he slowly removes his jacket from the banister and then, when he reaches inside, presents a bottle of chilled Schlink Haus Spatlese wine with great flourish. *How did he know?* she wonders. The only time she remembered drinking with him was at happy hour almost a year ago. He seemed to be enjoying dancing with Alpha too much to pay attention to what she was drinking. A smile spreads across her face while she leaves to put the wine in the refrigerator.

"Okay, the phone is working, you order the pizza and I'll be down in a few minutes." She needs to get away from him. "It's too soon," she tells herself, "just a few minutes to collect myself." River knows it's only a matter of time before she and Adam make love, just not now. Something about taking this where it has always seemed to be headed scares River; it always has.

She races upstairs and busies herself, spreading the sheets on the bed, leaving him downstairs cleaning the floor and putting away his tools. She almost finishes the bed and waits upstairs until the pizza gets there when she hears his footsteps on the stairs. She quickly leaves the bedroom and meets him at the top of the stairs. Her heart is beating so hard and fast she is certain she hears it and wonders if he does. *Why fight it?* she wonders.

"I'm finished up here," she trembles.

He takes her hand and holds it briefly before she pulls away and heads downstairs. "What is taking the pizza delivery so long?" Then the doorbell rings.

They sit on the floor in the dining room and finish the last of the pizza and wine. Adam has eaten almost the whole thing himself; River has a hard time forcing down one slice. After her third glass of wine and feeling tingly, she lets him force her onto the floor next to him where they look out at the moonlit lake with the little white gazebo.

"I bet it looks better with the light off."

He reaches over and turns off the lamp there on the floor. Through the wall of windows, the full moon sends a beam of light into the room. River, relaxed from the wine, folds into Adam's arms as he pulls her to him. It feels natural and easy, being close to him. She likes his muscles, his bigness. He looks down at her, and she feels a warmness settle deep inside her. Adam touches her face, softly tracing her nose, her eyes, and her lips with his finger. His wet lips kiss her forehead and then travel down her body, undressing her as he goes. She tries to help him, but he won't let her. His mouth is warm and soft, and he lingers as he kisses her in her most private places.

"I been waiting a long time for this," he whispers in a voice thickened by desire. River looks down at his face, dark with emotion, and all she wants is him. She feels her body begin to reach for him, and she almost peaks, but he stops, allowing her to retreat from orgasm. Her hand goes down to do what has become natural when he gently takes it away. "Let me baby, just let me," his voice deep and guttural, arouses her even more. Once again, he brings her to the beginning of orgasm, and there again he stops, resting his head on her stomach.

"Not again," she whispers, "please, not again."

Slowly, he pulls his heavy body atop her and whispers into her ear, his words wrapped in his hot, wet breath, "This is your night, baby." He makes love to her slow and long, just as she'd imagined he would. Her voice sounds foreign to her as moans she can't control grow louder, sounding as if some animal has crept into the room with them, and she is glad he covers her mouth with his, quieting what surely would have been a primal scream. She lays there in his arms, contemplating the lake, the gazebo, and the moon, and wonders how many other women are thirty-three before experiencing their first shared orgasm.

≈Alpha's Training is Over≈

Alpha, as usual, is there at the curb when River's Audi turns the corner onto her street. "Been waiting long?" she asks as Alpha settles into the seat.

"No, it's fine, I like mornings. The only cool part of the day." Alpha has taken well to her job and both River and Daryl are happy with her progress.

"So, you and Daryl report to Tony, right?" River studies her face and wonders where this conversation is headed.

"Well, yes. Why do you ask?"

"Well, do I report to you or Daryl?"

"We haven't discussed it. We're not that structured, Alpha. Probably me. Why?"

"No reason. That's good though, I always get along better with women."

River's curiosity changes to concern. She wonders if something has happened between Alpha and Daryl. In the beginning his visits to their office had increased with Alpha's arrival, but now he seldom comes to the office. And recently, Alpha's moods seem to change almost hourly rather than daily.

"Do you go out much, Alpha? Do any of your old friends know you're back? Maybe an old boyfriend?"

"No," is all she says. Then she turns her back to River and stares out the window at the cars sharing the Gulf Freeway with them. The remainder of the drive to work is silent, except for George Duke playing "Peace" on the radio.

The day is almost over, and Alpha smiles a third hello when Adam stops by the office. River is sure it's Alpha's short dresses that were responsible for Daryl's increased visits and she thinks it's probably the same for Adam. Daryl walks into the office as Adam is finishing some measurements before leaving, and River notices that Alpha doesn't smile so quickly for him.

"Are you ladies ready for tonight?" Daryl asks, looking directly at Alpha.

"I guess." She smirks.

Tony's Bistro has grown from three to five restaurants and Alpha is assigned two. Daryl is clearly her champion and she has learned quickly. Tony and Daryl invited River and Alpha out to dinner to celebrate Alpha's one-year anniversary.

"We'll meet you guys at six."

"See you there," River tells Daryl, with hopes the evening will be a short one.

The wine before dinner relaxes everyone, and Alpha's mood improves greatly. She removes the pink eyelet jacket and reveals a low-cut black dinner dress. River knows the dress is short without needing to look.

"You like?" she leans in and asks Daryl and Tony, giving them both long looks.

"Yeah, it's nice," Daryl grins.

Tony seems as embarrassed by the question as River is. "It's pretty. You and River both look very nice."

River is glad to see that Alpha flirts with all men, not only Adam. She makes a mental note to talk to her tomorrow concerning her inappropriate behavior. River sees Alpha as two totally different women. She is hot or cold, more often cold. Some part of her wants, or maybe even needs, to know men want her, and she seems to always be hard at work getting their attention. Then she either laughs at them or hates them for wanting her. River calls it Alpha's little cat and mouse game she's seen her play with Daryl. Tonight, she is playing this game again and River doesn't know what to make of it, especially with Tony being there. In the beginning Alpha had seemed relieved she didn't have to ride to work with Daryl. But then she seemed pleased when he stopped by the office and had lunch with him almost daily. River wonders what changed when Alpha seemed to cool, and Daryl stopped coming by the office completely. Alpha disturbs her thoughts when she raises her glass to River and announces as they end dinner, "I'm a real employee now and I just signed a lease on my apartment Saturday."

"That's great. Where is it?"

"It's really close to where you live," she answers. "Now you won't have to drive so far to pick me up. And I'm going to start paying for gas, too, since I got a raise. I'll probably be getting a car pretty soon." She smiles in Daryl's direction.

~ ~ ~

Alpha barely settles into her apartment before inviting River and Adam to dinner, "For all those times you've fed me," she smiles. With no way to refuse, River accepts the Thursday invitation and tells Alpha it will have to be an early night, determined to find a way to limit the time she and Adam spend with her.

River selects a chardonnay from the wine rack and puts it in the refrigerator to chill. The front door slams and she winces, which announces Adam is downstairs. He is almost living there now. She calls down to him that he needs to hurry and change for dinner. River is finishing her makeup when he walks into the bedroom. *A pretty woman*, he thinks, realizing how lucky he is to have her. He knows there are plenty of men who are a lot better off, and a hell of a lot smarter than he is, who would be glad to take his place. *Hell, Greg's just waiting in the wings for me to fuck up*, he thinks. He tries to ignore that River's brother has not spoken one word to him on the few occasions they were together. Ernest, a man of few words naturally, found no reason to get to know this guy who, to his thinking, is clearly beneath his sister.

"Hey pretty lady." Adam smiles while softly swatting her behind. "You know I ain't too big on these social things."

"Don't start, Adam. I've put this off twice before. We have to go." She fastens her earrings and starts to leave the room. "And please, stop saying ain't."

"Okay, okay, gimme a break. I hope you see I'm trying, don't want to mess up."

"Don't worry. It's not a formal dinner. Use the utensils from the outside in, don't make that sucking noise with your teeth, and you'll be just fine."

She smiles, and he feels better. *She has the best smile in the world*, he thinks, and hurries to get dressed while she goes downstairs to wait for him. The wine is wrapped, and River is waiting at the door when she smells Adam's cologne before he comes down the steps. "Something else I need to work on," she whispers, "too much cologne." They walk the six blocks to Alpha's apartment.

Alpha is a vision in pink when she opens the door. The pink lounge gown she wears is cut low and displays her ample cleavage. River wishes she'd worn something other than the dark brown dress with the draped neck. It makes her look like a nun, she knows, compared to Alpha in all pink. Pink skin, pink gown, pink lipstick, and a pink ribbon holding back blonde hair that River swears looks pink in the candlelight. Instinctively, River's hand goes up to check her pageboy and finds every straightened and slightly turned-under hair is firmly in place. She feels a bit better.

"Come on in." Alpha takes the wine and kisses both River and Adam on the cheek.

River takes two steps inside the room and stops in her tracks, unable to believe the apartment is furnished so completely and expensively. Alpha floats into the room, bringing wine with fruit, cheese, and crackers arranged on a tray.

"Let's start with this. Dinner's almost ready," she beams. River has often given serious thought to Alpha's frequent and extreme mood swings but has rarely seen her as frenzied as she is tonight. It doesn't help River's mood when it becomes clear that Adam will be the only man here tonight.

"Okay Alpha, you've been back in Houston for more than a year. I'm just gonna have to fix you up with a guy," River tries to joke.

"No time for a guy, River. I've been so busy at work."

"Well, now that you've learned the office, maybe you'll start getting out more?"

"Maybe," she answers as she leans over and slowly refills Adam's glass, her ample breasts threatening to spill from her dress.

Alpha's just being Alpha, River tells herself. She becomes more concerned with Adam's drinking. *We've been here less than thirty minutes, and he is on his third drink.* Finally, she is ready to accept that he needs help, that his drinking is a serious problem. She promises herself they will talk about it tomorrow.

"Dinner is ready! Let's eat," Alpha announces with a flourish, raising both her arms in the air before she leads River and Adam to the smoked glass and chrome dining table. Boiled whole new potatoes, carrots, and short cobs of corn surround three steaming whole lobsters. Alpha finishes the table with salad, melted butter, and hot, crusty bread.

"This really is great, Alpha!" River thinks it is nice for her to make such an effort. She had expected something much simpler for a weeknight.

Glad when the evening is over and relieved when Alpha tells her she doesn't need to pick her up anymore since she's bought Daryl's wife's old car, River makes her way to the door. For the third time, and trying hard to hide her anger, she tells Adam they have to go, glaring at him as he slowly drains his glass and staggers to the door. River kisses Alpha good night and considers the amount of money she's recently spent, the apartment lease, the furniture, and now the car. Then she is brought back to the more immediate problem of Adam and his drinking. She watches him having a very hard time walking back to the townhouse, and River thinks it serves him right. *Why does he always have to drink so much?*

"We'll definitely have a long talk tomorrow," he hears her say as he struggles to make the six blocks home. *Fuck her*, he thinks, *and the horse she rode in on.*

"When you started being a damned matchmaker, River?" he mumbles as he stumbles, almost falling.

81

≈Tomorrow's Revelation≈

The sun streams into the bedroom and awakens River before the radio clicks on. She knows it will be hard to shake Adam awake, as it always is after he drinks. She studies his face as he sleeps, he looks peaceful, and River thinks the only time he ever really seems at peace is when he is asleep. She knows some of the demons that drive his drinking and wonders what she can do to help. Not a subject to begin while getting ready for work she thinks, and then she says softly, "Tonight, for sure. Tonight, we'll talk." Again, she shakes him, hard this time, but he doesn't respond. River sits on the edge of the bed and looks around her room. Things seem out of place and she feels that all too familiar feeling of something bad lurking around a corner, a feeling she's had much too often since she's known Adam.

River's bedroom suits her, and she wishes that she could spend the day here alone. She walks around the room, taking it all in. It is soft and quiet in hues of apricot and peach, a place where Adam's snoring does not belong. The morning sun slips through the deeply pleated sheers, casting a warm glow. A brass headboard almost reaches the ceiling and dominates the room. On the bedside tables are very large, matching, brass lamps. Beyond the brass footboard, half as tall as the headboard, is a wall of custom cabinetry with open shelves that Adam built. *He can build anything*, she muses. Doors with brass pulls hide the television and stereo. River has filled the wall unit with her most treasured volumes, as well as the art objects she's collected over the years. Suddenly, while she studies the volumes on the bookshelves: *Song of Solomon, The Ways of White Folks, Mozart*, the complete Zora Neale Hurston collection, River realizes she's never seen Adam read anything, not even the sports section of the newspaper.

For the third time, she shakes him, hard. "You better get up or you'll be late." He stirs a little and reaches for her without opening his eyes. It would be easy for her to fall into bed beside him, in bed is always good for them. Only a sad life, going nowhere, can be spent in bed, she tells herself.

She pulls away from him and heads for the shower. Just as she's covered her body with gardenia-scented bath gel, Adam pulls back the shower curtain and steps in, shoving his hardness into her back. She reaches for the towel bar, but Adam lifts her from her feet and pulls her to him. He gently kisses her behind her knee. Then he kisses the bottom of her foot. She's never been kissed there, and she doesn't want to leave lovemaking, the only place where she and Adam seem to be safe. It seems to her that sex is all she and Adam share that is good. She forces herself out of the shower, and tries not to think of Anna Julia Cooper, whose writings inspire and challenge her. Today those words force her from the shower when she recalls how Anna wrote that sexual love had become the one sensation giving "movement and vim" to the life she was leading. Then she remembers that Anna also wrote that it had not been enough.

The fogged mirror clears, and River's soaked hair drips on her shoulders, she didn't realize her shower cap had come off. "Damn." Since she's permanently relaxed her hair, it's easier to style than when she had to press it to make it straight. Still, it takes some time, and now this means she is going to be late for work. She wishes for her afro, just wash and go.

"Oh well, it's Friday," she mutters.

Rushing into her office, River opens the door and is surprised to see Alpha at her desk, updating a spreadsheet. "What happened, too much wine last night? Or did something, or somebody, keep you up?" Alpha's smile doesn't spread quite enough to be real, River thinks.

"No." River looks away quickly; uncomfortable with what she knows Alpha is thinking. "Just couldn't get it together. We had a nice time last night, and dinner was great. Although, I can't believe all your furniture. Your place really looks nice." She puts on the coffee and looks hard at Alpha.

Alpha's smile disappears, her face goes blank, and she doesn't answer. River takes two coffee mugs from the cabinet and continues as Alpha goes about her work. "I like to do one room at a time. Not so many bills to pay. But it must be nice to have everything done, nothing left but the bill to pay."

That tight smile returns, and Alpha says, "It's not mine to pay. It's Daryl's, so I did the whole apartment. You know, strike while the iron is hot." Then the tight smile grows into a grin.

River isn't sure that she understands, at least she hopes she doesn't. "What? You mean it's not your furniture? It's Daryl's?"

"No, it's mine." Alpha finally looks up at River who is standing at her desk and repeats, "It's mine; Daryl's just paying for it." Then another cold, hard grin troubles her face and scares River.

River reaches and pulls a chair closer to Alpha. She sits down close to her.

"Daryl is married with children. One who's seriously ill," she whispers.

"I know that. You know I know that." Alpha doesn't soften her voice or restrain her grin.

"You're friends with his wife, his daughter." River's head is beginning to ache. She massages her temples. Alpha continues to add numbers to the spreadsheet. "I hope you don't mean what I think you mean. Do you Alpha?"

Alpha looks up from her work, glares at River, and says, "It means one thing. He's paying for my furniture." Alpha appears thoughtful, and then almost laughing says, "He's not even that good in bed. Been after me since I was a teenager, and he's not even good at it." Then she laughs out loud.

River looks at Alpha, as if she is seeing her for the first time, searching for the right words to say. "I don't believe this," she mutters.

"And guess what?" Alpha's amusement seems to grow. "He balls with his socks on." Then she laughs and says loudly, "Quick Draw McGraw Daryl!"

"Alpha, don't do this. Don't get involved in this, please."

Alpha grows silent, stone faced. She wipes tears from her eyes that have gathered there from her uncontrollable laughter.

"Think about his kids. His wife. Tony'll probably fire him if he finds out." River's voice rises, unintentionally. "You don't need this kind of thing. And at work, too. God, Alpha, you're friends with his whole family!" River continues, talking to herself as much as to Alpha. "I can't believe he'd do this to his wife. And his poor daughter. How can he do this to them? Alpha, you don't need this kind of problem."

Alpha, still wiping at her eyes with the back of her hand, fixes River with steel-blue eyes, and calmly says, "I don't have a problem. It's his wife, his children, and his job. Sounds to me like it's his problem." She flips her long blonde hair around and starts to leave River's office. Then she turns back to River and says, "And I can always get another job."

River has a real headache now. "I can't believe he's doing this," Alpha hears her say, and angrily whips her head around to glare at River.

"Grow up, River! Quit being such a goody two-shoes. He's just like any other man who'll do whatever he thinks he can get away with. A man will do just about anything with just about anybody!"

"He's such a fool." River continues to talk to herself, having given up on rubbing away the headache.

Alpha ignores River. "I've got the receipt, too, with his signature on it. If he tries not to pay, then I've got news for him."

"You've got the receipt?" This is beyond River's understanding. What a fool, she thinks. He must think Alpha really cares for him, and she couldn't care if he lives or dies.

Alpha stands at the door to River's office. "Yep, I took it while he was sleeping. Three minutes and he's snoring. It just pisses me off, how easy it is for men." One final, hard flip of her hair and she closes the door behind her.

River stands up and slowly rolls her chair back to her desk. While she looks for Excedrin, she wonders how someone so young has become so hard and tries to recall anything Alpha has told her about her family. Her father had divorced her mother and married the woman with whom he was having an affair. River remembers thinking that Alpha hadn't forgiven him for that. She tries to remember if she'd ever heard Alpha say anything good about anybody in her family and realizes she has not.

In Alpha's eyes, her mother is "a weak fool, who lets men walk all over her like she is steps." Her mother's new husband is "a snake, who will screw a hole in the ground." The nicest thing River can recall she's ever said about anyone in her family is that her stepmother "knows how to use what she's got to get what she wants." River is certain that was not intended as a compliment.

Alpha's changed attitude now makes sense to River. She thinks back on several times when Alpha's behavior bordered on, if not subordination, then certainly, rudeness. Daryl, by becoming involved with Alpha, has created an impossible work environment. River feels things coming undone. That distant sense of doom seems to be edging nearer than ever before. River wants to talk to someone about it, someone to help her sort it all out. Tony is out; she knows he sees her as someone who can take care of problems, not a complainer. Then she thinks of Greg, and it doesn't seem strange to her at all that not once did she consider Adam. Instead, she decides to call her sister. She can always depend on Vallie Lynn.

≈A Quiet Time≈

The next few months are quiet, and even though Adam seems to be drinking very little, River still feels as if she is performing a balancing act that is about to collapse, juggling Adam, Alpha, and Daryl who, at any moment, will come crashing down on her. She and Alpha settle into a relationship that, while not as friendly as before, still pretends to be. *Maybe*, River thinks, *I can help her*. They spend a few of their lunch hours shopping after grabbing a quick sandwich, but no longer is there the occasional movie. Adam seems to be winning the battle with whatever he is fighting and is drinking less or hiding it better. Still she wonders why Adam has only been out twice in the last month when, at least, twice a week out with the guys had been his previous habit. Another change in his behavior that confuses her is his infrequent visits to her office, telling her he is just busy when she asks. *It's better*, River thinks, *less distractions for everybody*.

It has been the best month in several, and tonight, River is preparing for tomorrow's club meeting. Although she and Adam are getting along well, marrying him doesn't seem the right thing to do, despite his almost weekly proposals. Neither does she want to keep living with him. Her parents are not happy about that. This is not something she wants to talk to Vallie Lynn about. She knows her sister doesn't care for Adam. In fact, no one in her family even pretends to understand why she is with him, so River decides to call Evaline. The Bayou Ladies Social and Charity Club will be voting on Evaline's nomination for membership at tomorrow's meeting, and even though River will see her the next night at club meeting, she decides to give her a call.

Glad she answers, River says, "Hi girl, you ready for tomorrow night?"

"I can't believe I let you talk me into this."

"What? You make it sound awful."

Evaline intentionally sighs heavily into the phone. "I'm not too excited about being looked over. What if I don't pass muster?"

"Come on, Ev. It's not like that, and you know it. And we really can use your computer skills."

"No, I don't know! It just feels uncomfortable, being sized up."

"They're really a nice group of ladies. If you feel uncomfortable, I promise never to ask you again." River sees no need to tell her friend that her light complexion, along with being great with computers, just about assures her acceptance. River is least proud of her club's past history of the brown-bag rule. That rule, if unspoken, still seems to be in place if you look at the members in River's chapter. None of them have complexions darker than a brown grocery bag. River fingers her hair.

Evaline sighs louder. "Okay, I wish I could say no to you."

River smiles and kisses into the phone. "Why don't you come over? I could use a little help getting ready for tomorrow."

"Can't. A couple of us are meeting the new doctor for drinks. Remember the doctor I told you about, Dr. Small? We're getting together at the San Luis tonight. She should be leaving the hospital around seven o'clock, so we'll meet a little after that. Why don't you come?"

"Oh yes, the ob-gyn doctor, I remember you telling me about her. How's she fitting in?"

You couldn't miss the pride in Evaline's voice. "Everybody's really impressed. Our first black doctor at County, and a woman. It's great, girl! I hear she's talking about opening a clinic for women on the west end!"

"I'd better take a rain check this time. I've got a lot to do around here. But tell her I'm looking forward to meeting her."

"Will do, and I promise to try and get there early tomorrow, okay?"

River smiles and thinks how excited Evaline was when they hired the first black doctor at the hospital where she works. "And it's a she," she beamed. Evaline had invited River over to meet her and the doctor for drinks once before. River, not too fond of the drive over the causeway, especially at night, agreed to meet them whenever they were going to be in Houston. For River, Galveston has not quite lived up to its potential to be the exciting and thriving tourist town she thinks it should be. River hangs up the telephone and adds creole marinade to the fresh, pink turkey breasts. Club meeting will be fun; it is always fun.

While she gets ready for club meeting she feels better since she has something other than Alpha and Daryl's affair, or what to do about Adam and his drinking, to think about.

"Oh well," she murmurs. "Things are getting a little better." With the recent change in Adam, River hopes, maybe, she is right about him. She sees in him the man he can be, the man she wants him to be, the man she needs him to be.

≈Club Meeting≈

R iver smiles at the sparkling table in her dining room and goes to answer the doorbell, hoping it will be Evaline, but knowing it will be Sue, the club president. An uneasiness about Adam's whereabouts nags River, but she forces it away. He'd said he would just stay upstairs and watch television during the meeting, but he isn't home. Both his truck and motorcycle are in the garage. Out drinking again with his buddies, or worse, with his father, she worries. She has a deep dislike for Adam's father and the hold he seems to have on him.

River answers the door, and Sue, always with an air of purpose about her, sweeps through the door. "It's beautiful!" she exclaims as she looks around the softly lit room. "And, oh my goodness, it smells so good."

"Thanks, Sue." River is glad she decided against having the party catered, choosing instead to serve her fried turkey breast.

"They won't miss one slice." Sue smiles as she takes a thin slice of the fried breast from the bone china platter and finishes it off in one bite. She'd forced River to share her secret of marinating the turkey overnight in creole seasonings before frying it in peanut oil.

The missing slice doesn't disturb the platter, which is flanked by potato salad on one side and cold green bean salad on the other, each served in matching crystal bowls. The china, crystal, and stemware are banded with gold, and River has placed golden flatware in its caddy on the table. Even though the fragrant seasoning of the fried turkey hangs heavily in the room, the scent of cayenne pepper tickling her nose, Sue can smell there will be sweet potato pie for dessert.

The Bayou Ladies is one of the many women's social and charity clubs that are an integral part of professional black society in the South in the late sixties and early seventies, an outgrowth of the many clubs formed after Reconstruction, led by the National Association of Colored Women. The early clubs adhered to the strictest codes of social and moral behavior, and while, unlike the earlier clubs, these later clubs don't build schools, they do remain active in civic and educational issues. River has been a member since the first year she and Greg opened the Paradise Palace. One of the Bayou Ladies' galas had been held at their club. Three of the most prestigious clubs had asked her to become a member, and River chose the Bayou Ladies Social and Charity Club after learning they take their betterment of the community oath seriously, still using the founding club's slogan, "Lifting as we Climb" as part of their ceremony. She soon becomes a favorite of the other club members and hosting tonight's meeting is her first since being elected entertainment chairman.

Sue plops down on the creamy navy leather sofa, crosses her shapely legs, and announces, "You know, River, you're wasted on a man like Adam!" River has heard this too many times from Sue and had hoped it wouldn't come up tonight. "It's like asking a man to appreciate Dom Perignon who only has a palette for Thunderbird!"

"You don't really know him, Sue, do you?" River lights the short, fat, gardenia-scented candles and starts arranging them throughout the room and wonders again where Adam is.

"Well no . . . but I've heard about his family, everyone has, and none of it's good, nothing like your family. And, if I'm being honest, you've changed lately, River. You don't seem to be as sure of yourself, as upbeat as you used to be, and I'm not the only one in the club who's noticed, either."

River, worried that her sagging confidence is showing, sits down beside Sue and takes her diamonded hand. "Things are getting better, Sue. Adam's had a rough life. He's had a lot to overcome, but he's a strong man. And it really is getting better. He has had it very hard, harder than you'd believe. We have to help our men. Don't we?"

"I guess. Just make sure while you're trying to help him, he's not better at hurting you. That's all." Sue walks over to the salmon mousse River has placed on the breakfast bar and thoughtfully spreads some on a cracker, convinced she is right about Adam. The doorbell ends any further discussion. Evaline is the last to arrive. Adam still is not home.

The first order of business is River's introduction of Evaline. Then the recipient of the Bayou Ladies' annual scholarship is selected from those recommended by the high school counselor. The young woman will receive financial and mentoring support during her college career. River's proposal to form a "Learning to be Ladies" summer program is adopted. Young black girls will be taught social graces during six weeks of the summer, and River is chosen to head up the committee that will get that started. It is after ten before River serves the sweet potato pie and coffee brewed with a hint of chicory. After lingering over coffee, the meeting is adjourned.

"How'd you like them?" River asks Evaline while they clear the table.

"It was fun, and I knew you guys did Thanksgiving baskets and Christmas dinners for senior citizens, but I didn't know about all that other stuff. I thought those social clubs were just an excuse to raise money for those notoriously lavish Christmas parties that you guys are known for."

"Maybe some of the clubs, not ours though. But we *do* like our Christmas parties!"

"You think they're gonna vote me in?"
"How could they not? Besides, we need a computer whiz like you." The two friends laugh easily together, but that laughter is quieted just after eleven when Adam stumbles in through the back door. They are putting the last of the dishes into the dishwasher. It is clear he is drunk, and River's heart sinks. She wonders how he can go for months without drinking, and then do this. Just when she's almost convinced herself he is winning the battle with whatever torments him, he proves her wrong. She decides to wait until Evaline leaves to say anything.

That damned Evaline, he thinks, as he stumbles to the refrigerator. *Seems she's always here, 'specially when I'm not. Damned yellow bitch!* He weaves while he stares into the refrigerator, his weight supported by the opened door.

"You want me to fix you a sandwich?" River asks while she takes out the leftover turkey and gently closes the refrigerator door.

"Yeah. If you got time and can break 'way from your

94

comp'ny," he slurs.

Evaline starts to collect her things. "I'm going, River. I'll call you tomorrow."

Adam finds a bar stool and sits down hard, misjudging the distance. "Don't leave 'cause a me. I'ma take my san'mich upstairs. So y'all can stay on down here and keep on running me down."

"Adam, please!" River wonders what this is about, where he's been, and how he got home, since both his vehicles are in the garage, and she didn't hear a car in the driveway.

He takes the sandwich from the plate and starts upstairs, then stops, weaves back to River, locks his elbows on the breakfast bar to support himself, and slurs, "Don't please me, Miss River. And one more thang; you can't turn me 'ta no house nigger. Un'erstand? You and no other godamn woman can clip my wings." The spewed turkey bits lay on the counter and floor.

He then makes his way upstairs leaving River, who senses something worse than he's been drinking is wrong, clenching and unclenching her fists, her nails biting into her palms, furious. He is such a different man when he isn't drinking, but now it is clear that, like his father, he will always drink. No matter how long he remains sober, there will always be a day or a night like this one, she knows. But this night is different, worse than any one before, and River is scared.

Evaline tries to avoid River's eyes when she opens the door to leave. "You all right girl?" She stands in the doorway waiting for a reply that doesn't come. "Earth to River!"

River smiles, and Evaline thinks it's the worst smile she has ever seen—never leaving her tight lips. "It'll be all right

I'll work it out, don't worry." She goes to the door and kisses her friend on the cheek. "Why don't you go on home? It's almost midnight and Jim might worry."

"Forget about that, no need to worry about me, I'm more worried about you. Jim and I both are."

River remains quiet, and Evaline understands. Then she dangles her keys at River and says, "I'm out of here." After failing to get a real smile from River, Evaline closes the door behind her. River's steps are slow and heavy as she climbs the stairs, picking up bits of turkey as she makes her way upstairs where she finds Adam sprawled, fully dressed, on the bed. She picks the partially eaten sandwich from the floor, stands looking at him, and says aloud, "Sue just could be right."

≈One Month Later≈

Things at work continue to change and Alpha seems to grow more distant by the day. River is at a loss to understand it and thinks it must be more than the relationship between her and Daryl. In fact, she and Daryl have been so discreet, if Alpha hadn't told River of the affair, she wouldn't have known. Even after Alpha told her, River thought she and Alpha had worked around it, but things between the two of them have become seriously strained. *Why?* she wonders. The only thing more confusing than Alpha's behavior is the change in Adam.

Adam hardly ever goes out without River. If she refuses to go with him, he stays home. He is also going through another of his "not drinking at all" periods, asking her almost daily to marry him. She is not convinced, however, that the comfortable period will last or that this time will be any different than the other times. It is Friday though, and she is looking forward to the weekend she and Adam have planned to the Austin hill country. She hurries home to begin packing and tries hard to force away feelings of gloom.

May is late for Texas wildflowers, but it has been an unusually cool and dry spring, which has caused the flowers to be late in painting the hill country in colors of blue, yellow, and orange. Luckily, the colors are holding. Anxiously looking forward to one of her most favorite road trips, she fixes dinner while thinking about the pleasant weekend ahead and smiles, musing how anyone who expects Texas to be flat will be surprised on their first drive up to the hill country along Highway 290. There they will find gentle rolling hills that, this time of year, will be covered with bluebonnets, firewheels, lemon mint, and Indian paintbrush. It always adds to her pleasure if the landscape includes a fenced barn or rustic cabin and a few grazing cattle, as it almost always does.

Adam, usually home before River, has not come home yet, and she worries. With him there is always a worry. The salmon steaks are becoming dry, so she sprinkles them with lemon juice and wraps them back in the foil paper. River's concern deepens. Dinner has been ready for over an hour, and Adam has never been so late coming home from work. It is almost seven o'clock and she decides against running her after-dinner errand. She goes to the garage and lifts the door, so she can put her car inside. There, in the garage, is Adam's motorcycle, parked next to his truck. His keys are on the garage floor next to the bike. River takes deep breaths, trying to slow her heartbeat. Her stomach trembles, and she wraps her arms around herself as she walks over to the truck and stares inside, as if it will tell her what is wrong. It's hot in the garage, but a hard chill shakes River, and she holds herself tighter. Maybe he's visiting one of the neighbors, she hopes. He's become friendly with several of them and that has pleased River since Adam didn't like that they were the only black couple in the subdivision and had kept to himself in the beginning. She looks up and down the street, almost as if she's misplaced him. The neighbor who lives across the street from them was gardening when River came home and is still working in his yard. She walks over to him and forces herself to smile when he looks up, noticing he doesn't return her smile.

"Hi, how are you?"

The neighbor stops his work, stands up, takes off his gloves, and extends a hand to River. "Just fine ma'am." Then he smiles and says, "You all right?"

River wonders why he asks. *Don't I look all right?* "Oh, fine, I'm just fine. Your yard is always so beautiful, but it looks like it takes a lot of work though." River keeps trying to convince herself that nothing is wrong. Maybe one of Adam's friends stopped by and he's left with him, she hopes.

"Yes ma'am. It takes a little work, but I like it." His tight smile leaves, and she grows afraid as his look grows serious. She tries to swallow, but her mouth is dry.

"I was wondering if you saw Adam when he came home this evening?"

The neighbor answers quickly, as if relieved he's got permission to tell what he's seen, his words almost running together. "Yes ma'am. It was right 'round five o'clock. I'd just come out. Your husband pulled up in the driveway with this car hot on his tail."

River takes a deep breath and tries again to slow her racing heart. *Husband,* she repeats in her mind.

"Must've been plain clothes police; car was unmarked, too. They had guns and I think they showed badges. Not sure about that, kinda hard to see from over here."

Guns? Policemen? What?

The neighbor interrupts her rambling thoughts and hurries on. "One of them held a gun on him while the other one handcuffed him. I'm sure about that, then they put him in the back of the car and pushed his motorcycle in the garage. Had a hard time getting the door down though, and then they peeled out of here, real fast. It really was something! Never saw anything like it!"

River stares at the man, unable to look away. She feels an urgent need to urinate, to rid herself of something foul, and backs away from the neighbor into the street. The horn of an approaching car stops her, and she turns and stares blindly. Her neighbor's words bounce around in her head. *Guns, unmarked car, handcuffs, husband.*

"Ma'am, are you gonna be all right? I can send my wife over."

River runs home, closes the door hard, and once inside starts to undress. Almost naked when she reaches the top of the stairs, she steps into the shower, scrubs her skin until it hurts, trying to wash something awful away. Jumbled thoughts clang in her head; *what should I do, who should I call? Maybe I can think after a shower. Maybe.* She keeps adding hot water to the shower spray while random thoughts, at breakneck speed, chase through her mind. She tries to organize them, but they are out of her control. Then she wonders if the water from the shower spray is too hot. While she concentrates on cooling the too hot shower, thoughts begin to fall into place, and when she steps out of the shower, she knows the first thing she must do.

"I'll call the police station. Which one?" she asks herself. "Information will know." She picks up the telephone, water dripping onto the carpet.

"Information. Number, please?"

"Yes, yes. Can you give me the number of the Houston police station?" She dials the number given to her.

"Houston Police." The female voice that answers is so lifeless, River at first thinks it is a recording.

100

"Yes, I'm River Smith. My husband was arrested this afternoon by two plain-clothes police officers. Can you tell me anything about it?" She wonders why she said husband.

"What's your husband's name?"

"Adam Jones."

"Address please?"

"The address is 1807 West Winds Boulevard." She's then put on hold and while she waits, she reasons she'd had to say she was Adam's wife if she hoped to get any answers.

The voice with no feeling returns, "Ma'am?"

"Yes."

"Yes ma'am, he was picked up. He's already been transferred to the county jail." River is unable to move, but she finds her voice. It surprises her, sounding nothing like her voice, much too high pitched.

"What's he charged with?"

"You need to call the county, ma'am. They have his records." She gives River the telephone number.

River takes deep breaths, tries to swallow, but finds her mouth as dry as cotton. She swallows water from the bathroom sink and then dials the number.

"How are you related to Adam Jones?" the new voice, male, that sounds more human, asks.

"I'm his wife," River lies again.

"He's held with no bond. You need to get a lawyer to find out about the charges. I can't give you that information."

River is floundering. "What can you tell me? Anything, please."

"I can just tell you that he's scheduled for a grand jury hearing on Monday. And that's more than I should've told you."

River looks at her watch. It is almost eight o'clock, and she knows only one lawyer. As desperately as she wants to, she knows she can't call him at this hour.

River feels heavy and she sits on the bed. "Is there any way I can find out anything tonight? Can I see him?" Grateful that the person stays on the line until she can speak, her higher pitched voice doesn't surprise her this time.

"Well, like I said, a lawyer. Or a preacher. His preacher, if he's got one, can come any time."

"Thank you." River hangs up the phone.

She drags herself from the bed, and despite what she's been told, dresses to go to the police station. In a hurry, she blows her hair almost dry and feels a little better once she combs it into her secure pageboy. Maybe she can convince them to let her see him tonight. She needs to see him, to talk to him. It terrifies her to think of him being locked away in some horrible place for something, whatever it is, for which he cannot be guilty; he must not be guilty. Dressed, River checks her pageboy in the mirror and closes the door behind her. The car backs out of the garage and stops at the edge of the driveway. She doesn't know where the police station is. Pressing the opener, the garage door lifts, and River pulls the car back into the safety of the garage. The door comes down hard and she sits there, clutching the steering wheel. Finally, she releases her clenched fists, slowly at first, and then as hard and as fast as she can, her hands pound the steering wheel until they ache.

"Why, Adam, why, why, why, why?" Her voice is little more than a murmur at first. It grows louder. She feels like she is tottering off some slippery edge, losing control, and as hard as she tries to balance herself, she can't. She slumps over the steering wheel, hands throbbing, and cries long and hard.

She doesn't know how long she's been in the garage, but she

feels exhausted. So, she pulls herself together, goes into the house, and calls Greg.

When she hears his voice, she cries the whole story to him. He waits for her to finish and then quietly says, "I'll be right there." He spares her the need to ask him to go and talk to Adam. He volunteers, and after all, he is a minister. He takes his ordination certificate from its frame and goes to River.

When Greg pulls into River's driveway, she is standing outside by the garage and, for the first time, he thinks she looks small and helpless. Like always, he wants to protect her, to rescue her from whatever is happening. He's never blamed River for leaving; he knew he'd lied to win her and had not known how to keep her, and even worse, how not to drive her away. He hugs her tightly, and she doesn't resist, wishing for a moment that she was back there and safe. He feels his love for her unchanged and brushes her forehead with a kiss.

It is after ten o'clock when they get to the county jail, and it takes almost an hour for Greg to gain clearance to see Adam. He is with him less than fifteen minutes when River, with her face pressed against the glass in the heavy metal door, strains to see Greg who is walking back toward her. She is trying to read his face in the distance, trying to see just how bad it really is. Her reflection in the glass distorts Greg's face but not her puffed and frizzy pageboy. She had not taken the time to dry it completely, and now nervously she tries to smooth it. Greg waits for the officer to open the door and walks to River. He kisses her forehead again. "Let's go."

Greg takes her hand and leads her outside, and for the first time in the fifteen years River has known him, his hand doesn't feel small. Even though her hands are swollen and painful, she draws comfort from the strength of his firm grip and allows herself to be led to the car. Neither of them speak, neither of them wanting to say or hear what must be told and heard. Inside the car, River sits quietly, pressed hard against the car's passenger door, as far away from Greg and the awful news as she can get. With a tight grip on herself, she looks at Greg.

"Just say it, Greg. Just say it."

"Adam's been charged with aggravated rape."

She holds herself tighter. "What does that mean? And who accused him of whatever it is?" Somehow, she knows who it is, but asks anyway.

"It means a weapon was used. The woman is Alpha Broussard. Hard to believe. That's your assistant, right?"

"Yes," she says, "yes, it is. Please, take me home." On the drive home, Greg tells her all that Adam has told him. It isn't much. Mostly that he didn't do it. Bail has been denied until he goes before the grand jury Monday.

River remains quiet and steels herself for whatever lies ahead. "Thanks, Greg, for everything."

"Don't worry, everything's gonna work out."

Greg holds onto her hand as she opens the car door with the other. He feels awful for her and wants to take her back home with him and take care of her. He hates Adam for River's hung down head as she walks slowly toward the front door. He wants to kill him.

Alone in the house, close to midnight, River sits at the kitchen table and stares at the ruined dinner on the counter. Then she fixes her thoughts on Alpha and all she knows and suspects about her and wonders aloud, "Why didn't she tell me?"

Even though she knows it's impossible to sort it all out, River keeps trying. Certainly, she had cooled to Alpha somewhat after learning about her and Daryl, but they still had lunch together sometimes, or quick shopping trips. River is confused, there is too much she can't fit together, and considering all she knows that is wrong with him, one thing she is certain of, Adam did not rape Alpha. She knows that for certain. She doesn't understand how she knows, but it is something that she doesn't have to convince herself of. Something happened, but whatever it was, it was not rape.

Armed with this one certainty, she pushes all other questions aside and sits down to decide what she should do next. She puts the kettle on for tea and then, abruptly, wondering if Adam has cigarettes, she stands and takes the teakettle from the stove, picks up her purse and keys, and walks swiftly to the car.

It takes her a while, but she finally finds Washington Street and the county jail, parks her car, and walks in. Passing again through the heavy metal door, she marches up to the same officer that she had left a little more than an hour ago. Her large hand fits easily around the four packs of Kool cigarettes she takes from her purse. She hands them to the officer and asks him if he'd get them to Adam.

"I'll see what I can do, ma'am."

River doesn't know whether Adam will get them or not, and, for her that really isn't important. She's done all she expects of herself tonight and whether he gets the cigarettes or not is out of her hands. She then focuses all her energy on what she can do until Monday at ten o'clock when the grand jury convenes.

At home again that Friday night, well past midnight, she catches her reflection in the hall mirror. River studies her image and tries to understand where she is lacking, where she isn't enough. She is a good person, and she is smart. She knows that. She thinks she is pretty until her eyes come to rest on her puffed-up pageboy. The night has been especially warm and damp, and

105

her hair shows its effects. Not only is it puffed up, but the edges show signs of kinkiness. She pulls her hands through her hair, trying to smooth it, when she notices that there is almost an inch of new growth. River walks into the kitchen, sits down at the kitchen table, and says aloud, "It's time for a retouch." She'll pick up a perm kit tomorrow and do it herself, she decides. There will be no time for a beauty shop appointment.

River checks the messages on her answering machine. One is from Vera, and River wonders if she's already heard about Adam. No need to wonder what she'd do if she were in River's place. Without a doubt, Vera would walk away and never give Adam a backward glance. River thinks she won't call Vera, but instead decides to return Evaline's call after she has tea.

As she stands in the kitchen waiting for the water to boil, River's reflection in the oven window holds her. For the first time, she wonders why she pays so much attention to her hair. Why, she wonders, does she need that damned pageboy? The teakettle whistles. She wraps her hands, still aching from the pounding she'd given them earlier, around the steaming cup of harvest peach tea, and walks wearily upstairs, refusing to look at herself as she passes the hall mirror.

≈Evaline and Jim≈

The telephone rings and Evaline looks at the clock and then at Jim. "It's half past one in the morning. Wonder who's calling so late?"

She makes her way to the telephone from the kitchen table where she and Jim are putting together a ship in a bottle from a kit they'd bought. They both enjoy their time together, and Friday nights are always late for them, when they usually finish more than one bottle of wine.

~ ~ ~

It had surprised Evaline to see how much Jim enjoyed the deceit their relationship required. They'd had their first serious argument a short time after returning from their first trip to France. They'd gone to visit River and Greg and brought along their photographs from the trip. River had been lost in the pages of photographs when, without looking up, she asked, "What was your favorite city?"

Jim quickly replied, "Nice," while a secret smile played at the corners of his mouth. His foot found Evaline's under the table, which she quickly withdrew and studied River's lingering glance in Jim's direction. Certain she read something in that glance, Evaline grew concerned. She hated lying to River.

Jim broke the silence on the drive home.

"I'm sorry, Evaline. I shouldn'a made that joke about Nice."

"That's right. You should not have."

"No need to be so upset. What's wrong?"

"Jim, I don't like lying to River. We don't lie to each other. I just don't think she'd understand about us."

"What's to understand? We're living together while I'm getting a divorce? Kinfolk always help each other out. Nothing to explain or understand."

Evaline's voice rose. "And what about your divorce? I never heard of it taking years to get a divorce! Especially with black people!"

"Look, it's complicated, lots of stuff to sort out between me and my wife. When my brother died, you and I agreed I'd move in here to help with the expenses. The divorce from my wife came months later. And besides, you're worrying about nothing, I don't think River thought a thing."

"I've been thinking, Jim. I don't need the expense of this big house. The rest of y'all keep crying about keeping the homestead! Maybe you think that just because you're the only man I've been with, I'll keep living like this. Who cares if we can't get married, you need to be divorced! Uncle!"

"Calm down, Ev. I'm working on the divorce and I promise, I'll never joke about that again. Okay?"

~ ~ ~

Evaline flashes an approving smile at Jim and the progress they are making with their ship. She reaches the telephone and says, "Hello."

"Adam is in jail, accused of raping Alpha."

Evaline doesn't speak until River finishes, and then whispers,

"I'll be right there, just as soon as I can get dressed. I'll be there."

"What a bastard!" Evaline yells while she dresses. "From the beginning I felt like he was trouble, but even I didn't think he was this kind of trouble!"

"What is it?" Jim asks. "You want me to come with you?"

"No, that's okay." She tells him some of what River has said before heading to Clear Lake. When River answers the door, Evaline tries to hold her, but River pulls away, she doesn't want comforting, doesn't want to be softened up. She needs to remain angry. Ready to fight whatever lies ahead. While she won't allow Evaline's sympathy to temper her anger, she welcomes her easy nearness. She did not call Vallie or Ernest because she knew their nearness would not have been such an easy comfort. "I'm just gonna ask this one thing, River. Why do you think you can fix this guy and his unholy mess? Or why do you even want to? Or is it that you need to?"

"That's three things. You gonna have a glass with me?" River tries to smile, while holding up the bottle of Merlot she's just uncorked.

"Sure thing. I hate this for you, River, but I hope you don't expect me to feel bad for Adam."

River drinks the first glass of wine like water and sighs heavily. "Ev, we don't even know what happened. Whatever it is, it might be his fault, but I need to keep an open mind if I'm going to get through this. If I'm going to do whatever I have to do, I need to be able to think maybe it's not. Adam is an alcoholic. There, I've said it out loud. But one thing Adam's not, is a rapist."

"How would you know? He might not be a rapist, but whatever happened, dollars to donuts, it's his fault. He's useless, totally! I don't know why the hell you put up with it. After all

109

you gave up for this guy. That's what I can't understand. And just what is it that you have to do?"

River sits on the sofa and looks up at the ceiling. "I can't let this happen to him, whatever I have to do. This is serious, Ev, and Adam didn't rape Alpha. I know it, you might not know it, but I do. You saw the way she threw herself at him that time at the Side Door."

"To hell with him, River, and her, he didn't have to catch her white ass. For the life of me, I can't figure it out. What makes you think you can fix everybody? You need to be thinking about you. You need to be thinking about getting out of this whole mess called Adam."

River drains the last of the wine from her glass and pulls her terry robe tighter about her. "First things first. Ev, I'd do almost anything to make this work, anything to make it right." She looks beyond Evaline's disapproval and whispers, "When I think of what my family must think, especially Daddy and Ernest." This is what pains River more than anything, she has failed the two men she admires the most.

Evaline and River talk most of the night. She feels comfort in Evaline's nearness, she always has, and it is only after River's fourth glass of wine, and the steadiness of Evaline's voice discussing what she should do, that she sleeps. The position that River is sleeping in looks strange to Evaline. Her arms are wrapped about her body, as if she is hugging herself. Evaline thinks maybe she is cold and covers her with the heavy throw hung on the arm of the sofa. Then she falls asleep on the comforter on the floor, next to River. Next to River feels good.

≈Two Days before Monday≈

After a shower, River stands on the balcony outside her bedroom and watches the rising sun drive away the mist that has settled on the lake. There have been good mornings when she and Adam stood here and planned for a future that now seems to River little more than wishful thinking. She blinks her eyes hard and fights back tears because this morning she can't see beyond Monday morning and the grand jury. Her throat aches but she refuses to cry.

The balcony door opens and there is Evaline, balancing two cups of tea and croissants on a tray. As much as she depends on Vallie Lynn, Greg, and Evaline, she wishes she could talk to her brother, but knows she can't. Ernest has little patience with human frailties, and River is trying to understand how she allowed Adam into her life, a sure reflection, in the light of what is happening, that she's failed somewhere. No matter, she reasons, for now he is a part of her life and she must see it through. What kind of woman would leave her man in a mess like this? Especially since he can't be guilty.

"Hey girl, so what's the game plan?" Evaline chirps, setting the tray on the glass-topped patio table.

"I don't know, Ev. Just going to play it by ear. I'll call Jim Bell a little later."

"Who's that?" The sweet aroma of peach steams from the cup Evaline passes to her.

"The lawyer who handled my divorce. You met him I think, once. You went with me when I met him at the San Luis for drinks, didn't you?"

"Oh yeah. You guys got to be pretty friendly for a while. I wish I could be more like you, River. It's like you never meet a stranger, and in just a few minutes, everybody you meet is your good friend, or wants to be. Looks like happy just flows out from you. And that laugh, if you could bottle it, you could make a million."

River looks up at Evaline, and something warm inside her stirs, comforts. "Okay, Ev. Enough with the flattery." River laughs out loud, and then says, "I don't know, Ev. Maybe I work harder at it, maybe I need to know that people like me."

Evaline wants to tell her how much she more than likes her, but instead says, "That sounds like a good place to start, with the lawyer. He can let you know what to expect, I guess. I'll hang out with you today if you want me to." River lingers over the aroma from the cup before taking a sip, fingers her hair, and wishes Evaline knew how hard, sometimes, it is to change what is inside her to the happy that comes out.

"No, Evaline. You've done enough, and I'll call you later after I make some calls."

"You sure?"

"I'm sure, Ev."

Evaline finishes her croissant and heads downstairs to the kitchen with the tray noticing that River has only crumbled the croissant and left the pieces scattered on the plate.

While River brushes her teeth, she hears her say, "Well, I think I'll hang around anyway."

112

"Evaline, thanks, but really, why don't you go home? I'm not sure what I'm going to do today, I just need some time to think."

"Well, just call me if you need company." She puts the last of the dishes into the dishwasher, grabs her purse, and runs upstairs to kiss River goodbye. River follows her downstairs, sits down at the kitchen desk, and tries to bring order to her day. She takes out a pad and writes:

1. Call Jim Bell.
2.

She is unable to come up with number two.

River looks at the clock, clearly it is too early to call. She decides to wait until nine o'clock. As much as she hates to disturb Jim on a Saturday morning, she is glad he gave her his home number. River brews coffee and watches the clock, still wondering what number two should be. At exactly nine, she lifts the telephone from its cradle and dials Jim Bell's number, relieved he sounds awake when she tells him who she is.

"Well, River. How in the world have you been? It's been a while."

"Yes, it has been. I'm doing all right, but I need your advice on something, Jim."

"What's that, honey?"

River hates having to say it. Thinking about it is bad enough; but saying it and hearing it makes what is almost impossible to believe the ugly truth.

"The guy I've been living with, Adam Jones, was arrested yesterday and charged with rape. Aggravated rape, in fact. He can't get bail and is going before the grand jury Monday."

"Uhm. I see. That's not good. What's his full name, River?"

"Adam Anthony Jones."

"Anybody been in there to talk to him? To hear what he has

113

to say?"

"Greg went in last night to see him. Greg's a minister now so he could go in. Adam said he didn't do it."

"Well, that's mighty good to hear about Greg. And about this Adam, that's what they all say, right? You got his social security number there, River? Did he say what *did* happen? Why the woman filed the charges? Why she'd tell that kind of lie?"

"No. It's Alpha Broussard, my assistant at work, who filed the charges. I was hoping you could help with his case." River fumbles through some papers on the kitchen desk and gives him Adam's social security number. He feeds the information into the computer on his desk.

River hears Jim sigh into the phone. "Looks like you've done all that can be done for now. He's probably said all he was going to say already. Probably too late for a lawyer to advise him now on what not to say."

"But somebody needs to go in there and let him know we're working on it. Someone needs to let him know all that's happening, what to expect."

Jim hears the fear in River's voice and feels bad for her.

"Well, you could get his minister to go in and see him. If he's got one." River hears sarcasm; she doesn't think it is intended.

"I told you Greg talked to him last night. I can't ask him to keep doing that for the whole weekend."

"Well, I don't think that even a minister can go in more than once a day. Do you think Greg would mind, even though he's not his minister? There won't be that much to tell anyway. All you have to do now is wait for Monday."

"Okay, but I need to know so much. What about this grand jury? You know, Jim, I'll pay for this consultation. Do I need to get a lawyer?"

River sounds desperate, and he wants to help. "Don't worry about that, honey. It's a hearing. Monday, the jury'll listen to the evidence. Then they'll decide if there's enough for them to take the case to trial and expect to get a conviction. If it goes to trial, that's when this guy'll need to have a lawyer."

"I see." Jim thinks River sounds as if she is speaking from a distance and thinks she's probably let the mouthpiece fall away. He likes her a lot and feels bad that she's allowed this guy to bring her to this. Then she sounds stronger, mouthpiece back in place he guesses, when she asks, "What'll happen at the hearing?"

"There are seven members on this jury panel. They'll listen to testimony from Adam and this, what's her name again?"

"Alpha."

"Yeah, and then they'll decide if there's enough evidence to bring formal charges against Adam. That's about it." He studies the information that has popped up on the computer screen. "Hold on River, let me take a look at this file that just came over."

He looks at the information on the computer screen and finds that Adam Jones is no stranger to the police. Most of it is petty stuff, but a lot of it is from years back, and he starts reading aloud from the list. The worst is a case of aggravated assault that had been dismissed when the female plaintiff dropped the charges, and that is the most recent, about a month ago.

"River, you there?"

"Yes, and I heard some of that. I just need to know what happens if other people want to give evidence? Will they get to talk to the jury members?" River is back, her voice strong and clear. "Should I go?"

"If you know something about the case, yes."

"How do I get my name on that list? Who are the members of the grand jury? That's what I need to know."

"Well, I can't help you there. They've probably already put that list together, only witnesses who have information about what happened. And members of the grand jury are kept under pretty snug wraps, no jury tampering allowed."

"There'll be nobody to speak for Adam? Just for Alpha? Is that what you're telling me?"

"That's the way it works, River. This is not the trial, it's a hearing to see if there's enough evidence to warrant a trial. If so, then both sides will present their witnesses at trial."

"If he needs a lawyer, could you take the case?"

"No, I'm not practicing law anymore, and when I was, it was civil law. You'll need one who handles criminal cases. Hold on, I've got a couple names here." He thumbs through the cards on his desk and gives River two names.

"I can't thank you enough. At least I have some idea of what to expect. This is my first time..." Her voice trails off into the distance again. "Are you sure I can't pay you?"

"I'm sure, honey. One more piece of free advice. I hope this all works out, for your sake, but I've got a feeling this won't be this guy's last run-in with the law. There'll be others, that's a pretty sure bet. This guy has a police record, it's old but it's a long one. River, one thing you need to know is you can't make a silk purse out of a sow's ear. And honey, I'm mighty scared you just might have yourself a sow's ear."

River thanks him and says goodbye. Sow's ear or not, she'll deal with that later, but for now she just knows Adam did not rape Alpha. Doing whatever she can to make sure she speaks before the grand jury has just become the number two on her list. River sits at the table with the telephone resting on her lap until the beeping sound reminds her that she needs to close the line.

River's brother has a friend who practices law in Houston, and River remembers his first name is Michael. But as hard as she tries, she can't remember his last name. Ernest had introduced them when he first moved to Houston shortly after she and Greg divorced, hoping he'd be someone his sister would date. She looks on every page in her directory, hoping to recognize his last name, but there is no Michael anyone. She curses herself aloud for not being able to recall his last name. What she is planning requires the confidential participation of someone inside the legal community, someone like Ernest's friend. River crumples the paper with the names of the lawyers Jim Bell has given her. Hating that Ernest will be disappointed in her more than she is in herself, she has no choice. She swallows her pride, picks up the telephone, and dials her brother's number.

≈A Brother's Help≈

Ernest is six years older than his sister, and they are close. Their parents required that of their children. It was clear early on, to everyone who knew him, that he would be successful at something. He always stood apart. He had demonstrated an early discipline, rationing his weekly allowance as well as his Saturday movie popcorn, so that it lasted the entire week. Never mind if the popcorn was too stale to eat by midweek. He was serious, seeming older than his age. While the other boys mastered the art of the swaggered gait, he memorized the lock code of the briefcase he'd asked his parents to buy for his fifteenth birthday. The briefcase was packed with the papers he often referenced as a member of the Consolidation Committee. This committee was formed by a team of classmates who were working on issues created by the recently combined black and white high schools in Hopewell, Texas, thanks to desegregation. Decisions had to be made concerning what the school mascot would be, what school colors they'd choose, as well as the school song. These were matters Ernest took seriously; the other members of the committee respected his calm, serious approach and soon voted him chairman.

Ernest received a full scholarship to Prairie View A&M University. After completing his undergraduate work and a two-year job assignment in Chicago, he was immediately accepted into the MBA program at Northwestern University. When River, not wanting her brother to leave Texas, asked why he didn't take a position in Houston, he told her he wouldn't be a corporate token. She thought he would never return to Texas to live again and cried when he left for Chicago. She'd been right, fifteen years later he was married, living well in New York, and following a strategically planned career path to senior management at Paine Webber.

~ ~ ~

Ernest is grinding coffee beans and picks up the ringing telephone.

"Hi. I was scared you wouldn't be home. I'm glad I got you." River tries to sound cheerful, but her brother hears something in her voice and waits for her to go on. She remains quiet.

"I got back from Hong Kong yesterday. Making coffee to help me over the jet lag. How are things?"

"I'm all right, but I need to get in touch with that friend of yours that you introduced me to, the one practicing law here. Is he still here in Houston? I just can't remember his last name." *Just get to the point and get it over with*, she thinks.

"River, are you in trouble? Why are you asking about Michael?" Ernest switches the phone to a more comfortable position and slowly lowers himself onto a kitchen stool.

"I'm fine. Adam's in a little trouble and I need some advice, that's all." The tremor in River's voice tells Ernest that his sister is not fine. The fingers on River's left hand begin to throb and she looks down to find that they are turning blue. She's wrapped the telephone cord around them so tightly there is no blood flow.

She unwraps her fingers and watches the color return.

"Oh, him." She hears the disgust in her brother's voice. "What kind of trouble and why am I not surprised? Must be serious if you need a lawyer." Ernest hasn't bothered to learn anything about Adam and has been hopeful he'd be out of his sister's life before he ever needed to. His impatience with human inadequacies has only intensified with age, and Ernest has refused to give Adam any serious consideration, referring to him as a joke when Vallie Lynn mentions him.

"I just need to ask him some questions." River can't bring herself to repeat the details to her brother. *What will he think of me?* she wonders.

"Listen River. This Adam character is not the kind of guy you need in your life. You know this! I know you know this! And you need to get yourself together! Hold on, I'll get the number." Ernest's voice is hard, cutting, and he wonders why River is drawn to men who, it seems to him, she has to pull or push along. He turns to the number in his directory and gives his sister Michael Jamison's name and telephone number. "Let me know if you need anything else, River. And get it together!"

"Thanks, Ernest. I'll call you later. Love you." Tears sting her eyes, but she fights them back, "And get it together!" ringing in her ears.

Ernest hangs up the telephone and pours himself a cup of coffee. He sits there and wonders why River had to get involved with somebody so soon after her divorce, but if she had to, why couldn't it have been somebody like Michael? Maybe he just wasn't needy enough, he decides while dialing Vallie Lynn's number to find out what is going on and if he needs to go to Houston.

River quickly dials the number her brother has given her.

Please let him be in, she prays as the phone rings. It is almost eleven o'clock and there is a lot to do between now and Monday morning.

"Hello," a voice answers.

"Hi, Mr. Jamison. I'm River Smith. I met you once a couple of years ago. My brother, Ernest Thomas, introduced us. Do you remember?"

"Oh yeah, I sure do. Well, how in the world have you been? I think you owe me a few return calls. And what's with all this Mr. stuff?"

River mumbles something about being sorry about that and then forces out all the sordid details to this almost stranger. He doesn't interrupt, only interjecting, "I see," every now and then. When River finishes and pauses, he asks, "What do you need from me?"

"Well, I need to know how to get my name on the list of witnesses scheduled to testify before the grand jury."

"From what you've said, you don't know anything about what happened that night. Is that right, or do you know more than you've told me?"

"Well, no, I don't really have any evidence. But maybe I could be a character witness or something. Just to give them a clearer view of things, help them to see the big picture."

Michael hears the determination in River's voice and tries to remember just how she looks. He remembers she had eyes that drew you in and a smile that held you there.

"The grand jury is just interested in gathering facts, just evidence relative to the charges, nothing else."

"I'm in a special place here. Not one I like being in, but I'm here." She feels sweat forming on her forehead and reaches up to brush it away, thinking it isn't that hot. "I know these two people, really well. How could the jury members not be interested in what I have to say?"

"I'm just trying to keep you from getting your hopes up about something that's probably not going to happen. That's not the way the process works."

"Yes, but sometimes things work out better when the process doesn't work, right?" The tone of her voice suggests to him she already knows the answer to her question.

"What does that mean?"

"Ernest told me about that inmate you defended. The one who either strangled or drowned that prison warden, I don't remember everything, but I think the warden was using him to run a scam from inside prison. I'm sure you remember, though."

Michael sits down in the chair he's been resting his foot on. "It wasn't the warden; it was one of the guards. What else did your brother tell you?"

"He said you got a list of prospective jurors. You had someone do intensive background searches, you knew a lot more about everybody on that list before jury selection took place than you should have, knew which ones to strike, which ones to keep. That wasn't the way the process was supposed to work, was it?"

Michael is impressed with her determination; she isn't about to accept no for an answer. He can tell. *Someone good to have in your corner*, he thinks.

"There were other circumstances that led to that acquittal, River. Just what do you want from me? Doesn't sound like it's advice."

"I appreciate the advice, I do, but what I really need to know is how can I find out who is on this grand jury? Who the minority members are, especially."

"Why?"

"I just want them to hear what I have to say. That's all I want."

"It's against the law for you to try to talk to any of them. You could be charged with jury tampering and get jail time, and a pretty big fine."

Michael stands up and walks thoughtfully across his carpeted living room.

"Do you know where my office is?"

"No, but I can find it."

"The corner of Louisiana and Jefferson. What time can you get over there today?"

"Any time that you say."

"Meet me at three o'clock." *What could it hurt?* he thinks. *Let her try, and it just might help. Sounds to me like another black man being railroaded anyway,* he concludes.

River paces drinking her tea, not knowing what else to do while she waits. She doesn't allow herself to think anything differently, even though she knows she is asking for a lot. She tells herself that she will soon have the names she needs. Why else would he ask her to come to his office?

At a little after two o'clock the Audi speeds along the Gulf Freeway and reaches downtown Houston in less than twenty minutes. She pulls into the parking lot of the building ten minutes early. River is surprised by how easily she recognizes Michael standing beside one of the three cars in the parking lot. She parks and walks toward his car.

River is prettier than Michael remembers, but he thinks the smile that he'd thought could light up a room is gone. She walks toward him with her hand extended and a stiff smile. He ignores her hand and gives her a hug that she allows herself to relax into briefly.

"Hi," he says and looks down at her. "I spoke to Ernest a little while ago and he told me to give you that hug."

She allows herself the comfort of his embrace, but only for a moment and then pulls away.

"Hi Michael, it's good to see you again. I thought you might talk to my brother." Her eyes fix on the manila folder in his hand. "Is that it, the list?"

Her smile relaxes some, erasing a few of the tired lines from her face when he takes the list from the folder and gives it to her. "This is it, but you didn't get it from me, understand?"

"I understand. I don't want anyone getting into trouble. I'm just trying to help Adam any way I can." River looks at the list of seven names with three of them highlighted in yellow. She points to the highlighted names and asks, "Minorities?"

"Yep, three on this seven-panel jury. Two black, one Hispanic. If they all vote to no-bill this guy, the other four could still send the case to trial, so don't get your hopes up. Sorry you had to wait." It had taken him a little while to remove any reference to his office from the memo. Friend's sister or not, he can't risk being implicated.

No time to think about what might and might not happen now. "Thanks Michael, I really appreciate this. When this is over, I'll have you over for dinner. This is the best thing I know to do, Adam's best chance." She walks hurriedly back to her car and leaves Michael standing beside his car, wondering what a woman with so much going for herself could see in this Adam guy.

"Just another good black woman hung up on trying to save another bad black guy," he says to no one as he drives away.

Back home, River studies the list and wonders how to approach the three minorities from the list. The kettle whistles, and after pouring hot water over the tea bags, two of them, she lifts the cup and breathes in deeply, closing her eyes to the warm aroma before she takes a swallow. "Mmmm, apricot mango," she whispers, feeling hopeful.

The first name on the list is Mrs. Elvira Dixon, a retired school teacher. River picks up the telephone and dials the number. Her hopeful attitude improves when she hears a voice almost sing "Hello."

"Mrs. Dixon, you don't know me but I'm River Smith. You'll be hearing a case Monday morning, and I'd like a chance to speak to the jury."

"Dear, if you have evidence to offer, you really should be in contact with the district attorney's office," the kind voice says. "How'd you get my name anyway?"

"I know some people." River hopes her comment gives her some clout and hurries on. "I don't have any real evidence. I want to speak, maybe like a character witness, on Adam's behalf. I just don't believe he did what he's charged with, and I know both these people, really well."

The voice changes a bit and becomes less sing-song, almost stern. "Young lady, you could get into serious trouble for making this call."

"I know, I know ma'am, but can you tell me just one thing, please? Do grand juries ever hear character witnesses?"

"What's your name again?"

"River Smith." The telephone goes dead and River wishes she'd had time to thank her. Then, she thinks, thanks might not be needed; maybe police cars will soon be speeding to her house to cart her off for jury tampering. She grows afraid, wondering if that was the reason the woman had asked for her name again. She pushes her fear aside, gathers her courage, and then quickly dials the second name on the list. Mr. Martinez is a Spanish instructor at a community college. After several attempts, River reaches him and quickly repeats everything she's told Mrs. Dixon. His response is the same as Mrs. Dixon's, just a lot more immediate. If she isn't sitting in jail before Monday, then at least two of the jurors know her name and that she wants to be heard. One more to go.

Despite numerous attempts, she's only been able to reach Reverend Wallace's answering machine. The kitchen clock shows nine-fifteen, and she decides it is too late to call again. She wonders what would happen if she was in immediate need of counseling. Would the pastor expect her to record her desperation on his answering machine?

Exhausted, River decides that she'll attend service at Reverend Wallace's church tomorrow morning and won't leave until she is able to speak to him.

Reverend Wallace is a big man whose flowing black robe makes him appear larger as he strides across the pulpit punctuating specific points with his index finger that he jabs toward his congregants. His sermon, delivered in a strong baritone voice, is based on the story of Job and his determination to hold onto his faith despite untold suffering. Like Job, River sees herself facing insurmountable odds. And just like Job, she too is inspired to "stay the course." She doesn't allow doubt to linger too long, nor does she allow herself to believe that the course she is on is the wrong one. After church she hangs back at the end of the line of members waiting to shake the minister's hand.

"Reverend Wallace, I'm River Smith. May I talk to you for a minute?" The hush of her voice leads the minister to show her into his study. River feels a kindness about him. "What is it, dear? You look familiar. Do I know you?"

"I don't think so." River wants to get it over with, so she hurries on. "I don't want to break any law or get anybody in trouble, but I need to speak at Adam Jones's jury hearing. You'll be hearing it tomorrow morning."

He stands and takes River's hand. Such a well-spoken and pretty young woman. He wonders about the case and what she has to do with it.

"We shouldn't be discussing this," he smiles warmly while speaking and urging her toward the door. "It was nice meeting you dear. I'll see you soon." He shows her out, while he wraps firm hands around hers, still sore and swollen. River hopes he means what she thinks he does and again, the weight of impending doom lightens.

Back home after church, she returns the calls left on her answering machine, everyone's except Vera's. She is pretty sure she's probably read about Adam's arrest and doesn't need to talk to her to know what she would say. River remembers something Vera told her when she ended her relationship with Jason. She'd said she would never be bloodied or bowed by staying any bumpy course too long, not even in the name of love. Jason's is the last call she returns.

"I guess you heard?" River doesn't wait for him to ask about Adam.

"What's going on with you, River? How'd you get mixed up in something like this, and why are you putting up with this bullshit?"

"Jason, I don't even know what happened, and you don't either. I'll figure this out."

"I told you what I thought about the guy the first time I met him. Serious drinking problem; it runs in the family from what I hear. I don't know if you want to waste a lot of time figuring that out."

"Thanks for calling, Jason, and I'll stay in touch. I appreciate it, okay?" River hangs up the telephone, thinks about Jason and Vera, and wonders how is one to know when long enough has become too long.

The rest of Sunday is a blur in slow motion; she can only think of Monday morning. Until tonight, River hasn't allowed herself to think about what possibly could have happened between Adam and Alpha, but now she is unable to think of anything else. Thoughts scattered and thorny as a bramble bush shove and prick through her mind. She prays for sleep, prays for relief from the torturing thoughts of Adam and Alpha together. She wonders how she had convinced herself that Alpha's behavior was innocent flirtations. And what else has she been wrong about? Adam? Sure, he drinks, but she found it easy to believe that Adam, knowing she was good for him, would never be unfaithful. But he has been, that's for certain. When and where? What happened between them? She closes her eyes and tries not to see them in the throes of passionate lovemaking. Did he kiss her before? What words did he whisper? Did he tell her he loved her? River can't force away the image of Adam's mouth on Alpha in all the same places he'd kissed her. No matter how tightly she presses her eyes together, she can't stop their lovemaking in her mind. They are there, Adam and Alpha asleep on Alpha's beautiful new bed, black and white body parts intertwined, and the vision won't leave. Adam told Greg he'd only been by her house once, the night of club meeting, to do some closet work. But that was more than a month ago. Why did Alpha wait so long to file charges? It makes no sense. It is almost five o'clock when she finally falls asleep just as day is beginning to break.

≈Monday Morning≈

The alarm jolts River awake, and she feels as if she's been drugged after having slept less than two hours. She sits for a while on the side of the bed, finding it hard to believe the past three days; none of it seems real. Through the apricot-colored sheers, the June sun brightens the room but does little to ease River's fear of what the day ahead holds. She stares at the clock and wonders if she'll be speaking before the grand jury in three hours. She wills it to be so, forces herself from the bed, and looks out past the bedroom balcony and into a beautiful day. The sun is bright, and the sky is cloudless. The sparrows and chickadees that are singing around the bird feeder flutter away when River opens the French doors and walks out onto the balcony. This is one of those early June mornings in Houston, when the humidity is hiding, the scent of just bloomed jasmine, magnolias, and gardenias hangs sweetly in the air, and the temperature is barely seventy. It is a beautiful day, almost beautiful enough to make her believe that nothing bad can happen on a day like today.

River doesn't want to leave the balcony and sits down in one of the wicker rockers with her eyes fixed on the white gazebo on the tiny island in the distant lake. The last morning mist clings like a veil on the gazebo while mockingbirds flitter about its rooftop. She takes it all in, closes her eyes, and inhales deeply the scent of the sweet flowers in bloom, but needing caffeine to put some life into her tired body forces herself from the chair. In an instant, a cardinal bird dashes up from the gazebo roof, splitting the tranquil beauty of a peaceful, cloudless blue sky with a flash of red. Jarred, she turns away from the intrusion and closes the patio door hard to the beauty outside, taking slow steps as she makes her way down to the kitchen and the ugly truth. After dumping three English breakfast tea bags into her soup cup, she watches the steaming water darken. So do her thoughts; she knows it can all go wrong. Neither the shower nor caffeine have been enough to make River feel better about what the morning holds. Adam might be headed to prison—this is the truth.

River has no energy for dealing with her hair today and wonders what her shampooed hair would look like if she'd just let it dry naturally and didn't curl it at all. The new growth is showing a little too much kinkiness, she decides, and wishes she'd retouched it yesterday. She reaches for the blow dryer and hopes the heat will help straighten out the edges. After blowing it dry, she adds a few loose curls that she combs out and gently turns under. She feels a bit better about things, more hopeful, with her neatly combed pageboy.

The navy Lilli Ann suit with the navy and red blouse that she chose the night before is one of her favorites, and just conservative enough. No makeup today, she decides, while she fastens the double-strand pearl necklace, a gift from Greg, around her neck and slips into navy pumps. It is eight-thirty when she backs the Audi out of the garage and heads for the Harris County Courthouse. The drive seems to have taken much longer than thirty minutes as she looks up at the big clock on the front of the drab, depressing-looking building. Nine o'clock. River repeats the same prayer she's whispered all morning. "God, please let them hear me and give me the right words to say." She notices Alpha's car in the first row as she makes her way inside, her knees watery at the thought of seeing her for the first time since Friday.

She is directed to room 112 at the end of a long corridor that smells of Pine-Sol. The echo of her heels on the black-and-white tile, freshly mopped, still looking wet, slows. There at the end of the hall are Daryl and Alpha. River had known she'd have to see Alpha, but she'd hoped she wouldn't have to sit in the same room with her. She collects herself as she reaches them, and even though she knows the smile on her face must look as out of place as it feels, she doesn't know what else to do. She isn't surprised Daryl is with Alpha.

"Morning." She hopes that the trembling she feels inside doesn't make it to her voice. "Is the door still locked?"

Alpha keeps her gaze fixed in the distance, her hostility palpable, and refuses to acknowledge River's presence. She notices Alpha's dress and wonders if she owns a single dress that has a decent hemline. The red dress that Alpha has on, not only is too short, but her heavy breasts strain against the sheer fabric, and as usual, she has piled on the makeup.

"Yeah, it's still locked. We're kinda early." Daryl sounds like himself, but River thinks he looks different. She's unsure of just how, but he seems to find it hard to look directly at her. And when he does, he can't hold her eyes for long. *What has Tony been told?* River wonders. She left messages on both Daryl's and Tony's answering machines that she had urgent personal business and would be in later this afternoon or Tuesday morning. Since the entire front office is here, she knows Tony has been told something.

The sound of the door being unlocked disturbs her thoughts, and River sees her prayer has gone unheard, as there is only one small waiting room where they will all sit together. She takes a chair away from the others, near the opened door. The heavy scent of Pine-Sol is making it hard for her to breathe. Barely in her seat, River catches her breath when she sees Adam being led into another room across the hallway.

Greg made one last visit to Adam on Sunday and delivered clothes River chose for him to wear to the hearing. He also delivered River's instructions to be clean-shaven, and she was relieved to see that he'd shaved his modest beard and moustache.

What does a rapist look like? Surely nothing like Adam, clean-shaven, in the tan shirt and dark brown slacks. Adam senses River's presence and turns to meet her eyes before entering the room. He quickly turns away, hating that she saw the handcuffs.

River fights back tears that have been threatening all morning but quietly loses her composure and cries when Greg and her sister, Vallie Lynn, walk into the room. She needed her family but had refused to ask them to come to the jury hearing. She was afraid to; it was too embarrassing, especially since she knew what they all thought of Adam. Without speaking, Greg hands River his handkerchief and kisses her forehead. She thinks he is such a good and decent man.

≈Grand Jury is Convened≈

They sit in silence for what seems like forever when finally, the bailiff walks into the waiting room and calls loudly, "Alpha Broussard." Alpha gives River a cutting glance as she follows the small man into the jury room, leaving River confused. *Why in the hell is she angry with me?* Surprised that Alpha and Daryl don't leave after Alpha completes her testimony almost an hour later, she's even more surprised when she hears the small man call loudly for Daryl Johnston. Vallie Lynn and Greg look at River, questioningly.

"What could Daryl know about that night?" Greg whispers to River at which she shrugs her shoulders. All during Daryl's testimony, while River steals glances in her direction, Alpha sits erect in her chair and keeps her eyes fixed on some distant object, silent.

When Daryl and Alpha leave twenty minutes later, neither of them looks at, nor says anything, to River. Anger wells inside her. *What is this all about and what in the world have I done to them? Does Alpha blame me for whatever happened between her and Adam?* And Daryl, she is still trying to figure out how he fits into any of this, when she hears the small man with the large voice call, "River Smith." Her sister presses her hand, and

Greg smiles at her and stands, ready to help her from her chair, but she's already following the small man. Relieved and afraid at the same time, she takes deep breaths to try and slow her racing heart as she makes her way to the jury room. She fights back nausea and her knees feel watery, but she steels herself, calls up her anger, stretches her body upward, and takes firm, deliberate steps into the jury room.

The room is small and poorly lit as one of the seven people, Reverend Wallace, sitting at the large round table speaks. "Good morning, Mrs. Smith. Please have a seat."

River senses that he is in charge. She sits down in the only empty chair, directly in front of Reverend Wallace, and takes inventory of the people seated at the table. There are three white men, one white woman, and she identifies the two people she's spoken to on the phone. River, now feeling a bit more at ease, looks across the table and meets Reverend Wallace's eyes, as warm as they were yesterday.

"Are you from Houston originally, Mrs. Smith?" River turns toward the question asked by one of the jurors who doesn't look up from the table while speaking, and who she thinks sounds as if he really isn't interested in her answer.

"Well, no. But we moved here when I was a child. I've lived and worked in the area since."

"Where do you live?"

"I just moved to Clear Lake. Before that I lived in Alvin Heights. I grew up in Hopewell, on Thomas Street. That street was named for my family." Then, both Mrs. Dixon and Reverend Wallace look at her, as if they, maybe, are seeing her for the first time. River can't know that at that moment they both realize they know her family. Reverend Wallace thinks he remembers a street being named for Mr. Thomas who was a deacon at one of the churches in the closely knit family of black churches in the surrounding area. Mrs. Dixon was teaching at Woodburn Junior High when the principal submitted that family name, one of the more active families in the black community, to the city planners to have a street named in their honor. She'd taught River's brother before she retired. "How do you know Adam Jones?" she asks.

"I met him a little over two years ago. He works in the maintenance department at the office building where I work."

"What do you do?" The question comes from the same man who did not look up from the table earlier; he still doesn't look at her. His disregard for her stirs her anger, and silently she thanks him. It gives her strength. River wonders why neither Reverend Wallace nor Mr. Martinez are asking her questions.

"I'm the senior accountant and office manager for Tony's Bistro."

"How well do you know Adam Jones?" Mrs. Dixon resumes her questions.

"We have an intimate relationship."

"How serious is it?"

River surprises herself when she answers they've been considering marriage.

Mrs. Dixon is studying papers on the table before her. She interrupts a juror who starts to ask a question. "Excuse me. You said you work at Tony's Bistro?"

"Yes."

Mrs. Dixon writes some notes on the papers she's been studying and passes them to Reverend Wallace, who still hasn't asked a question. The room is quiet while Reverend Wallace makes notes on the paper Mrs. Dixon passed to him. River studies Mrs. Dixon, unable to decide if she is friend or foe when she firmly says, "Tell us what you remember about the Saturday night of April twenty-fifth." River wishes for the sing-song in her voice that she heard yesterday.

"I spent most of the day getting ready for a dinner party. I was hosting a club meeting that night. I'm a member of the Bayou Ladies."

"Where was Adam during the party?" Finally, a question from Mr. Martinez.

"He was home most of the day. I don't know where he was that night."

"When'd you see him that night?"

"About eleven. My girlfriend and I were cleaning up after the meeting when he came home and went up to bed."

One of the male jurors took up the questioning. "Was he drunk?"

"He'd been drinking. He drinks, maybe too much, maybe he was drunk." River moves beyond her lie and repeats every detail that she can remember about that night, and often losing her composure, finding it difficult to control her tremors and hold back tears when she tells of Adam's strange behavior when he stumbled into the house. She fights hard to keep away the images of Adam and Alpha that surface, assaulting her thoughts. She is determined to stay focused. Then a swift, strong tremor shakes her hard.

Reverend Wallace sees her tremble and feels a need to help her. He smiles at her and then quickly steers the questions in another direction. Something in this young woman has touched him. *She could be the daughter I never had*, he thinks.

"Tell us what you know of Alpha Broussard."

River thanks the minister with watery eyes. Relieved that this question is easier, she answers, "We hired her about two years ago. We've worked together closely."

Mrs. Dixon asks, "Do you consider her a friend?"

River is unable to answer immediately and is forced to think about the question for a while. "Not what you could call a close friend, but a lot more than just casual. We've done things socially; we've had personal discussions."

Another juror asks, "What do you know about her personal relationships?"

River carefully tells what she knows and finishes by telling how Alpha has furnished her apartment with Daryl's help. She decides against repeating Alpha's crude reference to Daryl as "Quick Draw McGraw."

Mrs. Dixon thinks she already knows the answer to the question, but she asks anyway, "You mean the same Daryl Johnston who was here today?"

"Yes, the same one." River notices the long look exchanged between Mrs. Dixon and Reverend Wallace, who then looks at the note she had passed to him earlier.

The juror who has refused to look up from the table finally looks at River and asks, "Did you ever notice Mr. Jones's attraction for Miss Broussard?"

The question and the tone of the man's voice scare River. "They both seemed to flirt with each other. I noticed it, sure, but never thought it was serious. Alpha seems to enjoy flirting with most men. And Adam…" Her voice trails off.

"Do you know if Adam carries a knife or not?" The question from the same man immediately causes River to reason that this must have been the weapon Alpha accused him of using in the *rape*. She searches her memory and recalls that she has seen a knife.

"There's a small knife on his key ring, I think."

"When was the last time that you saw him with it?"

River is certain now that this is the *weapon* that had been used in the *rape*. "I've only seen him use it to clean his fingernails. It's a small thing. I think it's called a penknife and," she stumbles over her words, "I can't remember the last time I've seen him with it. I think it's always on his keychain." She is having a hard time staying focused and wonders how Alpha could have considered that thing a weapon. *Did he threaten her with it? How could he have even been there?* She fights against her questions and tries to focus on those being asked by the jurors. On the verge of tears and exhausted, she needs fresh air. The small room is hot, and the strong odor of Pine-Sol is closing in on her. She is having trouble breathing; her eyes are burning. Chronic asthma tightens her chest, a symptom she hasn't felt for years, and she feels as if she's been there for hours. Thankfully, Reverend Wallace speaks up, "Well, I think that we've asked about all we need to."

River starts to stand when he quickly asks, "One more thing; tell me this, Mrs. Smith. If Adam is no-billed, are you certain you'd marry him?"

The question forces River back into her chair. Uncertain about just what no-billed means, she reasons it must mean that he could be cleared of the charges. Would she marry Adam is a question River has never been able to answer for as long as she's been in this relationship. Those times when she tried to convince herself that she would marry him, something always happened to make her think, no, not yet. Now, she is confronted with the question again, and she believes her answer to that question will weigh heavily in whatever decision the jury will make. She can't be sure, but for her, Adam's freedom from charges based on what she believes to be a certain lie is worth a maybe lie. She looks directly into his eyes and whispers, "Yes sir."

He smiles at her and says, "You're excused. Why don't you wait outside for a few minutes?"

"Thank you." River leaves the room with a straight back, her head held high and her knees feeling less wobbly.

Greg stands and takes her hand when she walks back into the room, neither of them say anything. They just stand there for a few minutes. Vallie Lynn looks at Greg and River and wishes they were still together. He was good for her sister. River then sits down to wait as she's been told and wonders for what. Greg and Vallie Lynn sit silently with her. Before long the bailiff appears, and this time he doesn't call out a name, but walks over to River and quietly asks her to come with him. Scared and hopeful at the same time, she follows the man back into the stifling room she'd left minutes earlier. Reverend Wallace is the only person in the room. He motions toward the chair she'd left earlier, and she sits down, still cold but damp from perspiration.

"River, I've got an offer for you, why don't you let me marry you? But only after you and Adam complete some marriage counseling. In fact, before anyone marries the two of you, you've got to have some counseling."

"Does that mean he's free to go? Does that mean that this is all over?" River had no idea it could be over just like that.

"Yes dear, he'll be released, probably late this evening or early tomorrow morning. There's paperwork to be processed."

"You mean it's over? Really? Just like that it's really over?"

"There wasn't enough evidence. Too much time had passed before she filed charges, and we had a problem with that. I don't even know how this case got to us. Somebody had some influence."

"You mean it's over?" River whispers.

"Understand dear," he fixes River in his eyes, "your being here, and the way you presented yourself, your testimony, turned the tide in his favor. I hope he knows what you've done for him. Even in the face of questionable evidence, which is what we have here, we might've been inclined to let the case go to trial. Cases have gone to trial with much less evidence than this one. Believe me, especially cases like this one."

"Yes, I'm sure. That's why I had to do whatever I could."

"It was in large part your belief in this young man that swayed the jury, and, just between you and me, Mr. Bell made a few phone calls too."

River stands and extends her hand, hoping she can keep the threatening tears away, at least until she is alone.

"Thank you, Reverend Wallace. Thanks for everything." He is surprised when he shakes her hand that River's hands surround his. He guides her to the door.

"No need to thank me. You did it. Just remember what I said about the counseling. Is it a deal? See that through and that'll be thanks enough for me."

River smiles broadly. "It's a deal. I'll call you next week. Thanks, Reverend Wallace."

"Good. That's very good. Now you need to go over to the office and see what you can find out about a very lucky young man's release." A look of surprise shocks his face when River reaches up and quickly kisses him on the cheek before she turns and leaves.

Reverend Wallace turns to Mrs. Dixon who has returned to the room as he picks up his Stetson, and they leave together. "With any luck, there won't be a wedding, certainly not one with that guy."

"Yes," she agrees. "I hope not. Not enough evidence to bind

him over, but I've got a feeling he's plenty bad news. Truly smells like trouble to me. But there is something about him. I can probably see a bit of what she sees in him." She shrugs her shoulders. "Maybe potential is what I sense. And I've got a feeling there's more to that Alpha story than we heard, too."

"Yeah. Probably so."

They watch River leave through a door being held open for her by an older man. "She'd better get used to opening her own doors if she chooses a life with that one," Mrs. Dixon says. Reverend Wallace nods agreement, waiting until they are outside before putting on his hat.

River learns that Adam will be released at twelve o'clock on Tuesday. She kisses Greg on the cheek and thanks him for everything. "Are you sure you can't join us for lunch?"

"No, I can't, I'd love to, but I can't." He takes River's hand and pulls her a few steps away from her sister.

"You don't deserve this, River. I'm happy you turned to me, and that I could help, but please, don't need me like this again. Don't have me feel again what it is like to want to really hurt another human being."

River holds both Greg's hands. "I can never thank you enough, Greg. I guess I just see something in Adam, something worth saving. And now that I'm out here in it, I need to see it through. I need to make it work and I hope you can understand." She turns and walks to her car, the blue Audi that years ago Greg had tied with a big yellow ribbon and left in the garage as a surprise for her, where Vallie is waiting.

River and Vallie Lynn drive to the River Oaks Grill for lunch without talking. They both order a chilled glass of Riesling and shrimp salad sandwiches on toasted whole wheat bread.

"River, there's something I have to say to you," Vallie Lynn starts before lunch arrives. "You know Mother and Daddy don't like to interfere in our lives, but we're all worried. You don't visit us like you used to. And what little we know about this guy you're with isn't good. In fact, to be truthful, it's downright awful!" The waitress returns with the wine and quiets the conversation.

"Vallie, I know it looks bad. But it's not as bad as it looks, he's not as bad. In fact, he's got a lot of good in him if he can overcome a lot of stuff in his past. There're some ugly demons back there. I know you guys don't like him, and he does too." She has expected to have this conversation with somebody in her family and is surprised it has taken so long.

"Who cares? And why do you want to be bothered with somebody who has demons to fight? In the beginning, you went through a rough time with Greg. As soon as things got good, you left. Is it you just like to suffer, River? I really don't understand."

"What kind of question is that, Vallie? What fool likes to suffer?"

Vallie Lynn looks at her sister hard. "You look really tired. You know Greg still loves you, and he'd take care of you, River."

"No, he wouldn't, not like I need. He'd look to me to make all the decisions. Everything would be, 'whatever you want.' I need to be with somebody I look up to. A strong man. Somebody whose opinion matters, someone I can depend on, you know, somebody like. . ." She falls silent.

"It doesn't look like you've found him yet, not to me, not to any of us, really. And no matter what you say, I know, not even to you!"

"I might not have known Adam as well as I should have, but I'm in it now, and I need to try to make it work if I can.

143

Especially now." They eat their sandwiches without talking for a while. River gives one-word answers to her sister's remaining questions, hoping to make it clear she doesn't want to answer any more.

"Ernest is worried too. I don't know why in the world you called him. You should have known better than to get him involved, the way he hates that guy."

"I didn't know what else to do. I needed his help, and I needed the attorney's number. Anyway, he hardly ever calls me anymore."

"Probably thinks Adam might answer the phone. And now, for sure, he'll never allow any of us to even speak his name. You know that. He's not too happy that you're causing Mother and Daddy to worry, either."

River falls silent again, determined to make it all work out, to prove to her family that she's been right about Adam. The drive to Vallie Lynn's is quiet, and when her sister opens the door to leave, River reaches for her hand. "Don't worry, Vallie. I'll sort it out and thanks for coming today. I love you. And I'll call Mother and Daddy." She kisses her sister's hand before she leaves the car.

"You know we're here for you, River, and remember this: there are no perfect wives or husbands, no perfect anybodys, not even you. But after you guys worked it out, it looked like Greg came close to a good husband. I think so anyway. And one more thing, perfect brothers don't always make perfect husbands, even if there were such things. Don't forget that. Just ask Ollie." Ollie is Ernest's wife.

"I love you, Vallie." River drives home and worries why she doesn't feel something more than relief. Then she realizes she will need one more day away from work and just as quickly realizes that neither Daryl nor Alpha will be pleased with today's outcome. She can't imagine what work will be like. "Too many questions," she whispers to herself. "I'll just have to take it a day at a time."

Home again, River ignores two more messages left on her answering machine from Vera and hates to have to leave one more message for Daryl that she won't be returning to the office until Wednesday morning. She needs to know what Tony has been told, so she dials his number. He is in the office, and she is relieved to learn he already knows some of what has happened, thanks to Daryl. He tells her they can talk more when she returns to the office, and then he wishes her his best. It is almost four o'clock. She is exhausted.

Sitting at the kitchen table, River thinks about all that has happened in the past four days and shakes her head in disbelief. The permanent relaxer kit on the kitchen bar stares back at her. Too tired to tackle her hair, she decides that she'll do it tomorrow morning. There will be plenty of time, for Adam won't be released until noon. Wearily, she rests her head on the table and falls asleep. Her rest is fitful, disturbed by thoughts of Willie McGee. She hears the sizzling sound from the portable electric chair that in 1951 fried his flesh and stilled his heart. Had he really committed rape? A female voice in the distance, a voice that sounds white, is calling out, "No! I'm sorry. No!" An hour later, in a kitchen grown dark, she awakes, raises her head, pulls at her hair, and heads upstairs to bed. As she climbs the stairs, she thinks of what Vallie said. Is she trying too hard to be right, to be perfect? She asks the dark stairwell, "What the hell is perfection anyway?"

≈Straightening Things Out≈

River wakes at daybreak. Again, she's hardly slept at all and the reflection in the mirror surprises her. She looks worse than she feels; grief-stricken. Hoping to erase the gritty redness, she reaches into the medicine cabinet, finds the Visine, and puts a few drops into her burning eyes. Her hair won't let her postpone the retouch. The kinky edges of the new growth look as if it doesn't belong on the same head with the already permed, straight hair. She drags herself down the stairs where she makes a cup of tea and, remembering to bring the hair kit with her, pulls herself back up the stairs. She holds up the steaming cup of tea and inhales the soothing peach aroma that mists her face before she takes a sip, and then she stares at the box in her hand. It is mild; she bought the wrong strength. Mild won't make it straight enough, she knows, and it won't last very long either. No time to buy another one, so she undresses and walks into the bathroom.

River turns on the shower and stares at the reflection that stares back at her from the fogged mirror that covers an entire wall in her bathroom. "Who am I?" she whispers. The familiar reflection is a study in roundness, which she attributes to her approaching thirty-fourth birthday, as well as not losing some baby weight that awakens the painful memory of her three failed pregnancies. She asks herself how she has come to this place of not knowing when for so long she has told herself she was proud and self-assured. Hadn't she believed it? She looks at her hair and wonders why she'd ever straightened it at all. Then she fingers the rough edges of new growth and reaches into the jar of permanent relaxer.

The neckline hair is the first area where she applies the thick white cream that smells of ammonia. Those were the instructions that she remembers from the first time she permed her hair. "Apply the cream to the neckline area first, where the hair is coarser." Once all the new growth has been covered and smoothed for the required twenty minutes, River steps into the shower and rinses her hair. Standing before the full-length mirror, she inspects her newly straightened hair when her eyes come to rest on her pubic hair. It is black, dense, and tightly curled. Does Alpha have straight pubic hair? Without a thought, she reaches over and applies the remaining chemical relaxer to her pubic hair. She smooths it gently and watches it as it grows straight. Then she turns the shower on again and rinses the hair free of the thick, white, stinky cream. Her pubic hair is now straight and a strange color of red instead of black. The perm has worked well; River's hair is now straight, all of it. River stares at her reflection in the mirror and sees her mother. In the eyes that stare back at her, her mother's eyes, River sees disappointment. Then the tears come, tears that rock her body hard and long. She hates her hair. She hates herself. "I'm sorry, Mother," she sobs.

Weighted with sadness, the remainder of the morning passes in slow motion. She dries and curls her hair, styling it in her straight and slightly turned-under pageboy. For the first time, the

147

hairstyle doesn't reassure her; not in the least.

She needs to hurry since Adam is to be released at twelve o'clock. River checks her appearance in the bathroom mirror while she quickly applies pink lipstick. The hot pink dress touches her body just enough, sliding easily over small breasts to hug the curves of her full hips. She smooths her hair while she slips on black sandals. A little Joy perfume sprayed between her breasts, and she is as ready as she'll ever be.

As the Audi speeds along the Gulf Freeway, River doesn't worry a bit about the directions; she will never forget them. She turns off the air conditioning and rolls down the windows. It's June, cooler than it should be, and she likes the salty wind on her face. She pulls into the parking lot and looks up at the county jail, ugly and cold, the color of clay. Her mind begins to race, and a sense of dread threatens. *I should be happy*, she thinks. "Might as well get it over with," she whispers and steps out of the car. The cool breeze is not enough to keep the perspiration from collecting between her breasts as she walks up the steps to the jailhouse once again. After she states her business, she sits in a metal chair and waits for Adam, fighting hard against the darkness that threatens. Thoughts that have troubled her recently, that she and Adam are just wrong together, that maybe she can't make it work, are all she can think of while she waits. Unable to reason them away, she feels her family is right, and she's made an awful mistake, pure and simple. So many firsts for her have been with Adam, including this, her first time involved with anyone accused of a crime, her first time at a jail. Then she thinks of a more pleasant first and wonders if she'll ever be able to make love with him again. At that moment the realization that she'd never had more than a watery hope for her and Adam, never a solid belief, drops on her.

His heavy hand on her shoulder surprises her. Lost in thought, she didn't hear his footsteps and looks up into his eyes and feels nothing more than the same relief she'd felt yesterday. Quickly, she looks away, not because like every time before when she was stirred, but because she feels nothing. No fire, no desire to feel his arms around her, his lips on hers. *Empty*, she thinks, *I feel empty*. When he bends forward to kiss her, he kisses the side of her face, missing her lips when she turns away and looks toward the door.

"Thanks baby. Thanks for seeing me through this. I'ma make it up to you. It's gonna be better than it ever was." She forces a smile and turns to leave without saying anything. Gently, she takes back her hand from him and tries hard to feel better, telling herself that the worst time in her life is over. She walks down the steps into the bright sun while Adam follows close behind.

River doesn't hear much of what Adam says as the Audi retraces its earlier path, thinking only that she wishes he wasn't there.

"Don't you agree, baby?"

"What?" Lost in her thoughts, she didn't hear him.

With a raised voice he repeats his question while he forces her hand from the steering wheel into his.

"I said we can fix this, make it better than it was. Don't you agree?"

"We'll see, Adam." She takes her hand away and places it firmly back on the steering wheel, not noticing a glint of anger in his eyes. Adam is confused but doesn't try to touch her again. *I'll just give her some time*, he decides. He takes stock of all that has happened, realizing it had almost all been lost; the smart, pretty woman who has a great job and loves him, the nice house and new car, all of it had almost been lost. It was about a month

149

ago when it struck him just how lucky he was. That was when he decided to clean up his act for real and never let anything or anyone come between them, but it had almost happened anyway. He realizes he's got to be careful and stay on top of things to make sure none of his mistakes will interfere with the life he wants to have with her. He wonders why it has taken this long for him to realize he really loves her. Any fool can see she is the best thing that has ever happened to him. He feels like kicking his own ass when he steals glances at her and feels a strange fullness in his chest when he thinks of all she's done for him. *She saved me! She is a smart, strong, tough lady, and now, on top of that, she saved my life.* He thinks about the visit he'd had last night in jail from that preacher on the jury and feels angry. He doesn't need him or anybody else to tell him how lucky he is to have a woman like River. He already knows it.

River presses the garage door opener and pulls the car into the garage, wondering why the drive home was much shorter than it should've been. It's early, no need to put the car away, but she needs to shut out the rest of the world, and the garage door comes down hard as she steps out of the car. Closing the car door, she thinks of how Greg had bought it, and left it in the garage for her to find. Life had been easy with Greg. *Was that the problem, had it been too easy? What have I done to my life?* she wonders. River feels herself losing control again, unable to rein in thoughts that are spreading like wildfire, unable to answer questions that are torturing her. There is something dangerous about Adam; she finally admits to herself. He seems to enjoy living life without rules. Has she mistaken strength for something more dangerous? How had she seen vulnerable sadness in him? Did last Saturday's newspaper report more accurately sum up what the last year of her life has amounted to?

Adam Jones was arrested, charged with raping a woman, and the woman making the accusation is white and works with him at Tony's Bistro headquarters. That was the report in last week's newspaper. River expected to feel more than relief to know the newspaper will now report the charge has been dismissed. Adam has been cleared of all charges. Why doesn't looking forward to that newspaper report bring her more than relief?

≈Home Again≈

When he walks into the kitchen, he senses River's body stiffen. River sees something cloud his face, a sadness that reaches for her, and she wishes she wanted to say something, that she wanted him to touch her, but she doesn't.

"Can I help you with something, baby?"

"No. Why don't you go and have a shower? This won't take long."

"Right. I'll be down in a few. Okay?"

Adam bounds up the stairs, feeling as light as a feather, and takes some steps two at a time. He closes the bedroom door, turns on the shower, picks up the telephone, and quickly dials a number.

"Hello," a soft female voice answers.

"I'm home," he rushes. "I can't talk right now, I'll call you later. But if she asks you about that night, tell her nothing happened, tell her I was drunk and I couldn't do it. I'll call you later, we'll work this out." Without waiting for an answer, he hangs up the telephone, steps into the shower, smiles, and takes a deep breath.

River is glad when he leaves the room. Not yet ready to hear whatever he has to say to her, she postpones it. *How much of it can I believe anyway?* she wonders. She hears the water upstairs and a vision of Adam in the shower creeps into her mind, warming her. And then, in a flash, there in her mind's eye is Alpha in the shower with him. She closes her eyes hard, but is unable to force them away.

Dinner is almost ready when the scent of Adam's cologne arrives in the kitchen ahead of him and River feels a hint of nausea. The grilled chicken breasts are sliced and tossed with the Caesar salad, but River, feeling sick to her stomach, is unable to eat. They sit at the table in silence while River watches him eat with his usual speed. Adam tells himself how much he loves her, how good he'll be to her, as he watches her clear the table, not noticing that she's hardly eaten a bite.

He wants to help, so he takes the plate from her and while putting it in the dishwasher says, "I'd be lost without you, River. Lost. I know what you did for me: you saved my life. I'll make this up to you." He means to be a better man. His mind is made up. He is determined to be a real man, as good as or better than her brother. Then he thinks of Harry and hates him for not being the kind of father Ernest's father must be, one who shows his son how to be a real man, how to hold on to a woman like River. He decides he will stay away from Harry. The visits to his parents' house will be few and far between. That'll make River happy; he knows how much she hates Harry.

River is surprised by words sounding like nothing Adam is capable of feeling, and certainly never saying, his voice softened by emotion. Her will to resist weakens. She stops clearing the table and lets him come to her and take her hands in his. For the first time in more than six years, since the day he vowed never to cry again, tears sting his eyes. The sad, hurting Adam she saw when first they met is back, and River, happy to see this Adam, reaches up and wipes away the tears. Adam pulls her into his arms and holds onto her, hard, until she murmurs, "You're hurting me."

He releases her but holds on to her hands while he kisses her softly as he leads her into the living room and pulls her onto the floor. Tears stream down his face and onto her body as he continues to kiss and undress her. River stiffens when he reaches inside her panties, remembering her newly permed pubic hair. Will he notice? She hopes he won't; he kisses her there and seems not to. He makes love to her, there on the floor, gently, as if he's afraid he'll hurt her. Soft kisses cover her face, and her tears mingle with his. He tries to wait for her, to control his climax, but he can't. "I'm sorry baby."

"Don't worry about it, Adam." The sadness she feels is overwhelming and she is glad it's over. They lay there on the floor and watch the sunset, neither of them sure of what to say. Adam needs to explain to River what happened. He needs to make sure she is still his.

"River, I made a big mistake in going over there. It was the night that you had the club meeting. Alpha had asked me if I could put some shelves in her closet. I shouldn't have gone over there. Can you forgive me?"

"Did you force yourself on her?"

"No, I didn't. I knew you'd be busy with your meeting, so when Joel stopped by, we went out for a couple of drinks. When he dropped me off at home that night, I saw your club members still here, so I walked over there to see about those shelves. I hadn't planned to go over there. It just happened. I probably wouldn't have gone if I hadn't been drinking, or if your club meeting didn't last so late. And she was all over me, trying to get me to do it. You know how she is."

River knows he is lying. He went there because he wanted to go. Drinking is always an easy excuse for everything. He always has that excuse. He didn't need to tell her that he'd been drinking.

"Were you with her, Adam?" She held her breath.

"No, River. Hell no! You know what happens sometimes. You know, when I been drinking. Well, that's what happened that night. I couldn't do it, no matter how hard she was trying, so nothing happened. But she was all over me."

River thinks back on the times when he tried to make love to her after he had been drinking and couldn't get an erection. She believed it was because she had resisted him so fiercely, refusing to be groped by a drunk, that he'd been unable to make love to her.

"Adam, I really don't know what to think. How could she accuse you of rape if nothing happened? Club meeting was more than a month ago. Why'd she wait so long to file charges? Something just doesn't make sense." She stops and looks at him, then spits, "And if you hadn't been drinking, I guess, you would've slept with her?"

"No! I was trying to get out of there. That's what I was doing. She was scared I was going to tell you about her, about how she'd been coming on to me, and thought you might fire her. That's what she said, that's why she did it. She kept calling me, asking me if I was going to tell you. I told her I wasn't, but I guess she didn't believe me."

River heads upstairs for a shower, then stops and without looking back at Adam, says, "Tomorrow you go to AA."

"No problem." He watches her disappear up the stairs. It's going to be all right. He's kept it together, at least for now. When River almost reaches the top of the stairs, he calls up to her,

"How'd you get that hair down there so straight? I like it like that, a lot." She hates him. She hates straight hair. Once upstairs, River sits down before her dressing mirror and thinks again about Anna Cooper, and whispers to herself, "Yep Ms. Cooper, you are so right, and just like you I feel my horizons extending, going way beyond sexual love." She roughs up that disgusting straight hair and steps into the shower.

≈Wednesday's Work≈

River doesn't feel rested and wonders if she slept at all when the sunrise creeps into her room and stirs her. Not moving, she wonders what the day ahead holds. She wishes she could have just one more day before facing this one. There will be Daryl and Alpha, not to mention Tony's request left on her answering machine for a meeting on her return. It is also the time of the month for financials, which, as always, means long hours for the next few days. Long hours alone with Alpha; River dreads the thought.

Adam is already up and dressed, anxious to get back to work and put this all behind him. River forces herself into the bathroom and is just about to step into the shower when he appears at the door with a cup of coffee. She smiles, takes a sip, and lets him kiss her goodbye. "I'll see you this evening," he yells as he runs down the stairs. Again, he thinks he is the luckiest man in the world and reminds himself of where he could have, too easily, been waking up today.

The front door slams and River, glad he's gone, steps into the shower, adding more hot water to the spray. Once dressed, with her straight and lightly turned-under pageboy firmly in place, she heads out to face the day. The mailbox hasn't been checked in several days, and River steps out the front door to retrieve the mail. She is slapped with the ninety-degree humid June morning. Summer in Houston seems to be eating away more and more of spring, shortening her favorite season. She hates the summers in Houston, but is glad the perm keeps her hair from shrinking. Quickly grabbing the letters from the mailbox, she hurries into the coolness of the air-conditioned car. Her reflection in the rear-view mirror reassures River her pageboy is undisturbed, still nice and straight.

River passes through Alpha's work area, which is a cubicle partially enclosed from the other clerks' open space, and she notices that even though Alpha is not at her desk, her computer is on. River decides that maybe work will be good for her, will give her something to keep her mind off Adam, and looking at the mail on her desk, feels she's been away longer than two days. She is going through a stack of papers when Daryl walks in.

"Glad you could make it in today." His voice has an edge to it.

River looks up at him. "Good morning, Daryl."

He continues to study the memo in his hand and doesn't look at River. Clearly, he is angry. River is sure he's not happy that Adam was no-billed.

"Tony wants to meet at ten."

River doesn't answer and keeps her eyes fixed on Daryl. She puts the mail back on her desk, leans back in her chair, folds her arms across her chest, and waits for him to look at her. *If he wants to have a conversation with me, damn it, he'll look at me*, she decides.

Looking everywhere except at her, Daryl mumbles, "Can you make it?" Silence hangs in the room. He walks to the door, turns, and finally meets her gaze, briefly.

"Can you make the meeting?"

"I'll be there."

Daryl leaves quickly, leaving the door open behind him where she can see Alpha has returned to her desk.

River collects herself and walks quickly toward her cubicle. Alpha looks up and unlike Daryl, greets River with an unblinking stare. "Morning Alpha. How about lunch today? We need to talk."

Alpha holds River in her frozen gaze and mutters, "Fine with me."

"I've got a meeting with Tony at ten. It might run late, so let's say one o'clock."

"Like I said, fine with me. Anytime."

Leaving her cubicle, River is certain Alpha really is angry with her. What the hell for? Back in her office, she thinks this day is turning out to be just as hard as she expected. A few minutes before ten, she takes her notepad and heads for Tony's office.

Even though he cares for River, Tony is a businessman. He knows some about the situation in the office, but doubts Daryl has told him everything. What he does know causes him to be concerned that River will leave, and he doesn't want to lose her. He knows she is responsible for how smoothly the office runs. River suggested and guided the transition from the simple accounting program, Peachtree, to the complicated but more efficient SQL system. Suggestions that she'd made during many of the business meetings had impressed both him and the newly hired Chief Financial Officer, Matt. Plans to expand his chain beyond Texas are complete, and Chicago is chosen to be the first city in which to expand. Tony wants someone from the Houston office, someone who has been there from the beginning and understands Tony's Bistro, to oversee the Chicago expansion. He decided that River would be perfect for the position, and now, with all the recent trouble, Tony feels that it will be a good way to get her away from the conflict in the Houston office, and "that Adam character," as his friend Jason refers to him, adding that he is "bad news."

River walks into his office and says, "Hi, Tony."

He stands and shakes her hand. "How are you, River?" He has always liked her hands, which, while large, suit her, don't seem out of place, and seem to announce the kind of woman she is—*I can take care of it, whatever it is.*

"I'll be just fine. Thanks for asking, I appreciate it."

"Matt and Daryl will be joining us. You've spent some time with Matt, right?"

"Yes, we've had a couple of meetings." River is confused and had expected this to be a meeting among just the three of them, where they would discuss the situation causing her absence and the recent court proceedings. She walks over to the corner table where there are croissants, coffee, and fruit, and looks out the windows at the view of the Post Oak and Galleria area, and then, considering Matt's attendance, wonders what the reason for the meeting can be. River catches her reflection in the window and instinctively starts to raise her hand to smooth and tuck under any errant strands of her pageboy. She stops herself, drops her hands, and turns away from her reflection.

"How does Matt like Houston? You know it'd be a perfect city if the summers weren't so long. Does he know what he's in for?"

Tony smiles. "Yeah, they can be brutal, but I think he likes the heat. Looks like he's a sun-worshipper."

Daryl and Matt walk in together. Daryl's much friendlier greeting than earlier doesn't surprise River. *He's so phony*, she thinks. Tony suggests that they get started and takes a seat at the conference table in the middle of the room.

"River, we've decided to make Chicago the first city for a Tony's Bistro. We're planning on opening two there. The economy there is thriving, and it's a city known for great restaurants." River takes a bite of the melon slice on her plate, listens intently to Tony, and wonders again why she's been invited to this meeting. While she is familiar with the Texas operations, she feels out of place in this expansion discussion, not having anything to offer. Matt smiles at River.

"Everyone is impressed with your understanding of what it takes to run this business, your organizational skills," he says between sips of coffee.

"Thanks, I do like my work." River looks at everyone around the table and wonders if they are waiting for her to say more. She is silent.

Tony speaks up. "I'd like you to relocate to Chicago and oversee the operations there." River is speechless, totally unprepared and without a clue as how to respond. "What? You mean temporarily? Until the restaurants are up and running?"

"No, River," Tony smiles at her. "It will be a permanent transfer, or a very long temporary one. You'd see to the renovations at the two restaurants. One is on Michigan Avenue, right in the city, and the other in Oak Park. You'd be responsible for everything. The whole operation. You'd hire help, of course, and I've already hired the architect to do the renovations."

River's hands instinctively go up to smooth her hair, tucking under the ends of her pageboy. She stares at Tony, unable to begin to understand all that it means, let alone answer.

161

Daryl chimes in, "It's a great opportunity, River. Do it right and the sky is the limit." River ignores him. *He probably hopes I'll try it and fall flat on my face.*

"This is a really big deal, Tony." River hears the fear in her voice and hopes no one else does. "It's a great opportunity and a huge responsibility. I just don't know. It's a lot to think about."

"If we weren't convinced you are the right person for this expansion, we wouldn't make you the offer, River. It is a big deal, you're right, and it comes with support and a promotion."

Daryl smiles at River. "I'd fight you for this if I could leave now." River looks at him and wishes he wasn't there. "But with my daughter being sick and all, there's no way I can leave."

"There's a lot to think about, Tony. When do you need an answer?"

"We need to know as soon as we can. If you decide against taking the position, we'll have to make other arrangements. Let's discuss any concerns you have though, 'cause I'm sure you're perfect for the job, River."

She stands and shakes Tony's hand again and thanks him for the opportunity. "Is a week too long?"

He smiles, telling her, "That'll be fine."

River walks back to her office tossing around questions. *Can I do it? What if I screw the whole thing up?* Then she tells herself she's done the same things here, only there she'd be alone. It scares her. Can she leave her family, she wonders, her family that she depends on so much? She's never been away from them, and her parents are getting older. She can probably handle that part of it, since Tony has assured her, she'll be back in Houston often for there will be frequent meetings at corporate headquarters. Still, she wonders if she can leave them. *Chicago, of all places, I've heard it's seriously cold there.* Thoughts crowd her, and then she thinks about what the move will mean for her and Adam. There is so much unsettled between them, and this just adds to it. She wishes she could talk to Ernest. She needs his sober advice. *Yes*, she decides, *I'll call my brother.*

The path through Alpha's cubicle reminds her of the more immediate problem with Adam. Suddenly, she feels overwhelmed with too much happening. She feels as if she is just being carried along, unable to change directions, not even sure what direction she should be headed in if she could. She checks her watch and scribbles a note on a Post-it pad, leaving it on Alpha's computer screen. *"I'm ready when you are."* She's only been at her desk for a few minutes when Alpha taps on her open door.

They walk in silence to River's car which, running late, she parked in the above-ground lot. On the short drive to the restaurant, she notices Alpha squirming and trying to raise her behind off the seat. Her skirt is too short to cover much of her rear, and the leather seat is hot.

"The sun really heats up those seats. Doesn't it?"

"They're hot as hell," Alpha answers. "It would've been better if we'd walked."

River looks to see if she is serious. The pained look on her face says she is. Serves her right. River smiles inside. She needs to learn to cover her behind.

"We're almost there. Nobody walks anywhere in Houston in June, not if they can help it. Especially not mid-day."

"Thank God." Alpha squirms as River pulls the car into the underground parking. They walk into Gilley's Steak House restaurant and ask for a quiet table. The hostess guides them to a corner table near the back of the restaurant and takes River's order for a glass of Riesling. Alpha asks for sweet tea.

The waitress is hardly out of hearing range when Alpha blurts out, "I'm sorry, River. I didn't want this to happen, but I had to do it. I just had to."

River is shocked by Alpha's sudden burst of emotion. Placing her hand over Alpha's, she squeezes it and asks, "What happened?" Before she can reply, the waitress appears with their drinks and takes their orders. Alpha orders a filet, rare, while River orders grilled shrimp. Again, Alpha hardly waits for the waitress to leave before she starts talking.

"Adam came over one night. He said you were having a meeting at your house. It was about ten-thirty and he'd been drinking. Said he wanted to look at the closet. He was gonna put some shelves in I'd asked him about, so I let him in. We talked for a little while after he looked at the closet, talking about how much it would cost." She pauses to take a bite of bread that she's dipped in olive oil from the bread plate. "Then he stood there cleaning his fingernails, and started telling me he wanted me as much as I wanted him. I told him he was crazy, that I didn't want him. He pushed me on the bed and tried to pull off my gown." River is stuck on her *gown*. Why didn't she have on a robe? "He kept trying to do it and telling me that you were trying to turn him into a pussy. That he'd do whatever he wanted to, a lot of stuff like that."

River feels sick being reminded of words she's tried hard to forget, realizing some of what Alpha is saying is true.

Alpha continues, "I asked him to think about you, but he just kept trying to do it. I started crying and then he cursed at me and left."

"But why'd you wait almost a month to file charges? I don't get that." She pushes the ashtray holding Alpha's still burning cigarette further away from her.

164

The waitress puts their lunch on the table. River asks for another glass of wine, looks at her food, and decides she doesn't want a bite. She has been able to eat very little in the past week.

Alpha takes one last long draw on her cigarette, stamps it out, and takes a huge piece of her rare steak chewing it hungrily. River looks away, nausea creeping up at the sight of the bloody plate. Her eyes come to rest on Alpha's package of Kool cigarettes, the same kind Adam smokes.

Before she swallows her food, Alpha continues in rapid speech, causing River to look away from the mass in her mouth. "I wasn't going to press charges at all, but he kept calling me, threatening me about what would happen if I told you." Alpha's speech slows, and she appears to brush away tears.

While feeling badly for Alpha, River wonders who is lying, she or Adam, and why? River takes a large swallow from her second glass of cool wine and forces down one of the skewered shrimp.

"I finally had to tell Daryl about Adam threatening me. I was really getting scared. I just wanted him to tell him to stop calling me, to knock it off. I thought he'd listen to a man. But instead of that, Daryl made me press charges and took me to the police station that same day. The policeman we talked to is his cousin."

"I don't understand why Daryl wanted you to press charges. And to say he had a weapon?"

More confused by Alpha's continuing mood changes, River tries to force away the thoughts that Alpha seems to be enjoying telling her story, as much as she is enjoying the steak. Minutes earlier she'd appeared to be near tears.

"You know," she says, and almost smiles, "Daryl's cousin asked me about a weapon. I told him he had a little knife, and he kept cleaning his fingernails with it. Maybe that's how they came up with it. I don't know where else they got that from. That's what I told them at the jury hearing, too."

River had been confused when several of the jury members asked about that little knife, so little you couldn't kill a gnat with it. She is angry now, but still she holds it in check. River learned a hard lesson in Alvin Heights, years ago, how to control her anger, not ignore it, but control it and use it later to motivate herself toward whatever she needed to do. Anger caused by Police Chief Manders and the mayor was responsible in large part, not only for her working hard to get them out of office, but for her finishing graduate school. This woman is talking as if this is no more than a traffic violation. Doesn't she realize if Adam had been found guilty, a big part of his life would've been spent in prison? This is a man's life here, her black man's life, and Alpha acts as if it is nothing at all. River doesn't want to ask, but she needs to know what she will say.

"Adam said nothing happened. Is that true?" For certain, River sees a smile playing around the corners of Alpha's mouth.

"No, he couldn't do it. Not because he wasn't trying, mind you, but because he'd been drinking. At least, that's what he said when he cursed at me."

River has never seen Alpha eat so much. She looks at her again and wonders if she is gaining weight; certainly, her face looks fuller.

"If that's true, why the rape charge? Aggravated rape at that. Didn't you know he could've been locked up for a really long time?"

Alpha delays answering the question. She slowly wipes her plate with a hunk of the French bread before she fixes River with those cold, steel-blue eyes, then says, "Like I said, it wasn't because he wasn't trying." She puts the entire piece of soggy bread into her mouth and smiles. "They have really good food here."

River has heard enough and is relieved she did all she could to save Adam. A sense of betrayal had plagued her since Friday, first by Adam, then Alpha, and now Daryl. She felt they all owed her more than they'd given, then remembers something her mother told her years ago. She'd said the only person who owes you anything, is you. Another of her mother's lessons she'd failed to learn was that no one can use you any more than you allow. She is angry she has allowed herself to be used, but wonders how Daryl could have done such a thing. He knew there had been no rape, and still was willing to see Adam locked away. She understands that in Daryl's eyes, Alpha has no part in this. Only that something happened between them, no matter what, and Adam had to pay.

The waitress brings the check that River quickly pays while Alpha, with her head tilted back, slowly exhales the smoke from her freshly lit cigarette and watches it trail away. Alpha pulls another hard drag on the cigarette with a smile of satisfaction on her face that remains while they ride back to work in silence.

River walks directly into Daryl's office and closes the door.

"Alpha said there was no rape, and that you knew it, but insisted she file the charge." Her voice is controlled, free of emotion.

"And?" Hostility thickens his voice. "He tried, didn't he?"

"But Daryl, aggravated rape? You know what that could've meant! And I know about you and Alpha. That's why you did it, isn't it?"

His face clouds. "No, I would've done the same thing if it had been you. He deserved worse than he got. What gives him the right to try to take what he wants?"

167

River loses some control and her voice rises. "Didn't you try with me? Not as hard, maybe. But didn't you try? And you've seen her with him. She's all over him any chance she gets. It's clear she doesn't mind being touched by him. Maybe that's the problem. Your woman wanted a black man. Is that it, Daryl?"

Daryl leaps from his chair and walks to the closed door. "It's over, River. He got off. Just be glad about that and don't worry about Alpha and me. Just let it be." He opens the door and stands beside it, waiting for her to leave.

River walks back to her office convinced Daryl only cares about himself, pure and simple. He doesn't care about his wife, his daughter, and certainly not about her. She wonders if she can work with someone as heartless as Daryl and as hollow as Alpha. And she doesn't even want to think about Adam. Chicago seems not to be so far away, and the cold weather might be a relief from Houston's summers. She feels a little less afraid of all the move could mean.

River works until late into the night, not wanting to see or talk to Adam. When she gets home, he is already asleep. "Thank goodness," she sighs, one more thing to think about today would be too much, so careful not to wake him, she crawls into bed.

When she catches the scent of his breath, she relaxes, thinking there is little chance she will wake him from his drunken slumber. With her back to him, she has just settled into a comfortable position when he turns to her and mumbles, "I was fired today." Then, just as if he's said little more than good night, he turns over and is snoring in minutes.

≈Galveston Beach≈

Two weeks later, Adam hurries from the job interview that River asked Greg to arrange for him at the plant where he knows the personnel manager. Adam feels good about it, and is almost certain the job is his, especially since he knows Greg will probably put in a good word for him. Before he leaves the plant, he calls River and tells her the only problem is the long drive from Clear Lake to Texas City. It took him almost an hour to get there, and with traffic, it could be worse. She reminds him to be thankful if he is offered the job. With that chore behind him, he straddles his motorcycle, shifts it into high gear, and speeds over the Galveston Causeway from the mainland to Galveston, anxious not to be late. He is determined to convince her today, or soon it will be too late, and everything could be lost.

Adam speeds across the Galveston Causeway Bridge over the bay. He feels as free as a bird, free from everything and everyone, nothing and nobody holding on to him. Only the blue sky above and the Galveston Bay below. Adam feels suspended in midair, touched only by the wind. He slows his motorcycle as the bridge descends onto Galveston Island. He wonders if, as they often are, the police will be waiting at the bottom of the causeway for unknowing tourists, or better still, defiant locals who fail to heed the speed limit. Sure enough, he is right. There they sit at the bottom of the causeway, waiting for their prey. He smiles at having beaten them at their silly game.

Broadway Boulevard is beautiful, and he drives slower than the posted speed, distracted by the island of huge pink and white blooming oleanders that divide the cars driving in opposite directions. Tall palm trees line both sides of the boulevard and stir gently in the island trade winds. At 61st Street he turns right and heads west to Seawall Boulevard and Gaido's Restaurant where they'd agreed to meet. His heart beats faster in anticipation. Even though the parking lot is crowded, he sees the car immediately and pulls in behind it. Galveston beach is always crowded during the summer months, but he easily finds a space for the motorcycle and walks into the bar area of the restaurant.

Trying to settle herself, Alpha finishes her second drink before Adam gets there. She doesn't know what to expect from this meeting. Will he be mad? He can be violent when he's mad. She's seen that and hopes to never see it again. Probably not, she decides, no matter what he said, she knows there is something good between them. When she sees him, she smiles and ignores that he doesn't return her smile as he walks toward her with his head leaning slightly to the side, a walk she's always loved. Already off the stool before he reaches her, she puts her arms around him. Aware of the looks from some of the people in the bar, she holds him tighter. *Let them stare*, she thinks, and to really give them something to see, she reaches up and kisses him on the mouth.

He stiffens and pullsaway from her, but she holds on to his hand and leads him to a booth in the corner. In the darkness of the corner booth, he allows a long kiss. Today is the first time they've been together in more than a month since Adam was arrested.

Alpha refuses to release his hand, reaching for the warm nearness of him. He studies her and tries to decide what will be the best approach. Deciding to try guilt, he looks at her with his almost see-through brown eyes.

"I can't believe you went through with what you said. I still can't believe you'd do that to me. That's some fucked up shit!"

Alpha has already ordered his gin and tonic, and the waitress is headed to their booth with the two drinks. When she is out of hearing range, he continues.

"Do you know I could be on my way to Huntsville Prison today, for a hell of a long time? How could you do some shit like that, Alpha?"

"I didn't want to do it. You kept calling me and threatening me if I told River. I got scared. You were acting crazy, like you didn't care about me anymore. I didn't know what had gotten into you, not calling me back. When I kinda mentioned it to Daryl, about what I should do, he wouldn't let me drop it and made me go through with it. I didn't know how to stop it," she hurries on. Pleading her case, she explains, "I didn't know about that aggravated part, what it meant, and then when I did, it was too late to stop it." Suddenly her voice turns angry. "Anyway, I told you that if you didn't do right by me, you'd be sorry. I meant that. I still do!"

The last night they were together, after refusing to have an abortion and threatening to tell River she was pregnant, he slapped her, hitting her so hard she fell back inside the opened door where she stood. He didn't look back when she screamed she'd say he'd raped her as he stormed away, hoping she'd fallen hard enough to do the job. He refused her attempts to talk to him since that night.

"I know I'm part to blame for this." He almost says "shit," but stops himself in time. "Can't you see the time is just all wrong? And of all the people to tell, why in the hell would you tell your ex old man? And you lied on top of it all!"

Alpha doesn't interrupt, only looks around occasionally to see if others can hear his raised voice.

"That was real stupid, Alpha, almost as stupid as you wanting to have this baby. I told you, we can have a baby later. After I get all this other shit fixed. This is just a bad-assed time. Now it's even worse. I don't even have a damned job. Can't you understand that?"

Adam's thoughts grab him, assault him, they are all he can see and hear. Listening to them, he is furious with himself. *How have I let this happen?* This is a question he asks himself daily, sometimes hourly. He'd only been with her three times and had decided that some white pussy wasn't worth his losing River. The very night he planned to end it, then she drops this shit. *How in the hell can she be pregnant? Why hadn't I used a condom? Damn what she said about not being able to have a baby.* He can't lose River. That's all that matters right now, and he'll do anything to keep that from happening. He's got to convince Alpha to have an abortion, and then he'll tell her to kiss his black ass and to go straight to hell.

He looks at her, his thoughts drowning out whatever she is saying, pleading, judging by the look in her eyes while she pulls on his hand. Crazy eyes, he thinks. *Yes*, he decides, *she is truly crazy wondering how she could ever have thought I wanted anything more from her than a roll in the hay.* And for that, she brought him to prison's door and is now threatening the best thing in his life, the life he wants with River. His thoughts grow louder. *Yes, hating her can be an easy thing to do. It must be a hell of a lot easier to knock somebody off that you really hate than it was to kill all those fucking Viet Cong. Shit, they never did a damned thing to me. But this bitch is fucking with me.*

Murder crowds all other thoughts from his mind. No matter how he tries not to, he keeps thinking how easy it would be to kill her. His hands wrap around her chubby neck, eyes bulging, as she gasps her last breath. And then, there he is digging a grave out on the little island in front of the gazebo. It strikes him as funny. Alpha's grave out on River's little private island, the one she loves looking out on so much, but when he thinks of the life he wants with River, then it isn't so funny.

Something about River keeps him anchored. Gradually, the murderous thoughts slip away, and he releases Alpha from his mind's death grip. River always makes sense. She was right to insist he take his collection of guns back to his father at the big house for safekeeping. He never saw anybody so scared of guns! She didn't need to know that he'd kept his favorite handgun, and besides, it was locked in his truck. Alpha shook his arm.

"Adam, did you hear me?" Hearing her high-pitched voice, he looks around to see if anyone is listening.

"What, what'd you say?"

"I said you don't need to have a job for me to have my baby. I have a job!"

"Alpha, just how long do you think you'll have that job if River finds out about this? I know your ex old man has some pull with Tony. Probably why my ass was fired! But don't think that River don't have some pull with the head guy too, 'cause she sure as hell does."

"You know she wouldn't do that. I know it, too. Little Miss Goody Two-shoes River!"

"Maybe not, but she could. Who can tell? Then, we'll both be sitting up here without a damned job. How the hell will it look for you to be pregnant by your boss'—?" the sentence lies unfinished, hanging in the air.

Alpha's face freezes. "Boss' what? You're not married to her. You could be living with me just as easy as you're living with her."

He drags his hand from hers, caresses her face, softens his eyes, and kisses her softly.

"Don't ruin it, Alpha. Help me work this out, please. Hell, what can I do without a job? If you just wait till I get this shit straightened out, we can have all the babies you want. The time's just not right. I need to pay back River some money that I owe her. I need to go through with this AA shit, so I can get my act together. Get a job I can hold on to, and just get my shit together, period!" He takes a breath and rushes on, "I'm going to them damned meetings with that preacher from the jury because River wants me to. The woman left her husband for me; damn, I owe her something, I can't just dump this much crap on her. I'm not that much of a dog!" Alpha takes back his hand, pulling it to her lap.

The waitress returns with two fresh drinks. Growing quiet again he takes his hand back from Alpha and almost downs the drink in two swallows. Alpha keeps reaching for his hand every time he removes it from his glass

"Right now, this is just more shit than I can handle. Can't you help a brother out? Damn, it's not like we can't have another baby later."

He notices her face soften, thinks he's on to something, and then he kisses her again, this time long and hard. "Help me with this baby. You won't be sorry."

She stares into his eyes, as if she can find the answer to why she has such feelings for him, real feelings. The last night they were together he had threatened to get on his motorcycle and keep right on riding if she didn't have the abortion. She hadn't really intended to go through with the rape threat. It was just that she would try anything to keep him in her life, and that was the first thing that had popped into her head. Then she lost control of everything once she told Daryl. That was also when she convinced herself he wasn't too crazy about River. How could he be if he could just ride away?

"Okay," she whispers. "I'll do it. Do you really love me, Adam?"

"Why else in the hell would I be here, trying to sort this shit out? I could'a just walked off. Could'a denied the whole damned thing. I'm not the only black man around. I'm trying to be a man about this shit, and it's pretty fucked up. I need your help here."

She releases his hand and slumps into the booth bench. "You'll take care of it? I don't think I can do it. And you'll be there with me the whole time? I want a real doctor, no dirty little back room."

"I'll take care of it. I'll call you in a day or two." He gets up to leave, but she pulls him back down.

175

"I reserved a room at the Sea Shore Hotel. I thought I'd spend the night on the island. Remember how it was that first time? Can you stay with me awhile?"

The Sea Shore Hotel was where they met the first time, and it had been pure magic for Alpha. The sliding glass door to room 301 faced the gulf, and left open the gulf breeze swept in. The water was rough that first night, and the sound of the waves rolled onto the beach played in symphony with the calls of the seagulls and her cry of ecstasy. It was a night she will never forget.

"Baby, I'd love to, but right now River is watching my ass like a hawk! Just give it some time, and we'll have a whole lot of nights together." He kisses her hard while thinking, *I can't wait for this shit to be over, so I never have to see this crazy bitch again.* He would like to stay on the beach, but not with her, and wishes River liked the beach as much as he does. But then again, he thinks, maybe not. Then it wouldn't have been such a safe place to meet Alpha the few times they'd been together, and who knew what opportunities his future held. It was good to have a place where he could get away.

They leave the restaurant holding hands. "Okay. Call me. I hope I can go through with it."

"I will, I'll call you, and I'll be with you all the way." He revs up his motorcycle and, excited by his control over the power beneath him and over Alpha, speeds out onto the Seawall Boulevard.

He had hoped Alpha would let his sister Ruth Ann, a licensed vocational nurse, do the abortion. Now he needs to find a doctor. "Damn the bitch," he cries out loud and speeds down the Seawall while the salty gulf breeze stings his face. Retracing his way, he turns onto 61st Street and heads back to the causeway. The ride clears his mind, and thinking about what Alpha has just told him, he decides Daryl deserves killing a whole lot more than Alpha.

Alpha watches Adam drive away until she can see him no longer, then she removes her shoes, crosses 61st Street, and walks the beach alone. The sand tickles the bottoms of her feet while she listens to the warm gulf water roll to the beach in soft, gentle waves and play with her legs. She wishes she could make Adam understand what having her very own baby means to her. She'd believed the doctor years ago when he told her she could never have a baby.

Memories of pain come back to her. She was only fourteen when pain doubled her in half and made her think she was dying, as her mother and stepfather rushed her to the hospital. It had been a ruptured tubal pregnancy which required removal of one ovary and its fallopian tube. The doctor told her mother the other fallopian tube was severely shrunken, and Alpha would probably never be able to have children. Her mother didn't ask who the father of her baby was. Her stepfather knew.

Since then, Alpha never used birth control. What was the point? Now, ten years later, she knows that doctor had it all wrong. She can have a baby! Now she knows that one day she'll have her own baby who will love her as she's never been loved in her life, except maybe by Adam. Their baby will be safe from all the things from which no one ever protected her. Then she remembers how much she hates her mother. Alpha decides this pregnancy has happened because she is meant to be with Adam. If they did it once, then they can certainly do it again.

Thinking of Adam, just as every time before, softens that hatred deep inside her that has hardened over many years and

177

many hurts. She knows she is foolish to question Adam's love for her. She is pretty; she is white; and she's never met a man yet who didn't want her. So why shouldn't he? What black man wouldn't? She wishes she had a girlfriend to talk to, someone like River. But she only has Daryl, and she knows now there is just so much she can tell him. All he wants is to get back into her bed, and she's through with him. Adam is her future, pure and simple.

While Alpha walks the Galveston beach, Daryl walks to his car after working late that evening only to find it in the parking lot with four flat tires. He knows immediately who is responsible and tries to see inside the car, but there isn't enough light. While he fumbles in his pocket for his car keys, he looks nervously around the dimly lit lot. Why did he work so late? Once he finds his keys, in his haste to open the door, he drops them from his sweaty hand. When he reaches down to pick them up, his heart is beating so hard that it hurts. "They need brighter lights in this damned parking lot," he mutters, and quickly scoops up the keys and hurries back to the office, his walk changing to a run every few steps. After almost an hour, AAA repairs the tires. He cranks the engine, which stutters and then stops. The sugar that was poured into the gas tank freezes the engine. The car is ruined.

≈The Abortion Plan≈

Adam's visits to the big house have become less frequent since he met River. She is uncomfortable around his family, especially his father who keeps the dogs chained in the yard. Of the many things River objects to about Adam's family, it is the chained dogs she objects to most, refusing to visit whenever she can find a reason not to, and that leaves Adam confused. "The dogs are well-fed," he argues. He thinks how different she is from any woman he's ever known: her collection of Barbra Streisand records, season tickets to the Alley Theater, even dragging him once to a Mozart concert that he thought sounded like noise. Relieved to see Ruth Ann's car parked on the side of the house, he pulls his motorcycle into the cluttered yard. His father walks out on the porch to greet him.

Harry's belly stretches his dingy-white t-shirt that is unable to completely cover a large part of his protruding belly. In his hand he has two paper cups filled with gin, straight up, and a fresh bottle in the back pocket of his worn jeans. Without asking, he presses one of the paper cups into his son's hand, as he walks up the steps. "Welcome! Been a while. Glad to see you still know the way here!"

Adam takes a big swallow and frowns.

"Ruth Ann home?"

"Yeah, she up in her room." Harry turns toward the house and yells to Ruth Ann.

"That's all right, I'm going up." Adam doesn't allow his father to call again as he bounds up the stairs to his sister's room. Without knocking, he pushes the already half-opened door wider, eases in, and sits down on the bed where, even though it is early evening, she sits, already dressed for bed. Neither one speaks for a while, the tension between them palpable. She knows something is wrong, considering it has been more than a year since he has been in her room. She turns in the bed toward him. "What's up?"

"I need you to help me get a doctor to do a' abortion."

She turns slowly and looks full-face at her brother. "What the hell are you talking about? An abortion on who? I know damn well it's not River!"

Adam takes another swig from the paper cup, frowning and coughing as too much of the bitter liquid floods his throat. "Naw." He stands and walks to the window. With his back to his sister he mutters, "It's Alpha."

Ruth Ann springs from the bed, rushes to the window, and pulls his arm toward her until she forces her brother to turn and face her. "You mean the white bitch who had your sorry ass arrested? That woman who works with River?"

Adam jerks his arm free and turns back to the window. "Yeah."

Ruth Ann speaks to his back. "I can't fucking believe you. You pretty damned stupid is all I can say. Just like your damned daddy. Fucking stupid!"

Adam spins around, sparks of anger flashing. "I don't need a fucking lecture. Can you help me or not? All I need from you is for you to help me find a doctor."

She stares at him with disgust etched on her face. "Yeah, I know this chick that's pretty chummy with the new black ob-gyn doctor at the hospital. She's an X-ray technician, and we talk over lunch sometimes. She's pretty connected. Maybe I can ask her."

"Do you know her good enough to ask? You only been there a few months. Can you ask her something like this without her asking a lot of questions? Without causing trouble?"

"Well, it's just a few of us black folks who don't cook or clean. We all know each other, somewhat. Besides, it's not against the law, abortions are legal now. All it takes is making an appointment at a clinic. I thought you were asking because you need it done in a hurry."

"How soon can it be done? How much will it cost? That's just what I need. Quick and quiet, that's it." Adam is excited. He wants it over as soon as possible; tomorrow will be just fine with him. His sister looks at him and wonders if there is any man anywhere worth a damn.

"How pregnant is she? I don't think they can do it after the first trimester."

"Probably a little over two months. Is that too much?"

Just as stupid as he is good-looking, she thinks, *not a fucking brain in his head*. "No, that's not too much." Ruth Ann turns from her brother and walks slowly back to her bed. She plops down with a loud sigh. "I'll see if I can get you an urgent appointment and call you tomorrow. Better yet, you call me when you can talk, when River's not around."

"What time?"

She turns her back to him and covers herself with the worn chenille bedspread. "I get off work at three, any time after that."

181

"Thanks, sis, I owe you one." He is at the door when his sister's words staunch his leaving.

"Adam, all that fighting against Daddy you do, maybe you're just fighting against yourself, 'cause from what I see, you're just like him!" He slams the door hard when he storms from her room. Being like Harry is the last thing he wants.

Ruth Ann thought if any of her brothers would make anything of themselves, it would be Adam, that he'd be different from their father. That somehow, he'd be better. Being better than Harry ought to be the easiest thing in the world, it seems to her. Adam always fought against doing whatever their father wanted him to do, standing up to him no matter what. She had hoped River could bring the good, if there was any, out of her brother, make him better. But in the light of things, being better than Harry doesn't seem to be where Adam is headed, Ruth Ann decides. "Men!" she spits into the empty room. "Fuck 'em all." Then she reaches under the bed for her almost empty bottle of vodka.

Adam, unable to wait, calls his sister at work a few minutes before noon the next day. She gives him the doctor's name, office address, and telephone number. "You better get her in there quick. She moved you up in the schedule, but there's no way she'll do it if Alpha's more than three months."

Once Adam convinces the receptionist he is making the appointment for his sister who is too embarrassed to call, he is told to have her there by five o'clock the next day. They will work her in. Trying to hide his excitement, Adam calls Alpha. "We got a five o'clock appointment tomorrow. With a real doctor."

"Tomorrow? That's so soon."

"Yeah. The doctor's office is on 8th Street and Broadway. It'll be easy for you to find."

"I'm not finding shit!" Alpha screams. "You can pick me up and take me. That's if I go at all."

"I'll already be in Galveston for a job interview. You'll have just enough time to make it if you go right from work. I'll be waiting for you there." *Can't lose my cool yet*, he thinks. *It's almost over.*

As promised, the next day Adam is waiting for her in front of the doctor's office when Alpha parks her car and gets in the truck with him. He pulls around to the unlit, back parking lot. "It's cooler back here," he says and kisses her quickly.

"You're coming in with me, right?" Her blue eyes, bright with tears, plead with him as her fingers worry the opal ring on her finger, a gift from Daryl.

"I don't think that's a good idea. Got to keep this quiet until we're ready to get together. You know I'll be right here waiting." He touches her face and kisses her, hard this time. "I'll be right here waiting for you." Alpha walks in alone.

"I don't need to be sitting up in the doctor's office with no white chick," he mutters when she is out of hearing range, "with no woman, white or black, but River."

Almost two hours later, Alpha walks slowly from the doctor's office. In her hands are hospital registration papers for outpatient surgery on Monday morning. Her eyes are red-rimmed and loaded with tears when she climbs into Adam's truck and reaches for his hand.

"So, when do we get it done?" He doesn't seem to notice she is near crying.

"It's scheduled for Monday morning at nine o'clock. I have to get to the hospital by seven o'clock to have all this done." She allows the papers to fall from her free hand onto the seat.

Adam doesn't look at the papers and barely notices the wetness collecting on the front of Alpha's blouse. "You think we can go by there now? Since we're over here. It'll save time Monday." He sees her face harden and reaches over to brush away a falling tear. "What all do you have to do, baby?"

"I have to have some blood tests. And this request is for a chest X-ray. The doctor will schedule things. She told me to go early Monday. So no, we can't go now." Her voice is brittle.

Adam is having a hard time pretending he cares about anything she's saying. He just wants this over, wants just one less thing to worry about. *Four more days*, he tells himself, *and all this shit will be behind me*. It is almost seven o'clock, and he's anxious to leave. With traffic, it will take him almost an hour to drive back to Clear Lake. "I just don't want it to be any harder on you. The sooner it's over, the better for you." He caresses her hands.

"It can't be any harder. Nothing can be harder, and nothing can make it easier. I hope you know that. I really do hope you know that."

"I know, baby, I know. And just like I promised, I'll drive you to the hospital Monday." He glances at the clock. "It's getting late, we better head home." Just then headlights from a car driving through the back parking lot shine inside the truck. Concerned about the lingering look of the driver, Adam downs his head, pries his hand away from Alpha's, and while shoving the papers towards her gives her a hurried kiss while he pushes open the passenger door. She stands in the gathering darkness watching him drive away. With the papers clutched in her hand, she walks through the darkness to her car left in the well-lit front parking lot.

≈The Doctor's Orders≈

Evaline is at her desk late on Friday evening organizing her schedule for Monday morning. The Clinical Laboratory and the Radiology Department are both located on the first floor of the hospital, next to the Emergency Room. Evaline sorts through the requests and removes those that are for X-ray. The request for Alpha Broussard causes her to pause, she thinks she recognizes the name and after looking closer at the form, she is certain. "It can't be," she whispers to herself. The procedure request is for an anterior and posterior chest X-ray. The surgical procedure to be performed is a "D & E." Evaline stares at the form and hopes she is wrong. Then she wishes she could give River a hug.

"How can it get any worse?" she asks herself. "How much more of this can she, will she take?" she continues talking to herself. Looking for any other plausible explanation she ponders what she should do. Maybe the father is that married guy River has been so upset about that Alpha is fooling around with. Maybe, if the father went with her to the office, maybe the doctor saw who it was. Evaline decides to call the doctor's office. Glad she and the doctor are friendly, she dials her home number when there is no answer at the office, praying she is wrong.

"Yes, they were still in the parking lot talking when I left around seven o'clock," the doctor explains. "The back parking lot was empty except for a truck when I drove through."

"Truck?" Evaline asks.

"Yes. Why are you so interested? It's probably just another black guy who thinks he has to sneak around to be with a white woman."

"Black guy?" Evaline repeats.

"Yes, I think he was black. I didn't want to stare in their direction when I left, but I'm pretty sure. That lot is pretty dark. And again, what's it to you?"

"I think this is the guy I told you about, the one my friend is involved with, that she went to court for."

"Oh no, I'm sorry to hear that. Maybe it's not him. I'm sure he's not the only black guy seeing a white woman."

"Yes, let's hope I'm wrong." She thanks her and agrees to meet soon for drinks. Evaline knows, as much as she hates to add to her friend's troubles, she has no choice but to tell River.

River remains silent long after Evaline finishes telling her what she already suspects. "River, are you all right?"

"Maybe it's not him." River's voice is childlike, little more than a whisper, and even though she knows she is lying, it's easier than the truth.

"River, I'm hoping the same thing. But, well, chances are it is."

"I know, Ev. I just don't want it to be. This is just too awful, and I don't think I can stand this, not one more thing.

What have I done? What in the hell have I done to my life? To Greg? To my whole family?"

Evaline removes the phone from her ear. River is talking and crying at the same time. Hardly understanding her, Evaline interrupts her, speaking calmly into the phone, "Come on now, River, you haven't done a thing but love the wrong man. Get a grip on yourself. Maybe it's not him. And even if it is, you're tougher than this. I know you are. You know you are."

"It's him. I know it's him. You know it's him." The crying stops, River's voice is strong again.

"Well, if it is him, and he went with her to the doctor's office, I'm betting he'll come with her to the hospital. No way can he know where I work or that I'll be doing her pre-op. So, I might see him. I'll call and let you know if he's with her. You need me to come over?"

Suddenly River is cold, and a chill shakes her. She feels herself spiraling down into something deep and dark.

"No, I'll be fine. Just call me Monday. I'll be fine, Ev."

River hangs up the phone, wraps a blanket around her shoulders, sits on the bed, and wonders if this is the way it ends. Alpha told her she would not be in to work on Monday because she was having some dental work done. Adam told her he was scheduled for orientation at his new job that day. She wonders how he will manage both. More than anything, she now knows that it is time. She must save herself. She doesn't see herself as the strong and independent person her mother raised her to be, who her sister thought had it all together. Not the woman who made her father and brother proud. *If this is true*, she tells herself, *I won't live with it, I can't; no matter how much saving the race Anna Cooper thinks we black women are tasked with*. Even though she's afraid of the huge

187

responsibility of the new job, and the almost paralyzing fear of leaving her family and Houston, it will make the decision on what to do about Chicago a lot easier. Once, just before Vera ended her engagement to Jason, she and Vera discussed what love meant. Vera declared she would never be "bloodied or bowed" in the name of love, and River had answered, "I don't mind a little blood for love, but I won't be bowed." Tonight, River realizes this has gone beyond a little blood.

Interrupting River's thoughts, the telephone rings. It's Evaline. "I don't know girl, you didn't sound all that good. I think I'll come over for a little while."

"No, thanks Ev, really, that's all right, you don't need to come over. Anyway, I hear Adam's motorcycle in the drive. Just call me Monday when Alpha gets there." River takes a long, slow breath, realizing Adam is becoming too heavy a load.

~ ~ ~

The sun creeps into River's bedroom at five-thirty Monday morning. She greets it with eyes wide open and doesn't move as Adam eases himself out of bed, trying not to wake her. She still hasn't moved when he returns to the bedroom thirty minutes later, dressed and ready to leave. While Adam makes noise, trying to stir River so she can see how good he looks and be glad she's stuck by him, she allows his goodbye kiss, anxious to learn whatever the morning holds.

River hears the door close and hurries into the shower, hoping the warm water will rinse away the scent of his cologne that's causing the sick feeling in the pit of her stomach. It doesn't. While she towels herself, she notices her pubic hair has become dense again and is beginning to curl, almost as if it had never been permed a little more than three weeks ago. She is glad to have it back. After a quick shampoo and blow-dry, River turns under a few loose curls with the curling iron and combs through the curls, styling them in her straight pageboy. Suddenly, she decides she is getting a little tired of worrying about her hair. She is tired of perms, and she is tired of that damned pageboy. At this moment, she decides to stop perming her hair. The scissors move quickly until she has trimmed away most of the already straightened hair, leaving behind hair that is short and somewhat uneven. She doesn't mind and arranges it as best she can. River is fed up with hair, straight or kinky.

In her office, River waits at her desk, unable to focus on getting any work done, just waiting for the call and notices how loose the black slacks she is wearing have become. She picks up the book on her desk. *Anna Julia Cooper: A Quintessential Leader*, by Janice Ferguson. It is Ferguson's PhD dissertation, and River has been reading it religiously for the last few weeks. Cooper argues those who benefit from the lack of adversity are not as healthy as those facing and overcoming adversity. *If that's the case*, River thinks, *I'll be pretty damned healthy once I "overcome" this nightmare.* She drops the book at the phone's first ring. The usually chipper Evaline can't hide the sadness in her voice when she whispers, "It's him, River."

"Thanks, I'll talk to you later, Ev."

River swallows the last of her coffee and walks into Tony's office with quick, steady steps. "I'm ready to discuss the Chicago offer, Tony." In less than an hour it is settled. She will be headed to Chicago in two weeks. She will need to make temporary living arrangements and Tony has already asked Relocon, an apartment locator in Chicago, to send information about the area and apartments in the city as well as in the many suburbs. River looks at the pile of color brochures Tony hands her, and a little excitement eases away some of her fear. She can hardly wait to tell her family of her decision. She knows her getting away from Adam is the news they have prayed for.

Once River's decision is made, she doesn't allow doubt to interfere. As with most things in her life, it is full throttle ahead, no matter how hard. For her, changing directions is the hard part, even when she believes she is headed in the wrong direction, but happily, she realizes she is getting better at that.

Greg is more relieved than excited about River's decision and has some equally unexpected news for her. He is getting married. A sudden flood of emotions assault River, all at the same time—sadness, jealousy, happiness. Uncertain about exactly what she should feel, she settles on happiness. Greg deserves to be happy. River knows the woman he is marrying. Someone who appears to love him more than she ever did.

≈Packing Up≈

River wonders where Adam is spending the remainder of the day after taking Alpha home from the hospital and hopes he's gone to his orientation. By two o'clock, Adam calls her office twice, leaving messages on her answering machine since she doesn't answer, telling her what a great job this will be for him. His only complaint is that it's a "hell of a drive." She is relieved he has a job. Before locking her office to leave for the day, River picks up the two large boxes she's taken from the storage room and heads home.

When Adam gets home that evening, two boxes, filled to overflowing with his clothes, are sitting in the entry hall. He quickly looks around downstairs for River, and not finding her, bolts upstairs. "River!"

"What the fuck are my clothes doing in those damned boxes?" he explodes when he finds her in the small upstairs office. The look in his eyes is one she hasn't seen before, foreign and frightening as he storms around the room and knocks things from the bookshelf. Is this madness? She doesn't know this Adam and has dangerously miscalculated the best way to end this relationship. Scared and not sure of what to do, she slowly turns away from him. He grabs the desk chair she is sitting in and twirls it around so she faces him, turning it with such force that it makes three rotations before he grabs it to stop its spinning. River grips the armrest to keep from being dumped to the floor.

"What the hell my clothes doing in boxes, bitch?" he screams again. This time, his caramel face, dark and angry, is almost touching hers, and she feels his spittle spray her face as he rants. River knows she is in real danger and summons all her courage, takes a deep breath, softens her voice, and slowly answers.

"Adam, I just need a little time away, not only from you but from all that's happened. I believe it will be good for us both. This has just been too much for me." She loosens her grip on the arms of the chair, and the tensed, aching muscles in her hands relax. "I need some time, just a little time, to sort everything out."

"How the fuck you think it'll be good for us? I'm in this for the long haul, understand? It won't be no leaving. Not no leaving and living, and that's for damned sure."

River does not move from the chair. She's at a loss and doesn't know what to do, and for now, doing nothing seems best. Adam's face remains inches from hers, so close she can feel the heat of his words. She doesn't know this person and grows more afraid by the second. He paces back and forth, stopping to glare and curse at her through his heavy breathing before starting his pacing again.

I'll see you fucking dead first!" he yells while some object in the room falls victim to his wrath and crashes to the floor. He stops his pacing and spins the chair around again with even more force than before. River grips the arms of the chair again and holds on tightly, trying to decide how she can calm him. Crossing the room in exaggerated strides, he stops at the chair again and fixes River with eyes she doesn't recognize. A menacing smile, more frightening than anything she's ever seen, slowly creeps across his face. He kneels on one knee and leans in close to River again; she feels his hot, wet breath on her face.

"You don't know who you're fucking with, bitch! Believe that shit, you don't have a fucking clue. I'm never letting you go! You really don't want to fuck with me! Take my word for that. I'll be your worst goddamned nightmare if you fuck with me!" Then suddenly, no longer smiling, he stands up and gives the chair another hard twirl, and yells, "Fuck!" as he hits the wall and drives his fist easily through the drywall.

River's breathing is shallow, too scared to take deep breaths, and she is beginning to feel lightheaded. She keeps telling herself to stay calm, just stay calm. Clearly, Adam is trapped in some violent temper fit.

She never takes her eyes off him as he marches back and forth while she tries to decide how to calm his rage. He continues to pace. Suddenly, he stops and with calm certainty says, "Do you know I'd rather see you dead than gone? Fucking independent bitch." He starts his march again.

Finally deciding on what, hopefully, will calm him, she softens her voice even more than before. "I'm not saying it's over, Adam. You know that's not what I'm saying. How can it ever be over between you and me? I'm just asking you to give me a little space. Just a little time. It'll make things better for us if I can just spend some time alone and sort myself out. I probably should have talked to you about it before deciding, but you know how much I love you, don't you?"

The cadence of his march slows. When he is almost stationary, she continues.

"Adam, do you have any idea what it's been like for me these

193

last few weeks? If you really care about me, about what I've been through, especially while you were in jail, you could understand just how hard it's been. You'd understand I just need some time, just a little time."

After almost an hour of marching and ranting, he sits down on the floor. He thinks about his time in jail. Maybe it has been harder on her than he knows, he reasons. *She's from a different world*, he tells himself, *one I don't have a clue about*. He takes her foot in his hand, and while massaging it, at times painfully, looks up at her and asks, "How much time?"

"It'll just be a month or so. No longer."

There is no reaction from him, so she keeps talking. She can see he is considering her proposal, and he hasn't returned to pacing. Then suddenly, reaching some unpleasant place in his mind, he throws her foot against the chair.

"And just what am I supposed to do for a month or so?" he roars.

She takes some time before she answers, time to give the pain in her foot to ease, as much as time to search for an answer. She hasn't mentioned the move to Chicago, and maybe, if she handles it just right, maybe she can use it to calm him. She is thinking as fast as she can, convinced that her life depends on the outcome of how she handles what is happening in this small room.

"Tony's asked me to go to Chicago and open those two restaurants they've been planning. I thought I could agree to take that assignment. It shouldn't take much longer than a month. And I'd have something else to think about other than what we've just been through. Since you've got such a long drive to your new job, maybe you could use that time to find us a new place, one closer to your work and not too far from my office.

Then when I get back, we can start all over again. A new start with all of this behind us."

His eyes return to a softer shade of brown, the red is gone. "You love this place. Why you want to give it up?"

"I only took a one-year lease, and it ends next month. Now the owner wants to sell it, so we were going to have to move anyway. With all that's been going on, I just haven't had time to talk to you about any of this."

That part isn't a lie. She is the owner, and she will be selling the townhouse. He appears calm now, so she rushes on. Still thinking and talking as fast as she can, she adds, "Finding us a place and learning your new job will keep you busy while I'm in Chicago. Just make sure the house has three bedrooms and a garage. I expect this'll mean a promotion when I come back to Houston, and I'll need a larger room for a home office."

"You sure about all this?" It is beginning to make sense to him, even though he suspects she has her doubts about him, and at times he wonders if she really believes what he told her about Alpha. Still, he knows women are easy, eager to believe whatever he tells them. But River, she is different.

"I'm sure, Adam. I've given up a lot for you and me. I've got a lot at stake here too."

Adam thinks about how ambitious River is and decides what she's saying makes sense. "Yeah, I can probably take care of that. Don't worry, I'll find us a good place. One where neither one of us will have too long a drive. Maybe I can find it before you leave. When will you have to leave if you take that job offer?"

"Don't rush. We want the perfect place. Besides, I'll probably have to leave in a few weeks so don't rush, we have time. He stands up and walks quickly to the bedroom, where he finds the newspaper on the floor on River's side of the bed. With more than a little searching, he locates the real estate section. *Maybe*, he thinks, *this is a good thing, this will give me the time I need to get Alpha out of my life.* His steps are lighter when he returns to the room where River sits, chilled and trembling inside, still afraid to move. "Let's see if we can find anything in the paper."

She takes a deep breath but realizes she will have to be very careful over the next two weeks. Now she needs to be certain Adam doesn't find out that it is a permanent move. River doesn't know how much of a chance there is in that since she knows Alpha is the only person from Tony's that he'll be talking to. She isn't sure just how much Daryl has told Alpha and, to be safe, makes a mental note to ask Tony to announce her move to Chicago as "temporary" until she is there.

The next day River makes a one-month reservation at the Chicago Hilton and Towers on Michigan Avenue beginning August first. Then she reserves her United flight to Chicago. She calls the realtor with whom she's discussed listing her home and gives explicit instructions. Don't discuss anything about the listing with anyone but her. Then, effective first of August, she agrees to the listing contract.

"Two more weeks," she calmly tells herself, "just two more weeks."

Adam keeps busy at his new job, which he really seems to enjoy, so that works in River's favor. When he isn't looking for a new house for them, he is helping her to wrap items she doesn't want to trust with the packers. Adam believes that the movers will put everything into storage in Houston until he finds a place to suit River. If he doesn't find one that pleases her before she leaves, he tells himself it won't be so bad to stay with his folks until he does.

One week passes, and while he sits on the living room floor packing away the stereo equipment, he notices Alpha's car drive slowly in front of the floor-to-ceiling living room windows. "Oh fuck," he whispers when she pulls into the driveway. He holds his breath, watching her as she backs the car out and slowly drives away. He calls to River upstairs, "I'll be right back. I'm going to get a pack of cigarettes."

Alpha is parked at the entrance to the subdivision and falls in behind Adam's motorcycle when he turns on to Bay Winds Boulevard. At the Holiday Inn, he pulls into the parking lot and finds a space behind the hotel. Using more force than needed, he knocks the kickstand into place and leans the bike on its support.

Alpha doesn't return his smile as he walks around to the passenger side of her car and looks in. "Get in!" Her face is red and twisted by rage.

"Bitch," he sneers under his breath. Still, he is glad she has the engine on and the air conditioning cooling the car. He doesn't know if it's the ninety-degree heat and humidity or the way his heart is racing, but he is dripping with sweat.

"Do you know how long it's been since I heard from you? What the hell is this about? I could've been dead!" she screams.

"We said I wasn't going to call you at work. I called you a couple times at home, but didn't get you."

Alpha stares into his eyes, long and hard, searching for something, love, truth, any little thing.

"We're trying to get things in storage before River leaves," he says with anger creeping into his voice. "I been looking for a house. It's been busy as hell, and I'm learning the ropes at my new job. Unless I want to stay a carpenter apprentice I got to impress 'em at the job. Give me a fucking break!" He takes a

197

long, hard drag from his cigarette.

Alpha reaches over and takes the cigarette from him. She puffs on it angrily. "That didn't stop you from calling to check on me. I did a lot for us, for you. Don't ever think you can forget it, understand? Not for one damn minute, and you know by now I mean what I say. At least I hope you do."

"Get off'a my ass. Be a woman and stop acting like a spoiled goddamned brat. Fuck!" He slaps the dash with his open hand, knocking off the picture of her dog. "I knew you was at work, doing all right, or I would'a heard it from River."

"It's always River. I'm sick to death of her. The sooner she's gone the better."

"Yeah, we'll be able to spend more time together then. Just lighten up for now, you acting like I'm the one leaving."

Alpha reaches for his hand and leans over to kiss him. "Don't say that. Don't even joke like that. Please."

He allows her a quick kiss, but pulls away. "Let's don't get started. We got plenty of time for that later."

"Feels like you're always pulling away from me. It doesn't feel good, Adam."

"Being with you the last few times ain't been too hot neither. I'm getting tired of all the shit, all of your damned whining."

Without looking at him, and in a guttural voice, she groans, "If I have to, I'll tell River about us, about the baby, about everything. How we agreed to tell her that nothing happened. And I know you're the one who fucked up Daryl's car, too. His cousin, that policeman, is watching your ass, so you better cool it."

At about the same time Daryl's car was ruined, her Doberman disappeared from her fenced backyard. Alpha refused to believe Adam had anything to do with it despite Daryl's insistence that he was involved. No matter how hard he tried to convince Alpha of it, she pushed the thought away. Adam knew how much she loved her dog. He wouldn't have done that—he couldn't have—she argued. The night he was going to leave it at Alpha's door, a policeman pulled him over for speeding when he wasn't. Glad the cop didn't search his truck and find the gun, Adam pulled over, opened the truck door, and let the dog out on the way home. Lucky dog.

"I don't know what the hell you're talking about," Adam complains. *The less she knows about me the better*, he thinks, deciding he's not telling her shit about Daryl's car or anything else. *Better his car than his ass*, he thinks, still harboring murderous thoughts.

"I don't appreciate you driving by my house. What the fuck is that about? And what do you think River would think if she'd seen you cruising by?"

"I don't care what she thinks. Besides, I live six streets over and I don't need to explain why I'm anywhere."

"I guess that's why you left that fucking note on my windshield a few days back. Because you don't care what she thinks?" He'd kept the note, though, and didn't know why, thinking then that it wasn't that big a deal. He and River will be in their new place soon, and Adam promises himself that Alpha will never know where that place is. He'd make damned sure of that.

"That's right. I don't care."

"You know, Alpha, a real woman wouldn't need to put this kind of pressure on a brother. She'd see all the shit he is trying to deal with and back the fuck off. Give him some time, some room." Her face softens, and he smiles inside, marveling in his way with her, a way that always works.

199

She reaches for his hand, holds it tightly, and pleads, "I just don't know what's going on. I just need to hear from you. The least we can do is talk. Is that too much to ask?"

"No, Alpha. That's not too much. Right now, I need to help River…"

"Fuck that bitch! It's always River!" Alpha screams, interrupting him in mid-sentence. Then, more to herself than to Adam she whispers, "I don't know why they had to change River's move from permanent to temporary, why she couldn't just stay in Chicago like she was supposed to at first. All I ask for is a phone call, and you sit here telling me about what she needs." Alpha is no longer able to hold back the tears.

"What'd you say? About River's move being permanent? At first?"

"Forget it Adam. Get out! I'm going home."

Maybe Alpha's not all that bad, but just not the woman for me. If talking is all it takes to buy me some time, then we'll talk. "Yeah. All right," he answers while reaching for the door handle. "Like I said, I called a coupl'a times. I guess I should'a kept calling until I got you. Sorry about that. Won't happen again. I'll call." He reaches over and quickly kisses her wet face while he pushes open the car door. He is almost home before he remembers he needs to stop and get a pack of Kool Lights and makes a U-turn in the middle of the street. "This was a pretty good use of my time, wasn't a waste at all," he mutters to himself. "Good to know I'm being watched." Then he wonders again what the hell Alpha meant by River's move to Chicago at one time being permanent.

Adam knows he'd be better off if he could find a way to tell River about all that happened with him and Alpha, but he also knows he needs to give it some time to get things back tight with

River. Then he'll tell her. "That's the only way, short of killing Alpha, to get that crazy bitch off my back," he tells the darkness, pulling into the garage. He pushes that thought away, knowing he'd be the first one they'd suspect if anything happens to her.

He smiles feeling better about everything as he walks into the house. River's going to Chicago for a month is turning out to be a good thing. It will give him some time to keep the whole thing from unraveling. He also hopes that with a little more time, maybe Alpha will set her sights on somebody else. "Yes," he mumbles, "I think I can make this all work out just fine."

≈Getting Away≈

River's flight is scheduled to leave Houston Intercontinental Airport a little after ten on Sunday morning. The packers arrive early Thursday, and the movers are scheduled for Friday morning. Adam will be at work, but just to be sure, River has given the same instructions to the movers as she has to the realtor. "Don't talk to anyone but me about anything!"

Unable to find a condo that pleases River in Houston, Adam is beginning to think they will probably end up getting another place in Clear Lake. He's been able to find another route that cuts his commute to work down to less than an hour. One hour is about the amount of time anybody should expect to spend getting anywhere in Houston, he decides. Besides, one thing River loves is the newness and neatness of Clear Lake. Adam awakes in their bed for the last time on Friday morning. He pulls River from the edge of the bed toward him.

"This is our last time waking up in this bed for a long time. This is messed up." He pulls her even closer to him.

"It'll be all right." She lets him rest his head on her stomach and tries not to tense up. "It'll be better when I get back. A promotion. A new start. Remember?" His head feels heavy and she tries to remember if it had ever felt heavy before.

"It better be! Living with the folks until I find a place is gonna be rough. I don't know if I can take Harry, not even for a month."

"Just keep reminding yourself it's only for a month. And remember how good it'll be when we get back together." She lifts his head off her stomach and sits up in bed. "I've got a long day, got to get started."

"I wish I could take off and help you."

Fear clogs River's throat, thinking how quickly everything can be ruined. "Just do a good job at work." She quickly adds, "And find us a place. That's all the help I need. Now you need to get dressed so you won't be late, got to make a good impression, right?"

He feels better about things knowing he's just made the best love to River that any man could, and he steps into the shower. Dressed, he goes downstairs and finds River at the breakfast bar with a cup of tea. He looks at the notepad with numbers in Chicago, and that uneasy feeling returns, stronger than before. One of the magnets that holds papers to the refrigerator reads, "Husband And Dog Missing, $100 Reward For The Dog." He's always hated that damned thing, and she knows it. It won't survive the move, he decides.

"I guess we'll sleep on the floor for a couple of nights," he mutters.

River looks up from her tea and the list she's making. Just two more nights, she reminds herself. "It won't be that bad. Besides, isn't that supposed to be good for your back?"

The hardest part has been those times when, like this morning, she pretends she enjoys the sex. She has not been able to have an orgasm with Adam since he was arrested, and she has no desire to masturbate. River wants nothing to do with sex. Having decided sex lay at the bottom of this nightmare, she blames herself for not being above it.

"Nothing wrong with my damn back." Adam stands at the door glaring at River, unable to shake that uneasy feeling. "What did you decide to do about the car? Where you gonna leave it?"

"I told you. At Vallie Lynn's house. They've got that three-car garage." *Just let him leave,* she prays, *before the moving van gets here. How will I explain its size?* she thinks.

"Well, all right. I just hope she starts it every now and then. Else the battery'll run down."

"Adam, it's just a battery."

"Yeah, I guess you're right. Still, if you leave it at my folks' house, I can take care of it."

"Are you kidding? Their yard already looks like a parking lot!"

He decides not to argue, glad at least the car will be in Houston and that she isn't taking it to Chicago.

"Make sure you get me a key to the storage place where they're taking the furniture. I might need to go and check on your stuff while you're gone." He kisses her goodbye, wishing he could get a grip on himself and stop feeling so jittery.

River listens to the motorcycle drive away and takes a deep breath. She and Adam could have stayed with Vallie Lynn and her husband, but she decided it would be too uncomfortable for everyone, knowing how they feel about Adam. She also knows if she'd suggested they go to a hotel, he would have insisted they stay at the big house with his parents. Spending any time around Adam's father made sleeping bags on the floor in the empty townhouse an easy choice.

The moving van pulls into the driveway at exactly eight

o'clock. After they load the last of the boxes, they lower a ramp from the rear of the van, and carefully drive the Audi into the van. When they are ready to leave, they tell River they should be in Chicago by Monday night for Tuesday morning delivery. She signs off on the listed inventory and watches them drive away a little after noon.

The beautiful townhouse is now empty, except for the two boxes of Adam's clothes and River's packed luggage. The realtor has a couple who is anxious to look at the house once it can be shown. That will have to wait. All River can think of is making it through the next two days, knowing it won't be easy. She sensed Adam's edginess this morning and knows it will only get worse. When Vallie Lynn's car pulls into the driveway, River pushes her worries away. She is happy to be spending the rest of the day with her sister and their parents.

Adam is unusually quiet while he cleans the garage that night. They have pizza, but unlike a year ago there is no wine. River drinks diet Dr. Pepper and Adam has only one beer. He has drunk very little since his arrest, and she hopes she'll be in Chicago before he starts drinking again, as she knows he will.

River tries to respond to Adam's displays of affection. He caresses her face while he traces her features with his fingertips, as if he's afraid he might forget them while she is away. She thinks of the first time that he'd traced and caressed her face, what now seems to have been such a long time ago, and she knows he loves her the best way he knows how.

A thought flickers—has she given it enough time? Her answer is a quick yes. He is wrong for her, too much like his father, and she doesn't have any more years, or days, to love or be loved by the wrong man. Still she feels sad for him and his inability to decide whether to love or hate his father, blaming him for his love of alcohol. The only thing worse, she imagines, is how awful it must be to have no respect for his mother, while at other times, wistfully, telling River he wished there were more women like her. River always wondered about that. She knows he has terrible nightmares about his time in Vietnam. There have been many nights when she's had to shake him awake from his thrashing. *Why wasn't loving him enough to save him?* she asks herself. Then she thinks of Evaline and thinks she could be right. "Do I really need to fix things, to fix people?" Then River decides for now she is what needs fixing the most.

"I'm gonna miss you, River." More than anything, Adam wants to be right with River and wonders if this is the time to tell her about Alpha. He wants her to know he's doing everything right, not doing anything that can mess things up for them. For the first time in his life he wants to be totally honest but decides it's best to wait until she gets back. He knows she has a lot on her mind, and he's already dumped enough on her to spend a lifetime thinking about. What he feels for River makes him want to be better. He wants to be a better man than his father. He remembers he didn't know how to answer when River, after getting to know Harry, asked him, "What good does he do?"

"Yes, I know. I'll miss you too. But we'll probably both be so busy the time will pass quickly, and then I'll be back."

"I'm never gonna let you go, never gonna give you a reason to want to go. I'll be a good man for you, River," he whispers. "You'll see." He gently forces her onto the floor.

She lets him kiss her neck. "Be good for yourself first, Adam. That's what comes first."

"I know. I understand what you're saying, but I'm gonna be so damned good you'll be glad you stuck with me. We'll show 'em baby, that we got what it takes." He kisses every part of her and makes love to her the best he can. She rewards his efforts with a fake orgasm. His fingers play in her hair afterwards, disturbing her attempt to sleep. He notices the difference in the texture of the new hair growth from the previously permed hair and kisses her closed eyes while smiling down at her.

"I feel your roots growing out. You gonna do something about that?" River knew the mild relaxer she'd put on her hair wouldn't last the normal six weeks. She hasn't decided on just what she'll be doing with her hair but is tired of that damned pageboy. She cut it again herself last week and now the pageboy is turning into a short bob.

She smiles back at him and says, firmly, "Thanks for letting me know. Not sure what I'm going to do about it yet." Then, out of the blue, she thinks of Vera and decides to give her a call.

River and Adam spend Saturday together looking for a house, and the day passes quickly. Unable to find anything that River seems remotely interested in, after they are back in the townhouse, Adam's mood darkens with the evening and grows worse by the minute. The last house they looked at was perfect, and he knows it. Thinking about what Alpha said about Tony wanting River's move to be permanent in the beginning edges him deeper into darkness. He watches her as she sits on the pale apricot-colored plush carpet in the bedroom, working on some papers scattered on the floor, and as hard as he tries, can't calm himself. It is barely eight o'clock, and he has nothing to do. He can't even watch television.

"River, why the hell didn't you at least keep a TV here, so we'd have something to do?" His raised voice echoes through every room in the empty house. He wants this to be a good night, and it bothers him that he can't stop worrying, can't hold it together and make the last night a good one.

If there was a television, then maybe he could think about something else other than what River did or didn't tell him. *Why in the hell is that bothering me so much?* "Why didn't she tell me?" he mutters to himself.

Without looking up from her work on the floor, she answers, "Adam, I have something to do." Immediately she knows that she's said the wrong thing as he turns and rushes downstairs to the empty living room. He begins pacing, as he had that last terrifying time she saw him lose control. His marching back and forth sounds even more frightening now with the hollow clicking of each step on the hardwood floors echoing loudly through every room.

She jumps up and rushes downstairs to join him. "Why don't we go to a movie?"

"Nah, I don't feel like no movie, nothing I want to see. Maybe I'll go have a drink." *It has been a long time since I've had any real liquor,* he thinks. *A good stiff drink will calm me right down.* "I'm going down to Gators. I won't stay long."

"Wait, I'll come with you." She rushes behind him, thinking if she goes with him, she can limit his drinks. She prays for just this one last night in peace.

"Nah. You work on your papers. I won't be long. I'm not too cool with this leaving, and I don't care what kind of promotion you might get. I need to think, not talk."

He opens the door, closes it, then walks back to River and stands there, glaring at her without speaking. Then he turns and leaves, slamming the door hard behind him. Her heart is racing, but she says nothing, hoping the drinks have their usual effect—deep sleep.

Gators is a thirty-minute drive from the house, and needing a drink badly, he stops at a liquor store on his way and buys a pint of Seagram's. He wonders how many gin and tonics he had at Gators when, at almost midnight, he heads home. It's only because it's been such a long time since he's had gin that he feels drunk, he tells himself, and that's why he's having to fight hard to control the truck. He lifts the almost empty bottle of Seagram's to his lips and spills most of what is left on the seat when he runs over the curb, fighting harder to regain control of the truck.

"Damned woman. I'm trying to be straight with her, and she's keeping fucking secrets. Wonder what else she and Tony boy been cooking up?" His slurred words bounce around in the truck with him, when again he misses his mouth trying to drain the last gin from the bottle. He jerks the truck over to the curb, curses, and looks in the glove box for the wad of napkins he keeps there. The spilled gin has soaked his pants and the seat.

"Brother don't stand a chance," he continues talking loudly to himself. "Somebody always out to fuck with him. If it ain't the white man, it's his damn woman. Lying bitch!" He stops fishing in the glove box when his hand comes to rest on the cold steel of the gun. He gently takes it out and looks at it fondly before sliding it into his pants pocket.

"Fuck the car seat. Let it rot, and fuck a damn woman," he yells out of the open window, and then he down-shifts the truck and speeds home.

≈The Cemetery Visit≈

River is in her pajamas asleep on the floor. She tried to stay awake but unable to calm herself, she'd taken one of the tranquilizers her sister had given her. She doesn't stir when Adam unlocks the door, walks to her on the floor, and sits next to her, studying her face for a long time while he fondles the automatic revolver. He stands up slowly and steadies himself before he slides the gun back into his pants pocket.

"Get up. Let's go for a ride!" he yells as he clicks on the overhead light. His loud voice bounces off every wall in the empty house and bolts River awake. She tries to understand why his eyes have that red hue of madness she's seen once before. She sits there for a few minutes, too afraid to move. Scared and confused, she rubs her hands hard across her face and through her hair, struggling to make sense of what is happening.

"Let's go for a ride," he repeats, but quietly this time, still in a struggle to steady his drunken imbalance. "Get up, let's go!"

"Let me get dressed," she mumbles, reaching for her clothes on the floor, hoping for time to understand what is happening. River needs time, but the look in Adam's eyes tells her there is none.

He picks up her robe from the floor beside her and throws it at her. "Just put this on. It's all you need. You dressed enough."

"Adam, it's late. We have to get up early, and I'm really tired."

"You'll have plenty of time to rest in Chicago. Since you just got to go. I want to spend some time with you tonight. Let's go." He stands with the front door open to what feels to River like the hottest night of the year.

Trembling hard every few minutes, River walks out into the darkness and tries to understand what is happening as she climbs into the truck. It is a moonless night, and where are the stars hiding? The truck slowly turns onto the Gulf Freeway, heading south. Adam drives without speaking for the first ten or fifteen minutes, and River doesn't say anything, afraid of not knowing the right thing to say. She can't think; terror has locked her mind.

"Are we going to Galveston?" she finally whispers. He remains silent, giving no clue to the madness driving him.

"It might be nice to walk on the beach tonight," her voice is stronger. "It'll be a lot cooler there than here on the mainland."

"You been getting real good at lying, River. You know damned good and well you hate Galveston, hot or cold." When he turns to glare at her, the truck hits the shoulder, and he struggles hard to get it back on the road.

River keeps reminding herself to take deep breaths, and while she considers herself more spiritual than religious, prays hard while he steers the truck back onto the road.

"River, why didn't you tell me your move to Chicago was supposed to be permanent?"

The cab of the truck reeks of his gin and cigarette smoke, and she knows this is adding to the dizziness she's fighting. She lowers the window to allow the escaping cooled air to take the stench with it, hoping it will help clear her head. She takes several deep breaths and takes time to collect herself before she speaks. She needs to make sure her voice doesn't betray her.

"Is that what this is all about?" She forces a laugh, louder and higher pitched than it should be. "Adam, there was no need to discuss that since I never once even considered it. How could I?" He glares silently ahead.

"I could never leave Mother and Daddy, especially now they're getting older. I told Tony that. What was the point in talking to you about something that I could never do?" she pleads.

He turns off the Gulf Freeway onto a dark road. River thinks she has never seen such a dark night and fights hard to control the tremors that move over her stomach and down into her legs. He refuses to answer her questions and drives without speaking until he reaches Greg's church ten minutes later. The truck turns into the parking lot and slowly creeps over a bumpy road to the back of the church, near the cemetery where, even though River didn't think it possible, it is even darker. Adam leaves the motor running and puts the truck in park. He then reaches into his pants pocket and fondles the smoothness of the pearl-handled pistol.

His eyes are fixed in the direction of the cemetery as he speaks with a flat voice, "I'd rather be over there than to try to live without you. Sometimes, you know what I think, River? I think the only time I'll have any kinda peace is when I'm six feet under. Right over there." He nods in the direction of the cemetery. "Don't you think it looks peaceful, River? Quiet and dark. Nobody at all to fuck with you."

River forces another laugh, this time less shrill, not so loud. "Well, yes, it looks peaceful, but we've got a long life ahead of us, a lot of years together before we need that much peace."

He turns from the cemetery and fixes her in an unblinking

gaze. She fumbles in the darkness to find his hand, unable to see anything inside the cab but his eyes. Her heart races, skips a beat, terrified of what she thinks the hardness is that she feels in his pocket. Still, she fights hard to keep calm, moves closer to him so she can see more than his eyes, and forces herself to speak.

"I feel sad too, Adam. I know what you feel, and I understand. It's just for a month though, and I'll be back so often, probably every week or so, that you won't have time to miss me. Don't make this worse than it is."

"I don't know, River. I just don't like it. Why do you have to take that damned job? You might get there and not want to come back." He looks back in the direction of the cemetery.

She reaches for the hand that is in the pocket where she's felt the hardness and gently tugs at it. It is closed around the hard object and doesn't budge.

"Adam, everything I love is here. Mother and Daddy are here. My sister, my whole family, my whole life. You think I could leave them? Do you?"

He pulls his gaze away from the cemetery and looks at River. The peaceful look leaves, and the tortured Adam returns, the one she'd thought she could save.

"You one of the smart ones. Who can tell what you might do? You probably think you too damned good for me anyway!"

"Come on baby, you know how I feel about you." She leans into him and kisses his neck, then his face, and finally his lips. She hears his breathing slow and become heavy. She reaches for his hand again, but it remains closed around the hardness in his pocket.

"Touch me here, baby, please." River caresses her breasts and steels herself for what she knows will be more of the sickening taste of gin and cigarette smoke still lingering in her mouth and making her nauseous. She leans into him and kisses him long and hard as her stomach rolls.

"River, I love you so much." He releases the gun and, finding River's breasts, drunkenly fondles them. She pulls him onto her.

"Help me with your pants," she whispers. He tries to help, finding it hard to support his drunken weight. Only seconds after entering her he becomes dead weight and is instantly asleep. She takes the gun from his pants and puts it into her purse. The hot July night is moist and sickly sweet, laced heavily with the scent of fallen and rotting magnolia blossoms, stirred by the misting rain that has begun to fall. River struggles to get him off her and vomits before she can free herself. She pushes open the truck door, stumbles out, and is racked with dry heaves. Exhausted, she leans against the truck.

Panic makes it hard to think, and she considers just leaving him in the truck and getting a hotel room for herself rather than going back to the townhouse. *Is there any way I can get to the townhouse or a hotel?* she asks herself. *It is much too far and too late to try and walk, and there is no way to get a taxi at this hour. Maybe he will sleep until the time for my flight to Chicago, but what if he wakes up and finds me gone?* she wonders. Who can tell what he will do?

River feels as if she will faint. Lightheaded, she needs to slow her heart that feels like it's in her throat, so she starts counting backwards to calm herself. Then she decides it will be best if she just sticks to her plan, reminding herself that she has less than six hours to go. She climbs into the truck's driver's seat and with the air conditioner on and the window down to force out the smell of Adam, gin, and vomit, she drives back to Clear Lake while Adam snores. Careful not to wake him, she pulls the truck into the garage and opens the door, eases herself out of the truck, and softly closes the door behind her. She leaves him there.

After soaking in water that is too hot for almost an hour, River stays up the remainder of the night. Only when it is almost time to leave, she shakes Adam awake. Dazed and unable to remember much about last night, he wakes up in the truck, not knowing what happened, but is certain they had not made love. After a shower, he tries to pull her to him.

"No time for that." Determined to avoid any confrontation, she works hard at avoiding his eyes. "Flight's not gonna wait for me. I need my coffee, and we don't have much time."

His hangover doesn't let him argue and, after cleaning what he thought was his mess in the truck, dresses quickly while trying hard to convince himself that he's been foolish to doubt River. He picks up the two suitcases to load into the truck. *Any fool could see how much she loves me*, he tells himself; *she's paid a lot to be with me*. The smell inside the truck makes him wonder why last night's gin made him sick. Knowing he'd been too damned drunk to make love to River on the last night before she leaves, he curses himself again and swears he'll never drink again.

One of River's favorite places is the coffeehouse on the corner of Nasa Road I and Saturn, so they stop there on their way to the airport. Even Sunday mornings start early in Clear Lake, and the jogging path around the lake is busy with runners. River loves Houston and Clear Lake, and is sad to have to leave it. She wants to hurry and get it over with.

"Let's go. I don't want to be late," she says as she finishes the last of her maple nut scone and cappuccino. They arrive at the airport in less than half the time River expected and are parking the truck when River reaches into her purse.

"This was on the floor of your truck last night."

215

"What?" Only then does he remember having the gun. He puts it in his pocket and follows River to the airport terminal, trying to remember how the gun got on the floor and when she had gotten it.

"I'm sorry baby, about keeping this one gun. I know I told you I'd leave all of 'em with my old man. I'll get rid of it. It'll be gone before you get back, even before you get to Chicago."

"Thanks Adam, I appreciate that." At the entrance to the airport she turns to him. "Let's just say bye here. If you go any further, it'll just be too hard, and the flight is leaving in a few minutes anyway. It'll be easier if we just say bye right here."

"Forget it. I'm going with you all the way. Here or there won't make a damned bit of difference; it's still messed up."

"With that thing in your pocket? That wouldn't be too smart, they have metal detectors at airports now. And if you go back to leave it in the truck, it'll make me late." She kisses him quickly, and before he can object, grabs the suitcases and in long strides walks away without looking back.

"Remember, you call me," Adam calls after her, "soon as you get to the hotel!"

"I remember."

He calls goodbye again, loudly this time, and she waves a goodbye without turning to look at him and disappears inside the terminal.

When she walks inside the airport, River is happy Adam is not with her. Waiting for her are her parents, Vallie Lynn, and Ernest. She is surprised to see her brother, who she'd thought was coming to Houston on business Monday. River doesn't cry when her parents and sister give her flowers—two yellow roses and a stargazer lily—her two favorite flowers. *Ernest came to the airport to say goodbye to me*, she thinks. Knowing how much her brother loathes Adam, and still, even though he might have seen him, he came to the airport anyway. River's eyes are bright as she blinks back tears. After spending breakfast with her family, where she is unable to eat anything having just eaten a scone, she goes through security clearance and boards the plane, without thinking to check her hair as she passes the airplane window.

Part Two

≈Chicago≈

It is almost one o'clock on the first day of August when River walks out of O'Hare Airport and over to the second island to wait for the car rental shuttle. A million miles from everywhere and everything she knows is how she feels, more alone and frightened than she had expected. Trying to hold back a need to cry makes her throat hurt, but she is determined she is done with crying. Tony has given her directions to the furnished office he's leased in Oak Park, a suburb west of Chicago. Armed with an area map and directions after the shuttle driver lets her off at her rental car, River heads to Michigan Avenue and downtown Chicago.

Accustomed to Houston's freeways, the Eisenhower Expressway is easy to find. River notices the exit to Oak Park that she'll be taking to her office the next morning. Even though she misses her family, she starts to feel free from Adam, and it feels good. She likes the feel of this city, too. It seems to wrap itself around her as the Eisenhower takes her underneath an elevated gold-colored building named the Chicago Stock Exchange. The tall buildings that surround her seem so close that, somehow, she feels embraced, protected by them. In Houston everything is so wide open. She thinks the city left her exposed and vulnerable, something she'd never thought before. As the Eisenhower reaches Michigan Avenue, River sees Lake Michigan and laughs out loud! She realizes what she had in her subdivision in Clear Lake was nothing more than a pond. She turns right onto Michigan Avenue and wants to drive slowly to take it all in, but the traffic won't allow it, forcing the rental car into the heavy traffic flow. Finding the hotel is on the right, she turns in and gives her bags to the doorman and her car to the valet. River checks in but decides against going to her room.

"I'm going exploring," she tells the desk clerk.

"I'll have your bags taken to your room, ma'am," he smiles. "It's a nice day for a walk. Enjoy yourself."

It is almost three o'clock when River walks out onto Michigan Avenue. She strolls down to Congress Boulevard and turns right, crosses Columbus and stops to stare up at two, almost forty-foot-tall magnificent bronze sculptures of Native Americans on horseback. They look to be posed for war, but neither of them appears to be ready for battle as one is holding only a small hub of a bow, and the other looks ready to throw a missing spear. River doesn't mind the pedestrians brushing past her while she stares up at the gigantic statues, maybe even more than forty feet, she thinks. She soon forgets about the missing weapons and is caught up in the natural, naked beauty of the Indians. She smiles up at them and walks into Grant Park.

Barely eighty degrees and it's August. River can't believe the weather. Where is the humidity? She doesn't know where to look first, at the rose garden in Grant Park or toward the centuries-old buildings strung along Michigan Avenue. Unable to decide which is more beautiful, both lose out when she finds Buckingham Fountain. The huge pink marble beauty spews water, how many feet in the air she can't guess, synchronized to rise and fall in rhythm with a Mozart symphony. *How serendipitous*, she thinks, *my favorite composer, fate is smiling.* With no desire to leave, she sits on a bench facing the fountain, enjoying the soft mist on her face, blown from the fountain by a gentle breeze off Lake Michigan. "There could never be a more beautiful city. This feels right," she whispers while the sounds of Mozart and the mist caress her.

After almost an hour she forces herself from her bench and heads north on Michigan Avenue. Once she crosses the flag-capped bridge spanning the Chicago River, she stops, marveling at the Wrigley Building, wondering if her eyes are fooling her when she sees so many varying shades of white terra cotta. The street sign reads Magnificent Mile, and River smiles again. She experiences pedestrian gridlock for the first time, as she makes her way around others on the crowded sidewalks. *In Houston*, she thinks, *you'd be hard pressed to find a single person downtown on any Sunday afternoon.*

River hasn't eaten a thing since coffee and the scone in Clear Lake, unable to eat a bite at breakfast with her family. Remembering the popcorn shop whose aroma beckoned when she passed earlier, she heads back in that direction. The line stretches at least twenty feet outside Garrett's Popcorn Shop, and River takes her place. After she listens to those ahead of her order, she decides the cheese and caramel blend must be the choice to make. She heads out of the shop wondering why the clerk has given her such a thick wad of napkins with her small mini-mix. She soon understands, enjoying the sweetest, and looking at her yellow fingers, the cheesiest popcorn she has ever had. She wishes she'd picked up extra napkins on her way out.

It is after five o'clock when she finally gets back to the hotel. She'd been wrong about beating back the need to cry and is surprised by the tears staining the front of her blouse. Unable to hold back the tears, she cries. She cries for all the people and places she's left behind, for all the dreams she's left there, too, and for her broken heart and all the hearts she's broken. She cries for more than an hour, body-shaking, snotty-nose crying. Afterwards, even with a dull headache and red, puffy eyes, she feels better.

≈The Letter≈

It's a little after nine o'clock Sunday morning when Adam, after leaving River at the airport, heads to the big house. He feels disconnected, unable to call River because she's told him she'll be going directly to the office, and hasn't set up telephone service there yet. He only has the number for the hotel, but she has promised to call him later and give him her office number, once she has everything organized. Then, feeling a little relief from the pressure of finding a place River will like, he decides to take a day off from house hunting and opts instead to stop by and see Joel, his friend since elementary school. They head to the pool hall on the corner and have a good day shooting pool, drinking, and spending time with the women who hang around. It is almost midnight when he pulls his truck into the yard at the big house and stumbles upstairs. Then, he wonders if River called and, if so, what she'd thought since he wasn't home. Gin dulls his concern, and soon he is snoring.

On Monday morning Adam's mother, who knows all about waking a sleeping drunk, shakes him hard. "Adam, you need to get up."

"What time is it?" He struggles to shake off the effects of too much gin.

"Five thirty. You better hurry up; you know it takes longer to drive from here to your job than it did in Clear Lake."

"Did River call?"

"No." She doesn't look back at him as she goes downstairs to her bedroom and continues, "I got something in my room for you. Now you don't need to be late, so hurry up."

"Okay, I'll be down in a minute." He dresses quickly, goes downstairs, and takes the paper from his wallet with the Chicago information.

"I'm sorry, the number you have dialed is not a working number…"

Adam doesn't wait for the message to finish and slams down the phone. *I must have dialed the wrong number*, he thinks, vowing again to stop drinking. "Damned gin messing with my sight," he mumbles and dials again. The same recorded voice answers again. He tries hard to fight back ugly feelings and speaking to the telephone says, "River probably just wrote the number down wrong. I'll call information; they'll have the right number."

"Information, city and state, please?"

"Yeah, Chicago, Illinois."

"What number in Chicago?"

"The Sebastian Hotel on Michigan Avenue." He waits, while he listens to his pounding heart and watches his breathing lift his shirt.

"I don't find that listing, sir. How are you spelling it?"

He looks at the paper. "S-e-b-a-s-t-i-a-n."

"I'm sorry, sir. There is no listing for a Sebastian Hotel on Michigan Avenue."

Now his heart is beating at a gallop, and he pleads with information to stay on the line while he spells it every way he can imagine, begging for a listing anywhere in Chicago. Still there isn't one. He is sweating, and despite his efforts to slow his heart, it feels about ready to leave his chest. He stands up from the kitchen table and turning in incomplete circles feels himself falling apart, and unable to rein himself in. His thoughts are fragmented, loud, and ugly. He stares down at the telephone receiver in his hand and jerks it from the wall. Sounds of breaking glass as he hurls the offending object through the kitchen window bring his mother and father running into the kitchen.

"What tha fuck you doing, boy?" Harry yells when he sees the telephone base hanging from the wall. Adam is pacing back and forth, not sure of what to do. His mother thinks her son looks like an animal that needs to be caged.

"Shut up, Harry." Shocked and unable to believe his wife would tell him to shut up, he wonders if his son is losing his mind. Unsure of what else to do, Harry grows quiet and glares at the broken telephone.

"I can't find the number! To the hotel! In Chicago!" Pitifully, his eyes plead with his mother. "Mama, I can't find River!"

She takes Adam's hand and leads him toward her bedroom. Each time he wrenches his hand away she takes it again, gently, and once inside the bedroom she closes the door behind them. His mother had hoped River would stay with Adam, but somehow had never believed she would. She didn't blame her when she stopped by last Friday to tell her she was leaving Adam and Houston for good. She had feared River was not the kind of woman who would stay with a man like Adam, so like the man she'd married. Still, she was thankful and forever in her debt because she'd stood by him during the grand jury hearing. She knew what River had done for Adam and had agreed that if she was leaving, then this was the best way, with distance and time between them.

"Sit down, Adam. Sit down and pull yourself together." The quiet in her voice calms him a little, so he sits down.

"Adam. You know if it wasn't for River, you'd be locked up now?"

"What'cha want with me, Mama? I don't want to talk about what could'a happened, about me being locked up. I need to go. I need to figure out what's going on with River!" He jumps up and heads for the closed door.

She blocks the door. "Sit down, Adam!" Her raised voice forces him back down. "Son," his mother starts, "River left a letter here for you Friday. You know she's been through a lot."

He bolts from the chair. "A letter? From River? Where's it at?"

"Just listen to me first! I don't know what the letter says, but whatever it is, you got to accept it. You got a good job at the plant, thanks to River, making good money, and you don't want to mess that up."

"Mama give me the damned letter. Right now!"

"All right, son." She keeps talking, not blaming Adam for cursing at her, behavior learned from his father, while she walks toward the night table. "Show her and everybody else you can make something of yourself, Adam. Stop all that drinking and running around. Read this letter and take some time to think about whatever she says." She gives him the letter and closes the door when she leaves the room, sadly wondering if her first born will end up like his father, and wondering, also, if she had hugged him more, would it have made up for his father's lashes with the razor strap?

Adam is afraid to open the letter and sits for a few minutes staring at River's writing on the envelope, hating her and loving her at the same time. He swallows hard and then hurriedly rips open the end of the envelope. It's hard to read since he can't stop his hands from shaking, so he lays it on the edge of the bed and begins to read.

Adam,

I believe you can be anything and do anything if you want it badly enough. What I don't know is what you want to be or do. You have a new chance at life. You have your freedom and a good job, make the most of that. Put this year behind you and move forward, and know that life is a gift to be treasured, giving more than we take.

I know all about you and Alpha, the pregnancy, and the abortion. You have a second chance, take it.

I could never be good for you after all we've been through. One day you'll find someone who is good for you. Just try and be good for her in return.

Don't try to reach me. It's best if we don't see each other again. Take care of yourself.

River

He folds the letter carefully and keeps folding it until it is little more than a wedge, and then he tucks it safely away, deep inside his wallet. He ignores his father's questions and his mother's pleading eyes as he walks out of the big house and climbs onto his motorcycle. He can't go fast enough, but he keeps trying while the wind blows away his tears and keeps them from blinding him.

"Somebody is gonna pay for this," he screams above the roar of the motorcycle. "I'm gonna fuck somebody up! I'm gonna fucking fuck somebody up!"

His day at work drags by while he tells himself he doesn't

give a damn about how impressed his supervisor is with his carpentry skills. He is in a black mood all day, unable to decide just what he'll do to Daryl and Alpha, or how to do it.

"Alpha can just kiss my black ass," he says often during the day, whenever he is out of anyone's hearing range. He vows to ignore every attempt she makes to contact him and promises himself never to speak to her again. "I knew the bitch was gonna tell River," he mutters to himself.

The day ends, and not real sure of what his plan is, he stops by the big house to get his gun and a drink before he heads to Houston and the building where he used to work. He pulls into the parking lot and realizes he doesn't know what kind of car Daryl bought. He parks his motorcycle and watches cars leave for almost two hours while he reads and rereads River's letter. He refolds the letter and wonders how he let it happen. Let her make his heart tender after he'd let it scab over, scarred from hurting all the years he can remember. How had he been stupid enough to think any woman could tough it out, had backbone enough to stick with her man, like his mother had? But he'd let River show him life through rose-colored glasses, believe that happily-ever-after bullshit, and this is the thanks he gets. Hell, he's been trying, all he needed was a little more time. They almost had it. Somebody had fucked that up, and he would make them pay.

His thoughts turn again to Daryl, and while he waits his mood and the evening darken. There are still many cars in the parking lot and no sign of Daryl. There is plenty of time to take care of him, Adam decides, and besides, he's drained the last drop from the bottle of gin. After tucking the folded wedge safely away in his wallet, he says to the hot, dark night, "Fuck it, fuck everything," and roars his motorcycle out onto the Gulf

Freeway. This night is the first of many nights when he will lie close with some woman, feeling alone, hating that woman isn't River. Then, while waiting for sleep, he tries to decide who needs killing more, Daryl or Alpha?

≈The Renovation≈

Sunday and Monday are the hardest two days River has known. She wonders why Adam couldn't have been a little like Greg, or why Greg couldn't have had just a little of Adam's fight, or why they both couldn't have been a lot more like her brother. To hell with what Evaline said, she wishes for a little perfection in her life. She wants her white picket fence. Miles away from everyone and everything she loves, she feels completely alone and wonders where she is headed, if this path she's chosen is the right one. As promised, she calls home frequently, and Greg tells River, just as they'd expected, Adam called several times asking for her number which he, of course, would not give him.

Tuesday turns out to be a little easier, and River has no problem getting to Buffalo Grove where she meets the movers. Happy to give up the rental car, and tucked securely away in her Audi, she feels more at home when she drives away, enveloped in the smell and the feel of the tan leather, and a hint of gardenia car freshener she'd slipped under the seat before they drove it into the van. As she speeds along the Eisenhower, heading back to Oak Park, she programs the buttons on the car radio to stations she's been listening to in the rental. She has been, however, unable to find a station that plays Zydeco, that fast-paced Louisiana music that has become just as popular in parts of Texas. She loves Zydeco. Even when the words of the song are sad, the music always makes her happy, makes her want to dance the sadness away to the Zydeco two-step. Stepping music seems to be what is popular in Chicago, judging by what the radio disc jockeys keep playing, but River slips in Buckwheat, the one Zydeco tape she has brought with her. When he sings, "Your Man is Home," she turns up the volume, moves in the seat to the rhythm of the accordion, and makes a mental note to have Vallie Lynn send her some Zydeco tapes. The beat of the music is catching, and before she realizes it, she reaches Oak Park and turns sharply left off the Eisenhower onto Harlem Avenue, headed to her office.

Each day in Chicago, River enjoys more than the one before. This change for the better started when Greg told her that after two weeks Adam stopped calling asking how to reach her. The time she spends in Oak Park proves her research before making the move to Chicago was right. While African American is one of the larger ethnic groups in Chicago, it remains a residentially segregated city. Most of the African Americans live either in South Chicago or on the far West Side. This is not the case in Oak Park, a city that actively planned for racial balance, more than simply tolerate many different lifestyles.

As the weeks go by, River quickly becomes an architectural buff since Oak Park is rich with architecture, especially Frank Lloyd Wright's prairie designs. After visits to Hemingway's museum, she begins to think what she thought after reading him in college didn't paint a true picture of who he was. Maybe he wasn't as tough as she had thought. She thinks of Adam.

The space Tony leased on the third floor of an office building on Lake Street is adequate, but River wonders if it will be large enough for both her and an accountant, once she hires one from the list Tony has provided. The first meeting this morning, however, scheduled for nine o'clock, is with the architect responsible for the renovations at the new restaurants.

At exactly nine o'clock, Stefan Ryjonski knocks on her office door. Stefan is of average height and weight, but his hazel eyes are much more than average. They take up too much of his face and whisper kindness. Stefan is first generation American-Polish, and River likes him immediately.

Since they work closely together, and working together is easy, almost fun, they soon become friends. He offers to show her the "safest" parts of the city for a single woman to live.

After he has taken her to what seems to be every apartment building in the downtown area, she finally finds the one she just must have and can afford to buy. Soon she'll be moving into an apartment on the forty-first floor of a high-rise building on Michigan Avenue, directly across from Grant Park with a view of her beloved Buckingham Fountain, one of the largest fountains in the world designed in a rococo wedding cake style. She learned that Burnham and Bennet, who are responsible for the beauty, were inspired by a fountain at Versailles.

Today she and Stefan are to drive into the city to inspect the completed modifications at the restaurant on Michigan Avenue. Clearly, they enjoy each other's company, and he frequently chides her for not considering him a serious suitor.

"It's not you, Stefan. Believe me. I'm just not ready for a relationship, with anyone. Work is all I want right now. You're right though," she smiles, "I've never considered dating a white guy. I'm a Southern girl!"

Pleased that he is attracted to her, she lowers the sun visor and checks her appearance in the car mirror, then she grows quiet. For the first time in weeks she thinks of her hair and decides it needs some attention. There is probably enough new growth there for her to cut off all the remaining permed hair. She is still determined to wear her hair in an afro and wonders if it will look a bit too nappy.

"Is it something I said?" Stefan interrupts her thoughts.

"What? Oh no, I'm sorry, I was just thinking." Then she flips the sun visor up.

River is finally getting around to hiring an office assistant and has scheduled an interview with Keisha Miller. Hers is the first name on the list. River smiled when she first saw the name, wondering if Tony had placed her first on the list because maybe with that name she could be black.

It is a few minutes before one o'clock when River returns to her office. She says hello to a young white woman who is sitting in the downstairs lobby, and tries not to stare at her curly, almost kinky hair. She has barely settled into her office when the receptionist calls to tell her that her appointment is on her way up. She looks through the glass window in her office door and is surprised to see the same woman she passed earlier in the lobby walking toward her office. She is an attractive, slim woman, and River wonders how she got her dark brown hair, which she wears in a short bob, to curl so tightly. River thinks it can pass for an afro.

"Are you Keisha Miller?"

"Yes, that's me," the woman laughs. "Go ahead and say it, I've heard it all my life. It's a black name, right?"

River laughs out loud and says, "Well, sort of." Feeling

comfortable with her, she continues, "You're the only white Keisha there is, I'll bet."

They laugh easily together, and River, with Keisha's work experience and the instant ease between them, knows she is perfect for the job. Obviously, Tony feels she is a good candidate as well, since something caused him to put her at the top of the list. River knows that very few things are happenstance with Tony.

After a few weeks, River finally accepts Keisha's offer to help her unpack and get settled in her new apartment, which means they spend several evenings together after work. River eventually stops questioning the ease of their friendship while, in her new apartment, she chops the onions for the potato pancakes Keisha is making.

"River, do you have a heavy skillet?" Keisha asks while she searches through one of the boxes marked kitchen. River opens a box and gives her the skillet.

"This is the best I can do. Heavy enough?"

"My savta thinks you have to have a cast-iron skillet to get these crispy enough. But if it's the best you got!" The hot oil sizzles when Keisha places several potato pancakes into the skillet.

River takes a pancake from the skillet and blows on it to cool it before taking a bite. "Savta? Who or what is that? My goodness Keisha, these potato pancakes are delicious!"

"Oh, that's what we Jews call our grandmothers, especially when you've got one as hip as mine. She's taught me a lot. And again, River, they're latkes!"

"Well tell your savta thanks for passing these on to you." River takes another pancake cooling on the platter and spreads it with sour cream.

"Yep, that and this!" Keisha passes her hand over her curly hair and frowns.

"What, you don't like your hair?"

"Just kidding. I love my hair, I love me, and it's a part of me!"

River spreads sour cream on the pancake on Keisha's plate, smiles, and says, "Yes, it is," before she reaches for another pancake. She is happy that Keisha is there.

The next few months are the busiest River can imagine, and she focuses on work, with only occasional lunch and movies with Keisha. She is glad not to have time or energy to worry about Adam since she is responsible for every detail of the renovation, which, she is proud to report to Tony, is on schedule and well within budget.

The restaurant on Michigan Avenue has been completely transformed and the interior decorators are almost done. River hasn't tried to hide her excitement. This is her baby. All the decorating decisions are hers. The walls are panels of deep, emerald-green velvet evenly spaced between panels of polished mahogany wood. Floor-to-ceiling drapes of zebra-patterned velvet edge the expanse of windows that look out on Lake Michigan, and that same fabric covers the backs and seats of the mahogany chairs. She has convinced Tony that a piano bar is essential, and River signed off on that charge last week. There at the end of the bar, stands a mahogany baby grand piano. Behind the piano is a small parquet floor for dancing. Tony has invested a lot in this restaurant, much more than any of those in Houston, and it shows. At River's suggestion, he's also transferred the chef from his best performing restaurant in Houston to the Chicago location. The grand opening is scheduled for New Year's Eve.

Everyone from the front office in Houston is expected at the opening in two weeks. River wonders if that includes Alpha since it has been weeks since she's heard Tony or Daryl mention her. Stefan and River smile at each other, proud of their creation, and then head out for a late lunch.

Driving home, River thinks of her apartment and smiles. Even living out of boxes, she loves it. There is a doorman who hails taxis and opens doors for you. Guests can only enter the elevators in the second lobby after signing the guest register and receiving permission from the resident being visited. River's Audi is kept in a heated garage with twenty-four-hour valet service. There is also a concierge on duty who arranges anything that the residents need, from twenty-one freshly prepared meals delivered weekly to your door to scheduling the staff massage therapist. On the ground floor are a grocery store, dry cleaners, fully equipped gym, and swimming pool. You never have to leave the building, and she draws comfort from that, still waiting to see her first Chicago blizzard. The view from her apartment, through floor-to-ceiling windows that form all exterior walls, while not being on the Magnificent Mile is, for River, nothing short of magnificent. It is like nothing she has ever experienced, and she loves it all. Looking to the north is the Chicago skyline where the Sears Tower and Crowning Glory building seem close enough to touch. Lake Michigan sunrises warm her east-facing bedroom, and many evenings she sits at her dining room table, watching a glowing red sun drop from view at sunset. At night she is often at her living room window gazing at the Crowning Glory building, shining brightly in the shadow of the Sears Tower, and thinks of her family. She is happy her sister and brother are coming to the restaurant opening. Her smile spreads when she sees Keisha's car in guest parking as she leaves her car with the valet.

Two days before opening night, River overhears Keisha call and make an appointment to have her hair permed.

"How many perm rods do they have to use to get your hair to curl so tightly?" River asks, laughing.

"None. This comes naturally. Remember? Thanks to my savta? Sometimes, I get tired of it and get it chemically straightened."

"What? When we talked about it, I thought you meant the color, or because you have so much of it!" River can't hide her surprise. "I just never thought a white woman would need a permanent relaxer to straighten her hair."

"Well, now you know." Keisha spreads her arms wide and bows deeply. They both laugh.

"Who does your hair? You think they could do mine? I was thinking of going back to my afro, but now I don't know, maybe I'll get it straightened."

Keisha smiles. "Sure, girl. Most of the women who go there are black. Some famous ones, too. I even saw Oprah there once. I'm one of the few white ones."

"Oprah, huh? Really? Where's this salon?"

"It's Yesia's on State Street. I'll see if they can fit you in." She makes an appointment for River the following evening.

≈Yesia's Round Brush≈

Excited and a little anxious, River leaves work early and drives to the city. Keisha is waiting for her, and since the salon is only a few blocks from her apartment, she leaves her car with the valet and they walk. Just as Keisha said, all the clients except two are African-American. The shop is huge with ten work stations and ten Egyptian male hairdressers at various stages of doing something to some woman's hair.

The receptionist directs them across the blond hardwood floor to a coat rack and asks them to put on one of the brightly colored nylon smocks. She directs Keisha to a smaller room in the rear of the salon. Nervous, River sits down to wait for her appointment and takes in the brisk activity. After one woman's hair is blown dry, using a round brush to shape it, her hair is curled with a hot curling iron. All the men have rat-tail combs in various bright colors sticking in their back pockets that they wield with great efficiency. The men use the tail of the comb to partition off and lift out a section of hair. Then, the tail is used again to catch the hot, falling curls and position them properly on the woman's head while the teeth of the comb are used to smooth the curls into the desired hairstyle. River takes it all in, and watching them, even with the eye of a novice, decides that the round brush is the critical tool in the whole operation. That brush holds the hair taut, lifting and shaping it, with the help of heated air from the blow dryer. Yesia, who will be doing River's hair, interrupts her analysis and calls her to his chair at the front of the salon, which looks out on busy State Street through a large picture window.

"So, for what you want me do here?" he asks with a heavy Egyptian accent and a smile.

"Well, I was trying to let it grow out enough so that I could cut off what little permed hair is left and wear an afro. No more chemicals or straight hair for me! But now, I'm not so sure."

Yesia inspects her hair and says, "It's nice. You don't need do some chemical to your hair, 'specially if you take it short. I fix for you. It's good?"

She relaxes into his chair. "It's good."

The scissors click furiously, hair falls around her, and as she looks at the hair on the floor, she realizes there won't be much left on her head after he finishes cutting off what's left of the permed hair. On her way to the shampoo bowl, she can see when she looks toward the wall of mirrors, she is right. There is little more than three or four inches of hair left. From the shampoo area she looks in another room and sees Keisha's hair growing straighter and longer as the chemical curl-relaxer does its job.

Back in Yesia's chair, he takes a small, round brush and turns her hair around it while blowing it dry. After he puts very few curls in her hair, he combs it through and spritzes it with holding spray.

"It's good?" he asks. The whole thing from shampoo to spray has taken less than twenty minutes. He gives her a large, pink-framed mirror and twirls her around in the chair so that, reflected from the mirrored wall, she can see the back of her hair. It is gorgeous, and it was so easy, and took so little time. She thinks about the almost non-existent humidity in Chicago, compared to Houston, and is certain it will stay looking good for days.

"It's good," she smiles, happy with the temporary gold highlights she asked Yesia to spray in her hair. She pays the receptionist and makes an appointment for the next week.

Then, she sits down to wait for Keisha and smiles, feeling innocent pleasure that it takes so much longer to do Keisha's hair than it did to do hers. More than an hour later, Keisha's dark brown hair is straight and hangs to her shoulders. They are walking back to River's apartment and River is certain she sees Keisha cast a longing glance at the woman they pass who has long, straight blonde hair.

"You think she has to straighten it?" River asks.

Keisha grunts, "Probably not." A few steps later she asks, "How do you think I'd look as a blonde?"

River looks at Keisha's dark brown hair that the sun reflects off, showing highlights of red and gold, and says, "Your hair is so pretty. I can't imagine why you'd want to change it. I've never thought of you as a blonde. Have you?"

"Sometimes I do," is her quiet reply.

River mutters, "Really? Hmmm." They don't talk the rest of the way home. River wonders if every woman struggles with her hair.

The winds from the lake pick up. Back home, River thinks her hair, though windblown, looks great, and she doesn't have a perm. All it took was Yesia's round brush.

≈Opening Night≈

Tony calls to say they are checked into the Chicago Hilton and Towers and that they'll pick River up at six o'clock. They will all ride to the restaurant together. River invites Keisha to leave her car at her apartment and ride to the opening with them in the limousine. Ernest and Vallie Lynn are in a hotel not far from the restaurant and will take a taxi. Ernest wanted to walk, but Vallie Lynn convinced him they weren't dressed to walk anywhere in Chicago, especially in December.

While she pulls on the black silk skirt, River wonders again if Alpha will be with them. The gold silk organza blouse matches the gold highlights Yesia added to River's hair. Excited about opening night, but uneasy about seeing Daryl, and maybe Alpha, she goes down to the lobby to wait. Keisha arrives just when Tony, in a black tuxedo, steps out of the limousine, and River and Keisha go out to meet him. River has spoken to him weekly, sometimes daily on the telephone, but this is the first time she's seen him in five months.

They climb into the limousine and River is relieved to see Alpha is not there, only Tony, his wife, Daryl, and Jason, who River hasn't seen in almost a year. Keisha is introduced to everyone and the ride to the restaurant is tense in anticipation of opening night. Daryl looks more than tense, River thinks, she thinks he looks sad. She knows he is having a hard time coming to grips with his daughter's death. She had died shortly after River left Houston. She was uncertain whether she should send personal flowers even though Tony had sent an arrangement from the office, then decided not to.

Daryl smiles and says, "You look great. What'd you do to your hair? I love it."

"It looks like Chicago agrees with me, and my hair." She returns his smile, and wonders if he means it.

The drive to North Michigan Avenue takes less than fifteen minutes. Stefan is waiting inside, and Tony greets him while smiling his satisfaction. The waiting list proves that advertising has been effective, for reservations are full until ten o'clock. The hostess takes them to their table by the piano bar where Ernest and Vallie Lynn are waiting, and River's heart swells when she sees the pride on their faces. Tony, happy with his decision to relocate River and the success of opening night, goes from table to table welcoming the diners who are served complimentary champagne. Daryl asks River to show him the new computerized inventory system, and he follows her to her office.

"Alpha left the company," he says immediately.

"Oh? When did she resign? She did resign, didn't she?" Daryl understands the look she gives him.

"Oh yeah, it was all her decision, even though things had gotten bad between us. Things started going bad after Adam was waiting for me one day in the parking lot. It was about a month after you left. At first, I was scared, thought about calling the police but decided not to. He looked different, kind of nervous. Whatever was going to happen, I just wanted to get it over with."

"I was asking about Alpha. Not Adam. I hope I wasn't

241

discussed in that conversation, and Daryl, there's nothing about him we need to talk about."

"I know. Just listen! And, no, he didn't even ask about you. Didn't ask for your number, nothing. But I told him anyway, right up front, that talking about you was off limits."

River studies Daryl. "I'm sorry about your daughter, Daryl. What are you trying to tell me?"

"Thanks, River. It's about Adam. He looked jittery, said he knew we couldn't talk about you, and that wasn't why he came by. Said he needed to put this behind him and wanted to know why I forced Alpha to press charges. He laughed at me, right in my face, when I asked him why he hadn't left her alone like she asked. Then he showed me a note she'd left on his windshield. I felt like a fool. I didn't know she'd been running after him all that time. Then he told me about her being pregnant and getting an abortion. I didn't know any of that."

"Is that what happened? Did you force her out because of Adam?" River feels anger for the first time in months, and this time she doesn't like it.

"No, I didn't want her to leave. She was doing a good job for us. Like I said, she made that decision on her own. I didn't have a thing to do with that. Things got bad between us after she saw Adam and me talking in the parking lot. The thing I had a hard time with, though, was the abortion. I was burying a daughter I'd have given anything to have here with me. How could she kill a baby? I don't know if she cares about anything or anybody. Not really."

"When I left Houston, I left this behind me and that's where I want it to stay. I've learned when something is all wrong and you can't make it right, you can't get stuck in it, you just leave it. I'm through with all of that, Daryl. Really, I am."

"Things are getting better for me too, River. At least my wife and I are talking now." He pauses at some thought that seems painful and then continues. "Before Alpha left the company, she mailed a receipt to my wife for some furniture I helped her buy. I stopped paying on it the day after I talked to Adam. Maybe that's why she sent the receipt to my house, who the hell knows." Silence hangs between them while he toys with the computer. River waits to give him time to finish whatever else he has to say.

"My wife asked me to leave the day after our daughter's funeral. But we're talking now. Maybe it'll be all right."

River touches his arm. That place inside her, that "thumping within" she's learned to honor from reading Anna Cooper's articles, softens her, and she caresses his hand. Maybe, she thinks, coming out on the better side of trouble is, if not the only way, the better way some life lessons can be learned, those lessons that ultimately teach us our true worth.

"I hope it will, Daryl."

"One more thing, River. I already told Adam that I regret what I did. I need to tell you too. Not just about the thing with Adam, but for the times I…" His voice trails off.

She smiles and stops him. "Thanks, I didn't know how much I needed that, and I appreciate hearing it. That's in the past, let's leave it there. We probably need to get back to the others, don't you think?"

"You go ahead, I'll be right out."

River leaves Daryl inspecting the computer system and heads back to her table. She thinks of Adam and finds it hard to see him as nervous and jittery.

The hum of conversation in the restaurant is smoothed by soft music from the piano. Jason sees River, stops signing autographs, for he still has fans, even in Chicago, from his Heisman days. He meets her as she is about to cross the small dance floor.

"How about a dance?" She thinks he looks older than he should.

"Are you alright, Jason? Still happily married?"

"Well, yeah, I'm married, and it's good," he answers. "I saw Vera a while back. Finally, I was able to get her to really talk to me."

River thinks Jason has lost some of his luster, in fact everyone except Tony seems to have changed, seems to shine a little less brightly than they had before she left Houston.

"So, you've put Vera behind you, huh? I always thought she was good for you."

"Yeah," Jason answers, "maybe that's the problem, maybe she's just too good. She can't let herself or anybody else be, you know, just plain human. Everybody's got to be better than that with her, at least that's how I see it. I hate I messed things up for us. I told her she needed to stop expecting everybody to be perfect, or else she might end up perfect by herself, forever." Then he looks in the distance and says, "You know, she just might be happy like that. I still miss her though. All this time since we broke up, I still think about her. I wonder why she didn't know I was doing better, doing my best?"

River hears little of what Jason says after "doing my best." Glad when the music ends, she gives him a soft kiss on the cheek and says, "I guess some people's best just might not be good enough, Jason." She takes his hand and heads for her table again. "I'm sorry, but I need to sit down. Do you mind? These shoes weren't made for dancing."

"Sure, River, sure."

On the way to her table, she thinks of Vera and decides she will give her a call. Stefan intercepts her just as she is about to make it to her chair. He doesn't ask, just takes her hand from Jason and leads her back to the small dance floor. His hand folds over hers easily, and he guides her gently, but firmly around the dance floor to a Zydeco two-step she taught him.

"I've got to sit down, Stefan, my feet are killing me." He leads her back to her table and whispers, "You're a looker, simply beautiful." She smiles and doesn't give her hair a thought.

In the limousine on the way back to her apartment, Tony smiles and says, "This is for you River," then he reaches into the limousine fridge and gives her a chilled bottle of Dom Perignon. "I thought I was doing Jason a favor by hiring you, but he did me a favor by asking me to hire you. We need to talk about your title and salary one day next week." He walks to the lobby with River and Keisha, and kisses River on the cheek while George, the doorman, looks in the distance while he holds the door.

River beams, almost giddy with happiness. She thinks of the Paradise Palace and its opening on another New Year's Eve so many years ago, and of the woman she is today, so different from who she was then. She and Keisha are about to enter the second lobby when Daryl catches up with them.

"Thanks River. For making tonight a lot easier than I thought it was gonna be." He grabs her hand and kisses it quickly, as if he thinks she'll take it back if given a chance.

Neither she nor Keisha are sleepy, still excited about how well opening night went. Back on the forty-first floor, Keisha looks at the few still unpacked moving boxes while River looks out on Lake Michigan, staring up at the Crowning Glory building to the north. Unpacking and organizing the apartment is just about finished and they are gradually bringing some order to River's apartment. Keisha opens one of the last packed boxes and, looking at a photograph, is surprised at how long River's hair once was.

"Why'd you cut your hair so short?"

River looks at the picture with the straight and softly turned-under pageboy and smiles. "It was too much trouble." She takes the picture from Keisha and places it on the fireplace mantle, between the picture of her mother and father on one side and the one of her with her sister and brother.

It is after midnight, and still River isn't the least bit tired.

"Let's walk around the lake, Keisha. We can bundle up, and it's not all that cold. What do you think?"

"Oh, okay, give me something to change into." They both change into warm-ups, and Keisha wonders if the damp night air will cause her newly straightened hair to lose its soft curl, or worse, turn into a frizzy mass. After changing into River's warm-up, she finds River's hair spray in the bathroom. *A few squirts will protect it from the moist night air*, she thinks. Keisha's hair glistens, and she stares in horror as her curls slowly fall away and her hair grows straight, heavy, and oily. She picks up the can and screams to River in the bedroom, "What the hell is oil sheen?"

River, unable to understand, comes running into the bathroom and can't hold back her laughter. Keisha is standing there with glistening, oily hair, holding the oil sheen spray in her hand.

"It's not funny, River, not even a little bit! Look at my hair. I thought this was hair spray. What the hell is it?"

River tries to stop laughing and says, "That's oil sheen spray and it's not for white folks' hair. My hair is dry and sometimes

I first spray it with oil sheen *then* the holding spray."

"Shit!" Kiesha curses while she pulls her glistening hair into a ponytail. "My hair is a mess. Come on, let's go."

River, still laughing, tosses the hair spray can to her. "I think this is what you are looking for."

Keisha throws the can back. "Why bother now? Come on, let's go," she says with a smile.

Bundled in their parkas, they cross Michigan Avenue to Columbus and walk through the pedestrian tunnel beneath the busy street, busy even after midnight. The Roman inspired architecture of the Field Museum and the Shedd Aquarium glow in the soft uplight especially designed to show them at their best. They turn onto the curved path that edges Lake Shore Drive and Lake Michigan. They walk north, Navy Pier with its Ferris wheel lights up the distant view. It is a cold, slightly damp night, and moonlight from a late harvest moon plays across the gentle ripples of Lake Michigan. They stay out longer than they had planned, and River is chilled. Thinking the walk wasn't the best idea, they almost jog back to River's apartment. "God, my *bones* are cold," River pants, wondering if she will be wishing for the warm Houston winters.

The Crowning Glory building with its lighted crown draws River and stays on her mind, as they jog to her apartment. She turns back to look at it several times, and by the time they reach her high-rise, she decides for sure it is the best building in the Chicago skyline. Although it's never mentioned along with the Sears Tower as a sight that should be seen, it is the building River always seeks in the nighttime skyline.

Back home, River waits with Keisha for the valet to bring her car.

"You and Stefan looked good tonight dancing that Zydeco,"

247

she says with a laugh.

"Yeah, he's a good dancer."

"Looks to me like he's good at a lot of things. You seem pretty happy these days."

"Don't start, Keisha," River replies with a smile, not ready to talk about how her and Stefan's relationship has grown. Then she kisses her good night after she refuses to stay over, telling River she needs her "serious" shampoo to "degrease" her hair.

Back on the forty-first floor, River stares out at the orange moon, and her reflection in the window is framed in the crowns of the Crowning Glory building. Again, she thinks of Vera and realizes her hair looks a lot like hers. She thinks to herself, *If buildings could talk, maybe that building would tell me how less magnificent the Chicago skyline would be if it wasn't there in the Sears Tower's shadow.* "I already know," she says out loud while she runs her fingers through her hair and, even after the long cold walk along misty Lake Michigan, thinks it is still perfect. "My crowning glory, Daddy, and no perm," River whispers. Before their walk, she and Keisha had celebrated with the champagne Tony had given her, and she pours the last of it into her glass, lifts it, and offers a toast to Chicago and the Crowning Glory building.

River glances at her portrait there on the mantle. She knows if she ever decides to wear her hair long again, she will have to get it straightened and smiles, whispering, "So what?" She looks out at the moon, the skyline, and the thousands of Christmas lights strung around Buckingham Fountain in the distance. That persistent lurking dread that has always haunted her remains faraway.

There is a quote by Sojourner Truth that River tries to recall. She can't remember it exactly, but Sojourner wanted us to know it is the mind that makes the body. "Body and hair," River whispers, "for black women, it's body and hair."

Things feel good. Her new city feels like it really is hers, and River smiles that, even without her picket fence, life is pretty good. In her bedroom she notices the message light on her answering machine is blinking. It is a message from her brother. He congratulates her on opening night and tells her that at breakfast in the morning, he wants to discuss her traveling to Brussels with him next month. He's just landed a very important client there, and since Ollie is too pregnant to travel, he hopes she'll help host the reception that he's planning for this client and his wife. River smiles. Life just got better.

≈One More Buy≈

More than a year has passed since River left Houston for Chicago, but to Adam's thinking it seems as if she left only days ago. Never a day goes by when he doesn't relive what could have been and what almost was, keeping her memory ever new in his mind. Adam sits in the living room of Alpha's small house, but it is River who he feels all around him. They were meant to be, he thinks, any fool would know that if they ever saw them together. If he had half a chance, he could make it right, if he could just find her and talk to her. He reaches for his shirt, feeling hot and sweaty, he'd just ripped it off minutes ago, but now fighting a chill he pulls its wetness around his shoulders. He swallows down the urge to vomit and mumbles, "Maybe I shouldn'a had that last little bit of gin, 'specially on a' empty stomach."

The urge to vomit is strong, and Adam forces himself from the sofa making his way to the bathroom. The reflection in the medicine cabinet mirror is of a man he hardly recognizes. The eyes he knew River loved are flat and dull, surrounded by dark circles. His face is sunken. The last time he weighed he'd lost forty pounds. He studies the pink panties and bra lying on the floor, as if trying to decide what they are or why they are there. A wave of nausea forces all thoughts from him, and dry heaves bend him in half. He falls on his knees with his head almost in the commode, as he tries in vain to vomit. Ten minutes later, exhausted and soaked, using the wall for support, he drags himself back to the bedroom and collapses across the bed wondering what in the hell is taking her so long.

Alpha's faded, brown Chevrolet creeps down the Gulf Freeway, staying in the slow right lane and keeping just below the posted speed limit, headed toward downtown Houston. It is early evening and Alpha's car blends easily with the flow of traffic, almost disappearing into the dusk as she turns off at the Scott Street exit. Why in the hell, she wonders, would Daryl's wife, or anybody in Houston with good sense, buy a car with no air conditioning, cursing the hot, wet air that blows in through the open window. Still, she reminds herself to be happy it hasn't needed much maintenance since she bought it. The car slows at the first stop sign, and Alpha strains to see into the distance, focusing on the scraggly tallow tree that sways between her and the next stop sign. She wonders why the breeze that moves the tree branches isn't making its way through the rolled-down windows and forcing away the hot sticky air in the car.

Alpha is comfortable with the Third Ward of Houston, the "Bloody Third" it's sometimes called. But they know her here, she feels safe. The car moves slowly away from the stop sign, and focusing hard on the tree in the next block, Alpha sighs in relief when she sees him standing beside the tree. She pulls the car over to the edge of the street, careful to avoid the deep muddy ditch that runs the entire length of the street and the children who skip along its hardened edge that serves as the neighborhood sidewalk. She knows they will play well into the night. She's seen them there on some of her late-night runs. The man beside the tree moves toward Alpha's car, and she reaches into the ashtray and pulls out three neatly folded twenty-dollar bills. The man slowly makes his way to her car while keeping watch on the surrounding area.

"What tha hell y'all doing, selling this shit? This yo' second trip this week. Nobody kin be smoking that much shit." He speaks and keeps a lookout, while passing his hand through the open window without bending to look in.

"None of your damned business what we do with it, long as I keep paying! Right?" She presses the folded bills into his hand while taking the small clear glass vial in one smooth motion. Inside the vial are ten irregular-shaped, dirty white "rocks," and she slips it inside her bra. "You worry when I start asking your ass for credit. How about that?"

"Right. See you soon. Peace out." He raises the peace sign with his right hand and walks back to his tree.

"Yeah, right, peace," Alpha yells as she slowly pulls away from the ditch and heads back to Adam. Calculating how much money she has spent this week, and today is only Thursday, she admits to herself that all of Adam's money and much of hers is going to keeping Adam in gin and crack. She has tried to convince him that they should move in together, then she could save on house rent since Daryl is of no help anymore, refusing to return her phone calls. Alpha is careful to obey every traffic rule and up until now, thankfully, has never gotten a ticket, or even been stopped and questioned. She wonders why, whenever Adam drives, they are stopped so often? It only takes her twenty minutes to reach the house in Pearville. Not as nice as the apartment she had in Clear Lake, but cheaper. She parks the car next to Adam's truck in the driveway of the small, rented house and unlocks the front door. When Adam isn't waiting, she grows afraid.

"Adam, I'm back. Where are you? Adam?" Her heart begins to race and her steps slow when he doesn't answer, fighting this fear that one day she will find him dead. Slowly, she pushes the door to the bedroom open and takes a deep breath when she finds him sitting on the edge of the bed, soaking wet.

"You got tha shit?" He reaches toward her without looking up.

Alpha sighs loudly and says, "Yes, I made it to hell and back just fine, and thanks for asking." She reaches inside her bra and throws the vial on the bed. "Can we talk before you start that? We need to talk."

Adam's movements are fast and jerky as he pulls the pipe from between the mattress and box springs. "Yeah, yeah, what you want to talk about baby?" His words run together. He places one of the dirty white rocks in the pipe and lights it quickly. Breathing in the bitter smoke, and after two deep hits, his body stops aching and a slow peace flows inside him. "What'cha need to talk about, my sweet baby?" Adam's voice is heavy, his words slow and thick, and his lids droop. He pats on the bed for her to come and sit beside him. "Come to Papa, baby, come on. Let's talk."

"Adam, what's the point? What good will it do while you're high? You never remember one thing we've talked about."

Adam pushes the pipe to her. "Here, take a hit. This'll calm your sweet little ass right down."

"Go to hell, Adam!" She turns away from him, slams the bedroom door behind her, and trods into the kitchen. Alpha takes a prescription bottle from her purse and wonders what lie she'll tell so that she can get a refill next month. The Prozac is lasting her only half as long as it should. The pink and green pills her doctor prescribed for depression, after she had the abortion, seem to be helping, not as much as at first, and only when she takes them twice a day, which her doctor warned her against. She swallows another one, bending under the kitchen faucet for a sip of water. Alpha opens the one-half gallon bottle of Seagram's and pours herself a little in a glass. She looks in on Adam who appears to be asleep, and then walks out on the small back terrace, worrying, as another year begins, why she hasn't been able to get pregnant again. She's just made herself comfortable on the chaise lounge when Adam slides the patio door open.

"Come on in here, Alpha. Look what Papa got for ya." She turns toward the door, and he is standing there stark naked with a large erection. She wants to go to him but doesn't move. He walks out into the blackness of the Pearville night and stands in the darkness, letting the warm, nighttime breeze caress his body before he moves to her and takes her hand. His movements are slow, and his senses dull as he leads her into the bedroom. Much later, exhausted, he sleeps while Alpha, covered in his perspiration, stares at the ceiling.

≈Stefan's Pain≈

Another year has passed and the second restaurant is up and running. River is in love with Stefan, and she is sure he feels the same. She hardly ever remembers he is white, or that she is black, just that they laugh a lot together, that they talk late into the night, that they dance the Zydeco two-step often, and that she feels loved. Promontory Point on Chicago's South Side has become the favorite place for their many long walks. Their lovemaking is quiet, satisfying, and always ends with his arms wrapped around her as she sleeps. "Spooning," he calls it. There is a quiet strength in Stefan, and River feels she can lean on him, that he won't disappoint, that she is safe. He treats her a lot like Greg did, but River thinks that Stefan treats her that way because he knows no other way, and it is not the effort it had been for Greg.

This is the weekend they have decided to tell his parents they are getting married. Stefan has told River that his parents probably won't be too happy about it, at first, explaining, "They might be a little bit prejudiced," but assures her that in time they will grow to love her just as he does. Stefan was amazed when River's family accepted him into the family right away, the very first time they met him, and wonders why it can't be as easy for his parents. To his way of thinking, if there was going to be any hating it should be the other way around. He doesn't know Ernest urged Stefan's acceptance, speaking to them before they met him, explaining how good he believes Stefan is for River and how happy they are. Stefan has convinced himself that in time, even with their initial displeasure when he first told them River was African-American, once his parents see how happy he is, how much he loves her and how good they are together, they will be happy for him.

Stefan wants tomorrow to hurry and come so they can start planning their wedding. River is uneasy, wondering just what they will say, thinking they probably won't say much of anything to her but, thinking of what Stefan has told her, will tell him how they really feel. Hopefully, they will be fine with it, but then a worry crowds her thoughts; *even if they accept me now, they could really hate me, once they learn I can't have children.*

After dinner, bundled in their winter parkas, River and Stefan walk along Lake Michigan, headed to Promontory Point. After driving there in silence, finally River breaks the silence.

"Stefan, I know you say our having children isn't that important to you, but are you really sure?"

"I've told you, Sweet, it's not. Besides, how can any doctor be sure about something like that? You've been pregnant before, you can be pregnant again."

"Maybe not, Stefan," she whispers, and burrows into his embrace, shielding herself against the frigid wind off Lake

Michigan and Stefan's desire for children. They continue their walk in silence.

At home they head straight to the bedroom, climb into bed, and fall asleep holding each other, both needing the other's comfort, both afraid to say anything more. Spooning.

The following afternoon, River finds Stefan waiting in the kitchen when she gets back from an errand. "Are you ready to get this over with?" he asks. They keep finding things to do during the day to postpone making the call.

"Come on Stefan, you're probably worrying too much. I'll win them over." His hazel eyes are almost brown, and he keeps rubbing his forefinger with his thumb, a sure sign he is in deep thought, worried, or nervous. The callous that was there when he and River first met is gone, but River can see the redness returning. *Maybe he is right to worry; maybe I should worry too*, she thinks, recalling how upset his mother had been because he hadn't called earlier on Thanksgiving Day.

River and Stefan were driving back from dinner in Wisconsin with one of Stefan's college classmates and didn't want to stop until they were home. It was late that night when he called, and his mother, worried, was in tears. River asked Stefan if he thought her hysterical crying was normal. He answered, "We've always been close. She worries, that's all." River doesn't answer.

"Here goes." They sit at the breakfast bar, and Stefan gives River the extension phone while he dials the number.

"Hello."

"Hi, Mom. What are you guys up to?"

"Oh, hi honey. I hope you're calling to say you'll be coming up for a visit. We need to see you, I haven't been feeling too well. Maybe you're coming for Christmas? Please?"

"Is Dad there? Did he take you to the doctor?"

Her voice rises. "I don't need a doctor. I just need to see my son!"

"Well, I'll be coming for a visit soon. Not for Christmas, but soon. Ask Dad to get on the phone, I've got something to tell you both."

Right away she starts screaming for her husband, and Stefan stands and starts a slow pacing while rubbing his forefinger with his thumb.

"Milos, Milos, come to the phone, quick! Don't give me bad news, Stefan, not on the phone. Come home so we can talk, face to face." He hears his father's voice on the extension.

"Is everything good, boy? Why you got your mama carrying on?"

Stefan has no choice but to ignore the question and hope they will understand. He walks over to where River sits and takes her hand. "River's on the phone with me. We want to tell you that we're getting married."

River can't make out what Milos is saying above his wife's screaming, asking God to take her now.

"Alina, shut up, I can't hear myself think." Milos' command quiets her but not for long. They both are talking at the same time. Well, Alina is really screaming more than talking.

"Don't do this, son," River hears Milos say. "Don't bring that nigger into our family. Do you want to kill your mother? Do you hear her? Do you hear what you are doing to your dear mother? Bong her all you want, but no marry!"

Stefan tries to reach for the extension, but River, on her feet, backs away from him, beyond his reach. He covers the mouth piece. "Please, honey, hang it up, for me, please, let me talk to them." He can't believe they are saying these things when they

258

know River can hear them. He'd thought they would be civil if not kind, knowing that she was on the phone and that he loves her. He never expected this.

"Mom, you need to calm down, please. River's on the phone, and you know it."

"I don't care. I don't care! I'm thinking about you," she screams. "No decent white woman will ever want you again if you marry that nigger. You'll be ruined for life!"

Alina stops speaking and is sobbing hysterically, so Milos takes this opportunity to add, "It must be she's putting something in your food, I know it, probably got a nigger spell on you. You need to get away from her. Stop eating her food, get away, quick!"

"What has she done to you?" Alina gains her voice again and screams, "Did she give you some kinky nigger sex, dammed nappy-haired nigger woman?"

That's when River lets the phone slide from her hands onto the floor and walks from the kitchen. In all her thirty-six years, she's never heard nigger so often in such a short span of time. One minute she is sad, and then she is back to that old familiar feeling of anger that always pulls her through tough times. *They*, she thinks, *in search of a better life, happily pick up and come to this country, my country, built on the backs of and enriched by the blood of my ancestors*. Then she thinks about the Middle Passage and all her ancestors endured.

Her anger rages. Tears falling, she thinks of her mother's youngest brother, her favorite uncle, the one who made a career of the army and was killed, a colonel in Vietnam. "How dare they!" she growls at the bathroom mirror. She doesn't take time to test the water from the faucet that she splashes onto her face. It is so cold it forces her to take a deep breath. She stops crying.

259

While she dries her face, she studies her reflection in the mirror and, replaying Stefan's mother's "nappy," focuses on her hair. Just then, Stefan opens the door to the bathroom and reaches for her. His eyes are red and wet. She wants to run to him but backs away until the bathroom wall stops her.

"I'm sorry, baby. I should have talked to them first. I can't believe they said those things, especially with you on the phone."

River wonders if he would have felt better about it if they had said it where she couldn't hear. "We can't marry, Stefan. Not now. Not with them feeling this way."

"We can, and we will. I'm forty-five years old, this is my life and I love you, River, I love you and your family. I never knew a family could be so close, and so easy. It'll work out, just give it some time, it'll work out, you'll see."

River feels as if everything is coming undone. She loves him and asks herself why can't that be enough for everybody? *Maybe in time it will be*, she thinks. She hopes Stefan is right and goes to him, rests her head on his chest, and decides to believe him, to believe that life will be fair. Then, they leave for a walk along Promontory Point as the sun is setting on Lake Michigan. That feeling of impending doom joins River, bringing doubt with it asking how could Stefan have not known how his parents would react? How could he have not protected her?

≈Back in Bayou City≈

The car limps into the yard of the big house, and the hungry dogs bark and strain against their chains. As usual, Alpha waits in the car for Adam to come out, not sure it is safe to step from the car before he is there to protect her in case the chains snap. It is late January, and the night is cold, damp, and moonless. She waits impatiently, giving the car horn a soft push. The porch light flicks on and Adam steps out onto the porch.

"Git out! What you waiting for? That dog can't reach that car and you know it!"

"Just come out here, just in case." When, as usual, she sees he isn't moving from the porch, she makes her way to the passenger side farther from where the dogs are, and steps from the car, then moves quickly to where he stands. She grabs his hand as soon as it is in reach. She'd tried to leave Houston but it didn't work, because that's where Adam is and that's where she wants to be.

Who was she kidding? There is no way she can stay away from Adam, no matter what her father warns. Adam lets her kiss him, and she follows him upstairs, glad Harry is not around, or at least not where she has to see him. The way Harry looks at her makes her wonder if she should buy longer dresses.

Adam has barely closed the door to his room when he asks, "You got the stuff?"

"Why didn't you come to my house? Why do I have to buy it, and then bring it to you, too?"

He kisses her, and she reaches into her bra and takes out the glass vial. Adam grins when he sees the pretty white powder inside. He is happy she buys the good stuff now, the stuff white folks use, instead of that cheap dingy-colored crack cocaine that is all he can afford, and he takes it hungrily. It was easy to give up the crack once she started getting the good stuff. She convinced him it wasn't as addictive as crack, and that maybe, he could stop using altogether. For a minute, he wonders if it costs a whole lot more, but then thinks that's not his worry. In the night table is the well-used tightly-rolled dollar bill. He takes it and snorts a line. He passes the rolled dollar bill to her, and just the same as the last few times, she refuses, telling him she is through doing drugs. He was puzzled about it when she made that big announcement, adding that she was through smoking and drinking too. True to her word, she hasn't touched a thing for over six weeks. It doesn't matter to Adam, more for him.

When he is feeling fine and mellow, he makes love to her in his room in his parents' house, across the hall from what once was his sister's room where the younger boys now sleep, and directly above his parents' bedroom. No one hears the sounds coming from the room, or if they do, they act as if they don't. No one, but Harry. And Harry hates that Alpha Broussard is always in his boy's room, making quiet noise, just won't leave his boy alone. He hears her too when every time, just before dawn, she creeps down the stairs just as quietly as she can. He watches her climb in on the passenger side, and thinks, if she is so scared of the dogs, why she keeps coming? He listens to her car complain before it turns over and backs slowly out of the yard, with the dogs straining against the chains and barking. Adam, not wanting to be late for work again, leaves not too long after her, with Harry still watching from his bedroom window.

The barking wakes Mary and she is not surprised to see Harry standing at the window, looking out into the darkness. "What's wrong, Harry? What's out there?"

"She was here agin. Why tha' hell that boy keeps seeing her, after all she cost him, I'll never know. She ain't no good for him. Bold as hell, too, keeps coming here, jes' can't wait for him ta come ta her place. Yeah, real bold, jes like a white woman. Feel like it gotta be however they want it to be. Can be wherever they wanna be. Jes' using my boy!"

"Using him for what, Harry? Looks to me like she's doing all the giving. Just for once in your life, try and stay out of it and let Adam sort it out. Stop trying to run everything and everybody." Mary pulls herself out of bed and hopes Adam or Alpha will find a place closer to Adam's job and move in together, so Harry can calm down. He hasn't been himself since Ruth Ann moved out three months ago and got her own place. It will be better for everybody, one less thing to worry about, one less thing to keep Harry on edge, especially considering she isn't that crazy about Alpha either; not compared to River.

"He ain't never been too smart at sorting things out, or he'd still have River. She could'a made something outta him, tha's

263

if anybody could. And if you don't know what she's using him fa," he glares, "you must'a forgot how it used to be fa you, when you was a lot younga."

Mary wants to tell him if he was a lot more of a lot of things, she wouldn't have any trouble at all remembering, but she knows some things are better left unsaid. Wearily, she goes to the kitchen to make coffee.

Harry's glare follows his wife as she leaves the room, and he thinks that since that day, when for the first time in her life she told him to shut up, she's been a little uppity in the way she talks to him. Maybe, it's time she be reminded of just what her place is, that maybe she's not happy with just one half-opened eye. Then he turns back to the window and wonders just what little Miss White Alpha would do if she finds somebody who can give her better than what she's getting from Adam.

≈Wedding Plans≈

River agrees with Vallie Lynn that the wedding should be in Houston where her family and most of her friends are. Since Alpha is no longer working for Tony, and she and Daryl are history, River can't see any reason for Adam to know anything about her being in Houston or getting married. Vallie Lynn asks why she cares.

"I don't care. I just don't want to risk him getting drunk and showing up. That's all."

The Rose Garden in Hermann Park will be in full bloom for a morning May wedding just before the summer heat makes an outdoor wedding impossible. River wonders about May's humidity and how her natural hair will endure one of Houston's most humid months with its tendency to curl tightly. Then she decides that it doesn't matter. Stefan told River he likes her natural hair. He didn't particularly like the way she wore it in the photographs he's seen, with her permed and straight pageboy.

It has been several weeks since River has spoken to Evaline, so she gives her a save-the-date call. She seems to be getting on with her life after Jim's wife, who it turns out he hadn't divorced at all, gave him an ultimatum, or he would be divorced. He decided to leave Evaline and return home, hoping she would continue to see him, but Evaline refused to even talk to him. When Jim left her, Evaline told River that considering she had gone almost all of her life without knowing she had an uncle named Jim, she can go the rest of it forgetting that she ever did. She answers the phone on the second ring and is glad to hear River's voice.

"How's it going?"

Sounding her usual happy self, Evaline chirps, "Hey girl. How's Chi town?"

"Just great. It's cold though, really cold."

"Yeah, but I thought you said you liked the cold weather."

River laughs. "I guess. Anyway, guess who's getting married in May?"

Evaline lets out a happy whoop. "You have got to be kidding! I'm so glad. The one time I saw you guys together, it seemed y'all just fit."

"Yeah, I just wish his parents felt the same way. It's just the three of them in this country, and I don't want to come between them."

"Well, you know what the Bible says, leave the folks and cling to the wife or hubby, or something like that. River, don't try to fix this, please!"

"Okay, okay! Just save the first Saturday in May. What else is happening with you?"

Evaline takes a deep breath and says, "How much time do you have? You probably won't even believe all that's been going on!"

"Just as much as you need." River sits down and looks out at Lake Michigan, ready to hear whatever Evaline, who suddenly sounds serious, is about to tell her. She knows Jim's leaving has been hard on her and River had worried about her. She is not prepared to hear when Evaline tells her that she and Ruth Ann have been living together for almost three months.

"What? And when were you going to tell me? Three months? We've talked a few times since then, and you never said a word!"

"Well, I just didn't know how you'd feel about it. Her being Adam's sister, you know."

Evaline explains that Ruth Ann finally decided to get away from her father and the abuse. He had always prevented her leaving by convincing her that her mother would question it if she left without a good reason. Harry knew she would rather die than have her mother find out about them. And, as usual, he threatened to tell her. Ruth Ann beat him to the punch and went to her mother and told her she was getting her own place. Mary didn't resist at all, and in fact was excited to help her daughter look for a place. In October, Ruth Ann moved away from her father, who was still trying to slip into her room only to find a dead bolt lock on the door.

"I'm glad she left. I always knew there was something weird about the way he was with her. I mentioned it to Adam once. He ignored me."

"Yeah. This happened about the same time that Jim decided to go back to his wife.

267

So, we kinda learned to lean on each other. At first, it was just eating lunch together in the hospital cafeteria and using each other for sounding boards before things started happening.

"What things?"

"River, I've always known I was attracted to women, and I know you've always known it. I just fought it, it didn't seem right, or I thought it wasn't, even way back when, well you remember when. Well, with Ruth Ann, it just feels right. It really doesn't matter what anyone else thinks, not even my family."

Gauging her words carefully, so as not to hurt her friend's feelings, River speaks softly into the telephone, "Well, I'm not that surprised about you. I always thought that maybe that was who you were, and I'm happy you are finally being true to yourself. But I never thought that about Ruth Ann, not once. Are you sure she's not simply confused after all she went through with Harry Jones?"

"Spoken like someone who knows nothing about the war we lesbians wage with ourselves, but I love you anyway, girlfriend. Ruth Ann and I talked about everything, we still do. She says she never knew she could be as happy as she is now, and I believe her. I hope she's being honest with me, and as hard as that can be at times, with herself. She told me she'd always wanted to talk to me, but since I was with somebody, decided not to. Then, when Jim left, well, like I said, things just happened."

"Well, I'm happy for you guys, but Harry can't be too happy about this."

"No, he keeps calling her at work. Lately called me a few times at work too, saying we need to talk. I told him I don't

have anything to say to him, that he should be happy Ruth
Ann's not pressing charges, which by the way, I think she
should. But she won't do it, she doesn't want her mother to
know anything about that. I don't know how in the world that
woman couldn't already know. Do you, River? How can that
be happening in a woman's house and she not know it? That is
beyond me! Anyway, I told him to stop calling both of us, or
everybody would know, including the police."

"Well! This really is something, I mean, really! I don't
know what to say, except I hope it works out for you guys.
Just be careful with Harry. According to Adam, anyone who
stands up to him can expect real trouble. And how's Adam
taking his sister living with you? Not well, I bet!"

"A lot better than he took Ruth Ann telling him about all
the years Harry slipped into her bedroom. He was still trying
to slip into her room, even after she put a lock I bought her on
the door, right up to the time she left. Bastard! I hate him.
For the first time in my life, I truly hate another human
being. But maybe I shouldn't worry too much about that. I'm
not sure he's human."

"Well, just be careful, and I mean it, Ev. As crazy as
you believe Adam is, and he is pretty messed up, Harry is
much, much worse."

"I'm not scared of Harry, or Adam, for that matter."
"Well, I'm scared enough for us both, and no need to flex
your macho muscles for me, Ev. Just be careful, and let's not
wait so long between calls."

"Will do, and that's a deal. Hey, I have to ask you, how
do you think me being with Ruth Ann will match up with you
and me being friends?"

"You mean because of Adam?"

"Yeah."

"Well, I'm sure it'll be fine. Just keep my wedding date to yourself; I'd just as soon Adam know nothing about it."

"I understand, and just for the record, Ruth Ann thinks a whole lot more of you than she does of Adam. She won't tell him a thing."

"Ev, just keep it to yourself, okay? Please? I hate to ask you to keep anything from Ruth Ann, but just this one time, okay?"

"You got it, girl. Talk to you soon."

River sits for a long while looking at the lake, holding the telephone, and thinking about everything Evaline has told her. "Who would have ever thought it?" she whispers to the empty room.

≈Stefan's Mother≈

February is the coldest month River has known, and still she thinks Chicago is the most beautiful city ever. Wedding plans are moving ahead, and it appears Stefan's mother has recovered from her "almost nervous breakdown." She is coming to Chicago and wants to talk to Stefan and River. They both are hopeful that his parents are beginning to accept their marriage. When River hears Stefan's key in the door, she hurries to meet him expecting to greet his mother. He is alone.

"Where's your mother?"

Stefan's eyes are dark, and he is rubbing the forefinger on his right hand with his thumb. "She said she was tired and will see you tomorrow, so I took her to my place."

"Well, how is she? Is she feeling better about our marriage?"

Stefan takes a thick stack of papers from his jacket pocket. "These are her doctor bills. She's on all kinds of medication for her nerves. So, no, Sweet, I don't think they are feeling any better about anything. At least, she isn't. I'd just as soon you not waste time trying to talk to her. Just give it time."

River takes his hand to stop him from rubbing a callous on his forefinger. "I'll talk to her, honey. I have to, in fact, I need to." River isn't sure if she can win her over, but she knows she must try and kisses him goodbye.

"Go home and spend time with your mother. I'll see you both tomorrow."

"Okay, Sweet." Slowly Stefan drives home, pushing against the anger he feels for his mother.

It was a sleepless night and River is up making breakfast when Stefan calls to say they are on their way, adding that it had not been a good night. River has just finished breakfast when the doorman calls to say she has a guest. River understands that Stefan didn't use his key, for his mother's sake, and wonders what the doorman thought when he asked to be announced. She is at the door before Stefan and his mother are and has the door open for them.

"Come in, Mrs. Ryjonski." River extends her hand, which Stefan's mother limply shakes. She is a big woman, not fat, just big, nearly six feet tall with long legs and arms. She has big hands, and the white sneakers she wears make her feet look huge. Her eyes are the same color as Stefan's, but dart about wildly. How, River wonders, can eyes so much the same, give rise to such different feelings? Stefan's eyes are peaceful, soothing, where his mother's eyes put her on edge. They dance around in her large face that is framed by dark brown hair that is stick-straight, cut short, and left unstyled.

"That's alright. I'll just stand out here. This won't take long, and you can call me Alina." A nervous smile worries her trembling lips, appearing, and then disappearing quickly.

Three other apartments open onto the hallway, and River looks at her in disbelief; no one stands in the hallway to talk. "It's really not comfortable out here, there are neighbors. Please, come in." She doesn't budge.

"Mom, come in please!" Stefan grabs his mother's elbow and pushes her toward the door.

She allows herself to be pushed inside but will not move beyond the foyer. "Well, like I said, I won't be long. I just need you to understand how much we sacrificed to come to this country from Poland, so we could give any child we might have a better life than what we left, a good life. You understand, I know. He won't have a good life and things will be hard for you two if you get together, maybe even dangerous. Some black man might get mad at you for being with a white man, or at him for being with you and, you know, hurt my son." She talks almost as fast as her eyes dance. That distraction and her accent make it hard for River to follow every word, but she understands enough.

"Don't worry about that, Mrs., oh, I mean, Alina. Don't worry about that, we spend a lot of time together, go to lots of places, and we've never had a problem. Nothing beyond a few glances."

Anger sends her eyes darting, dancing faster, and she begins wringing her hands. "Don't you understand? You're just not right for my son. You've already been married and divorced. The church won't recognize your marriage. And I just don't see how you'll fit in with his friends. You'll just ruin his life." Her voice is getting louder, and River wonders if the neighbors can hear her. Stefan must wonder the same thing because he cautions his mother to lower her voice.

"Alina, we love each other, and we're good together.

273

We've met most of each other's friends, and we all get along just fine. Don't worry, we're going to have a good life. I promise you, we will be happy."

Anger wipes the nervous smile from her face, and something close to hatred settles there. Her eyes stop dancing and drill into River as she yells, "It takes more than kinky nigger sex to…" River flinches, as if she's been struck, and Stefan steps between River and his mother.

"That's enough, Mom! You're going to have to leave. You can't talk to River like that. You said you wouldn't." He turns and reaches for River. "I'm sorry, Sweet, I didn't think this was a good idea. I tried to tell you." He kisses her quickly which is more than his mother can bear, and she tears from the apartment and starts pressing the down elevator button frantically. She makes it downstairs, where Stefan has parked his van in the curved driveway directly in front of the building where George sometimes allows him to park if he isn't going to be long. River leaves Stefan in the foyer and is glued to the wall of windows, staring at the driveway below where there is Stefan's mother, running and sliding in the snow, almost falling before she reaches the van and pulls repeatedly on the door. When she finally realizes it is locked, she starts screaming, knowing that Stefan did not follow her down and is still on the forty-first floor. Stefan joins River at the window and takes her in his arms.

"You'd better go down to your mother, Stefan, before George has to call the police." River pulls away from him, leads him to the foyer, and closes the door with him standing there. He wants to be on the other side of that door and pushes harder against that ugly feeling for his mother that stirs in him as he steps into the elevator.

River, scared, telephones her brother, wondering what she should do. He listens, and says very little, just that he is sure she and Stefan will sort it out and decide what is best.

"Best for who?"

"I don't know Stefan that well, but I don't think he'll let his parents tell him how to live, River. It's up to you two." For the first time, after talking to her brother, she doesn't feel better.

The next two weeks pass with Stefan's mother continuing to call River's house when she can't find Stefan at his. Then, without as much as a hello to River if she, rather than Stefan, answers the phone, demands that River, "Put Stefan on the phone." Not even with a please, River tells her sister. Then one day River isn't in the best mood when Alina calls with her usual demand.

"Hello, Mrs. Ryjonski. If you can't be civil, and at least say hello to me when you invite yourself into my home by calling here, you need to find some other way to get in touch with Stefan." Then, without giving her a chance to reply, she hangs up the phone, runs her fingers through her hair, and feels better, not quite so angry.

It is hard for River to tell what Stefan is feeling, only answering "No" when she asks if he's talked to his parents. He seems happy and is excited about the wedding, but River worries that the callous on his finger is back and getting thicker. Then one evening the telephone rings and it's Stefan's mother.

"Hi River. Don't hang up! I just want to apologize about my telephone manners."

"What?" River stammers, unable to say more. She can't believe the kindness she hears in Alina's voice. River mumbles, "I appreciate that, but Stefan's not here."

"I know. I just spoke to him at his place. I really want to talk with you."

River is hopeful and softens her voice. "Yes, Alina, what is it?"

"You know, we have a little money, and my husband and I talked about it. We'd be willing to give you all we've got, every cent. It's about $250,000. It's yours, all yours, every dollar of it, if you'll just leave our boy alone so he can have a decent life."

River gently hangs up the telephone and stands there, looking out the floor-to-ceiling windows toward the Crowning Glory building. She is unable to see the lights of the city in the distance or Michigan Avenue below partly due to the thick snow that is falling and partly because tears cloud her vision. She knows she has no future with Stefan. That it is impossible. Then, she wonders, fearfully, to what lengths they will go if she refuses their offer. What else might they be willing to pay someone else to do? This thought is almost enough to make her want to stay and fight, but she knows there is no way Stefan's family can be a part of her life. She feels a knot in her chest that brings with it a dull ache. When she wonders how she will tell Stefan, the pain grows. How can she walk away from a man she loves, and who returns that love in full measure, a man who makes her feel safe and cared for?

She stares out at the whiteness, and a smile edges onto her lips when she thinks back on their first trip to Europe. She and Stefan had been swimming in the pool at the Hotel Solange in Paris when, laughing hysterically, she lost her temporary bridge.

Crowning Glory: River's Journey

She didn't have time to feel embarrassed about her two missing teeth, when Stefan, without a thought, dove to the bottom of the pool and retrieved the bridge. He smiled and kissed her with her two missing teeth while he closed her hand around the rescued bridge.

River is smiling when she tastes tears, and the knot of pain in her chest moves to her back, right between her shoulder blades, and settles in deeply. Then she grabs her parka from the hall closet and heads for the elevator. She doesn't answer the doorman when he asks her if she needs a taxi, she simply walks out into the frigid day and heavy snow.

Keisha swings the door wide for River, who never comes by without calling and whose eyes are puffy. Surprised, she asks, "What the hell is wrong?" She pulls her in from the cold and knocks the thick snow from her parka.

"You feel like a walk along the Point?" River wants to keep walking. She's already walked more than a mile in the blinding snow before hailing a taxi. When Keisha bought her condo in the North Kenwood neighborhood, which was booming with gentrification, she introduced River to Promontory Point and it became one of her favorite places. No matter what the season, if birds were nesting, or the hundreds of monarch butterflies were migrating, the trees changing with the seasons, or just the sound of the lake caressing, or crashing against the retaining wall of boulders where she would often sit, she loved it all. Even when the snow falls as heavily as today. The Point has remained one of her and Stefan's favorite places for their many long walks together.

"Sure, let me get dressed." They drive to the park without talking, silently Keisha waits for River to tell her what's wrong.

The winter wind, after traveling across frozen Lake Michigan, tries hard to cut through their parkas when they exit the passenger tunnel that runs under Fifty-Fifth Street and enter the park. The lake is frozen white with dark water breaking through in several places where the sheet of ice thins.

"I can't marry Stefan. They offered to pay me, pay me a lot, to leave their son alone." River just blurts it out loudly, the wind making it hard to talk. The cold air hurts her lungs and forces River to wrap her scarf around her mouth.

Keisha stops walking. "What? You have got to be kidding! If not, I hope you told them to go straight to hell, quick, fast, and in a hurry! And I also hope you told them you were going to tell Stefan. Which, I hope you are!" She is beyond angry. She is outraged.

"You know that's the scary part, Keisha. I did think about telling Stefan, but I can't do that. Do you have any idea how badly that would hurt him? And he'd hate them."

"And they deserve to be hated if you ask me!"

"Yeah, but he doesn't deserve to hate them. That would be too painful. He adores his mother."

"And you don't think it's going to be painful if you end the relationship?"

"Even if we get married, I can't see how it would last. How could it survive those people? There's no way. It wouldn't survive. Stefan's too close to his mother to be happy, really happy, if she isn't happy." River believes that Alina, for as long as she lives, or maybe even more so if she dies, leaving Stefan feeling like a guilty son who'd abandoned his mother, would forever be a dark cloud over any future she and Stefan might have. She also thought of her inability to have children.

"Let's just walk, Keisha. I don't want to talk."

278

Crowning Glory: River's Journey

Both their faces are numb when, twenty minutes later, they turn away from the frigid lake and head back to the car, thankfully, with the wind off the lake at their backs. "I probably would take the damn money, and then tell them to go straight to hell. You think they'd tell Stefan? Hell no! Now that's all I have to say about it." Keisha is shouting, making certain River can hear her through the wool scarf she has also wrapped around her mouth against the frigid cold.

River says nothing, feeling terrible about herself for thinking of doing that very thing. She'd thought there would be no need to tell Stefan anything about his parents offering the money, or about her taking it, it could be their nest egg, and it would teach them a lesson in the process. Maybe later if they were, if not kind, at least civil to her and Stefan, she'd give it back to them. In the car with the heater blasting, she whispers, "I could never do that, Keisha, neither could you."

"Hummph, don't be too sure about me, girlfriend. Just don't be too sure about me."

The snowfall is not as heavy as it had been earlier, and River wonders why everything can't be as beautiful as the city that glimmers in the distance through the light snowfall.

≈Car Trouble≈

Aroused, Harry waits quietly after the soft noise from Adam's room upstairs stops, before he eases out of bed, so he won't wake Mary who is sleeping soundly. Like many nights before, he stands at the window, looking out and waiting. It isn't long before he hears footsteps easing down the creaky stairs. The dogs don't bark when Alpha steps out on the porch into the damp, dark morning and nervously looks around. Then, she remembers that Adam had fenced the dogs in the backyard earlier that night, so she hurries to her car, still entering on the passenger side. The engine strains but doesn't start several times before she smells gasoline and realizes she has flooded it. She decides to wait rather than go back inside and risk the dogs or Harry, and turns off the key. Adam will be down shortly on his way to work. Then the porch light flicks on, and Harry comes out followed closely by Adam.

"What's wrong, girl? I can smell that gas all tha way to tha house. Pop the hood." Harry speaks before Adam has a chance. In the dark, using a flashlight with a fading glow that Harry provides, they both peer under the hood.

"I never had any trouble starting it before. What's wrong?" She is looking to Adam, but Harry answers.

"I heard you out here cranking it to death. You probably just flooded it, tha's all. Just give it a rest, then give it another try."

In the lifting dark, Adam strains to see the time on his expensive watch, a gift from Alpha. "I can't wait, Alpha. I can't be late again. They already wrote me up twice."

Nervous eyes plead with him. "I need to get to work, too. What if it won't start?"

"Don't worry, girl." Harry slams down the hood. "If it don't start, we'll git you to work."

Before she can answer, Adam straddles his motorcycle and hurriedly says, "Thanks, Old Man." Then to Alpha he yells over the roar of the motorcycle, while walking it backwards so he can turn it heading out of the yard, "Daddy'll take care of the car and see that you get to work, too. You don't need to be late neither. I'll call you later." Then the motorcycle speeds away.

After waiting a few minutes before trying to start the car again, Harry gives it another try. The car refuses to start, and Alpha worries that she will be late for her seven o'clock shift.

"I'll take you home, so you can get dressed and won't be late. I'll have this wreck fixed by time you git off. Git on in the truck."

"Maybe Mrs. Jones can take me while you work on my car." Alpha stands beside the car, willing it to start.

"Git in the truck, girl. It's too dark to see under the hood," Harry growls. "Besides, Mary won't be none too happy if you be asking her to git dressed this early." She climbs into the truck and hopes the sun will hurry and light the darkness. Mary steps onto the porch as the truck turns out of the yard.

Alpha doesn't know this dark road and wishes Harry would slow down so he can avoid the bumps but decides against saying anything. Twice, by grabbing the dashboard, she avoids bumping her head when the truck hits two deep potholes that pitch her up from her seat. The second time she doesn't release her grip on the dashboard and continues to hold tight. Harry takes another turn and the bumpy road darkens, any light from the moon or stars unable to penetrate the gray fog that remains settled around the tall trees that line both sides of the narrow road.

"I don't know this way, Mr. Jones." Her voice trembles. "Could we get back on a main street?"

"You said you wuz running late. This here back way is shorter." Harry is straining to see as the road darkens, challenging the truck's weak headlights, no match for the deepening darkness.

Alpha looks behind them and wonders how long it will take her to run back to the better lit road they turned off from. She sees only blackness. The truck slows and turns onto another road that is little more than a grassy path. Just when she decides to take her chances with the blackness, she hears the click of the door lock, and then the truck stops. Alpha's hand goes for the lock, but Harry pulls her, forcefully, to him before she can reach it.

"Jes' be still, girl, you and me need to have a little talk!"

"It's so dark, Mr. Jones, please, let's go where there's some light to talk. We can talk at my place while I get ready for work, please." Panic is scrambling her thoughts and causing her heart to race. Her breathing is shallow. "Please, Mr. Jones, this is crazy. Stop this, and we never have to mention it, I promise, never. Please!" Her head begins to feel light, but she wills herself not to faint and starts to take deep, long breaths.

"Calm down, girl, just calm yo ass down." He throws his heavy leg across her thighs and pulls his hand through her hair. Tears roll down her face, and with her free hand, she pulls her scarf tightly around her shoulders. "What he like so much 'bout you, can't leave you alone, this yella hair? Is that it? Been wonderin' if it's yella all over." He pulls his hand through her hair again, this time hard enough to bring out a few blonde strands. Alpha doesn't scream. She is trying to think of a way out.

"Please, Mr. Jones, stop this. Adam will kill you! You know he will. You know he already hates you. I swear I won't say a word if you'll just let me get out of this truck. Please!" She is straining, trying to reach the door lock, but can't.

"You don't know shit 'bout me and my boy. Adam don't give a damn 'bout you, jes all that shit you bring ta my house for him ta suck up his nose. Disrespectin' my house like that. Think I don't know? Think he'd give you tha time o' day if you wasn't bringing him that poison?"

"Please, Mr. Jones, let me go. Please! I'll stop bringing it, I swear." It is getting cold in the truck, but she feels wet and clammy.

"Please, my ass. You should'a jes' left 'im alone. Messing up him and River jes' 'cause you like black dick." He reaches over and grabs her left breast and squeezes it so hard that she cries out in pain. "Let's jes' see how much you really like it."

With her free hand she tries to slap him, but he blocks her hand. "I'll have you arrested." She is panting with fear, exhausted from trying to free herself from the heavy weight of his thigh pressing hard against hers. "I swear. I'll have you arrested. I swear I will!"

"And who gon' believe a thing you say 'bout a black man? You got a histr'y 'bout lying 'bout black men, don't you girl?" Then he laughs, angrily.

Again, Alpha reaches for his face with her free hand, this time making contact, but unable to do much more damage than a long scratch on his right cheek before Harry grabs her arm and forces her down on the seat, pressing his knee into her arm to keep her from moving. Then his full weight is on her, and before the scream can escape her mouth, he forces the red scarf wrapped about her shoulders into her open mouth.

"Why you keep fucking with my boy? Almost sent him to the pen, too. Since you can't stay away from him, so crazy 'bout black dick, I got something for you. See how you like this?" Breathing hard he frees his pants, his lust fueled by hatred drives him hard, and seeing that she is naked under her raised dress excites him. The more she fights the more excited he becomes.

Muffled sounds strain to escape the red scarf. She brings her knees up, aiming for his testicles. He forces her legs down with his free hand and, to hold her still, brings his knee to her stomach and presses down hard while he continues to work his pants down. The more she twists beneath him the harder he presses down with his knee. She tries to explain to him, tries to tell him, to make him understand, but the words can't escape the red scarf. She can't fight the feeling of lightheadedness then, thankfully, she faints. When she regains consciousness, Harry Jones is shaking her, telling her to get up and straighten herself up.

"Now, how was that, girl? Better'n you thought it could be, I bet," he leers with sweat trailing down his fat face. Alpha moves like a robot in slow motion. Unable to see through the steamed windows, she fastens her coat about her, hoping it will warm her and stop her body's violent shaking.

Harry pulls into the driveway at Alpha's house. "I hope I don't have to 'splain to Adam how all this happened, how you came on ta me and how it wouldn'a happened if you had'na kept after me. I hope I don't. Now, go find yourself another black buck to fuck, and leave my boy alone. You done caused enough trouble at my house."

Unable to stop her body's hard trembling, and sick to her stomach, Alpha stands in the tub and adds more hot water to the shower spray. There are no tears, just low guttural moans, like some mortally wounded animal. The water collecting in the tub has turned red and she knows why. Then Alpha becomes silent, her eyes following the bright red blood that trails down her glistening white thighs. She sits down slowly in the tub and, with her hands, cups the murky red water trailing to the drain, trying to hold on to the baby that surely she knows is there somewhere. Alpha thinks of God, wonders if there is such a thing, and if so, why he is punishing her. Then she quickly reaches down to close the drain to save her baby, and wonders why whatever God there is, allowed her to be brought into this world at all, why she couldn't have turned her mother's bath water red. She wants to die. She's always wanted to die a little more than she's ever wanted to live, but never as much as she does right now. She eases herself down into the tub and sits in the murky red water for almost an hour trembling, but unable to force herself out of the coldness, unable to leave her baby.

Back at the big house, Harry replaces the distributor cap in Alpha's car. Mary hears the car start up and comes out to bring her husband a cup of coffee. "You got it going, I see. What happened to your face?"

"Scratched it on that girl's car hood, looking under her car. I don't want no coffee," Harry mutters, without looking at his wife.

Mary studies the scratch and turns away from him. She pours the coffee on the ground and walks slowly toward the big house that this morning looks old and ugly to her.

Alpha is still sitting in the tub when she hears a car pull into the driveway. Fear jolts her from the tub, and she hides behind the bathroom door, trembling and terrified by the knock at the door. *Is it Harry?*

"Girl, I got your car going, thought you wuz in a hurry to git to work!" He knocks again, harder this time. "Girl, you go' answer this damn door or what?"

She is unable to move, her breathing shallow. "I'm go leave yo car here, keys under the seat. Girl, I know you in there. You better git ta work," she hears him yell. Then, after she hears his truck drive away, she pulls back the covers of her bed and climbs in. She doesn't think to call in sick at her new job.

≈One More Goodbye≈

River dreads dinner with Stefan tonight and is glad to be distracted, as she always is, by the beauty of the centuries-old buildings that line Lake Shore Drive. The evening sky is heavy with dark clouds, the color of purple-hued smoke and loaded with snow. They hang low around the skyscrapers whose windows are brightly lit as she drives north along the winding drive to Riza's Restaurant. The city is still aglow even though the Christmas decorations have long been dismantled, and for a moment, passing Buckingham Fountain, still draped with thousands of white holiday lights, River feels less sad.

No matter what the season, Riza's Restaurant on Navy Pier never disappoints her, offering its diners sweeping views of Lake Michigan and Chicago's lakefront, at times referred to by the locals as the city's front yard.

River and Stefan love dining there during the summer, when just before the Wednesday and Saturday evening fireworks display starts, the lights in the restaurant are dimmed so that the twenty-minute fireworks show can be better appreciated. *No more beautiful fireworks spiraling down into Lake Michigan for Stefan and me*. She sighs.

River finds it fitting that the view out the glass walls of the restaurant, while beautiful, is cold and dark. While she sips her wine and waits for Stefan, she wonders why some people seem to live such easy lives, and hers has always been anything but, always requiring an extra effort. She wonders if she'd stayed with Greg, would others have seen her life as charmed? Evaline certainly had. She thinks maybe she should do just as her sister suggests and leave the decision to Stefan about what to do about his parents. But Stefan will never leave her, she knows that, even though if somewhere in his truest heart he wishes things were different, that she wasn't black or that his parents didn't mind that she was, that she'd never been married, and that there was no question about her having children. Staring out on frozen Lake Michigan, River feels a chill, unable to see forever with Stefan, not since she last spoke to his mother.

"Hey Sweet, am I late or are you early?" River looks up from her thoughts and smiles. He wishes for that full-faced smile of hers that he hasn't seen since his mother's visit.

"We're right on time." She returns his kiss and tries not to notice the glance in their direction from the woman at the next table. In Houston she would have expected some stares. That was the South. Somehow, here in Chicago, she expected things to be different and that there wouldn't be stares, not even glances.

"I ordered your drink." In a few minutes the waiter sets his Black Russian on the table and takes their usual order, River the filet of sole, and Stefan the crab cakes, which they always share.

How to start? she wonders. There is no easy way, just start, she decides. She lifts her glass and announces, "A toast, Stefan?"

"Sure Sweet, to what?"

"To us, and what we almost had," she whispers. The Merlot

288

goes down easily, and she feels foolish, wondering if she could be any more dramatic.

"Don't start again, River, please. We've already had this talk, more times than we need to." Stefan fondles his glass nervously, his eyes growing a deep shade of green in the candlelight.

"Not this one, Stefan." She empties her glass, gets the waiter's eye, and lifts her wine glass. The waiter brings her new drink, and she, unable to look at him looks at the wine glass and says, "I'm not going to marry you, Stefan." They've had many discussions about why, maybe they shouldn't marry, but she's never said this before; never been so definite.

"Come on, Sweet. You will marry me. We will marry each other. We love each other. Don't let my folks mess this up."

"It's more than your parents. It's me, honey. It's too much for me. You know I probably can't have children, and I know you want your own, that you wouldn't want to adopt. You told me so. It's all just too much for me. You wouldn't have your parents. There'd be no children, just me." She continues in a flat tone. "I can't be your whole life, Stefan, waiting and wondering when you'll begin to resent me, maybe even hate me, for all in life you've given up for me. It's too much. I can't live with that fear every day. Thinking I'm not enough."

He pulls his chair closer to River, pushes his drink aside, and takes her hands. "River, you are the most important thing in my life, just having you is enough, it'll always be. What can I say to make you understand that? My parents will come around, just give them time, you'll see. Please don't do this, River. Just let things play out." His eyes glisten in the dimly lit restaurant, but River's tears dampen her face. He dries them with his dinner napkin.

"Believe me, honey, they will not come around, they will

never come around, I'm sure of that." She wants to tell him about their offer to pay her to disappear from his life, and knows if she could, he'd be just as certain as she is that they will never come around, but she can't.

Stefan wonders if some part of him is not as sad as it should be, then he brushes the thought away. "How can you be so sure, Sweet?"

Once the waiter debones the sole and sets their plates before them, they both stare at the food, neither of them able to eat. "I'm sure, Stefan. Just take my word for it, I'm sure. I'm not going to see you anymore after tonight. I'm sure about that, too."

He holds onto her hands when she tries to pull them away. "What happened, Sweet? Have you talked to my folks again?"

She wants to lay her head on his chest and feel safe enough or brave enough to tell him everything. She wants to feel his arms around her and believe him when he promises her that everything will be all right. She wants to turn and scream at the woman sitting at the table next to them who continues to glance in their direction. Instead, she takes another drink from her glass and whispers, "Stefan, this is the way it has to be. There's no other way. My mind is made up."

"What about our plans, Sweet? Remember how pretty I said our babies would be? What about all of that? I don't want to wait any longer; I'm already forty-five, not getting any younger here!" He tries to smile.

She wants to scream at him, but instead says softly, "Stefan, please. Why do you keep saying that?" She is glad she decided not to have this talk at home, or she would be in his arms now, hoping he would hold her and make it all go away. But it will never go away, so she looks out at Lake Michigan and repeats, "There's no other way, and I can't talk about this anymore. I have to go, Stefan." She tries to stand but he holds her in her seat.

"If I agree, Sweet, can we still see each other, just as friends, have dinner or a drink sometimes?"

River wishes he'd resisted a while longer, but at the same time is glad he didn't. She thinks of Evaline and wonders if she is right, that she has some unhealthy need to fix things. Then she wonders if she is just afraid of not being enough. Never enough!

"We can still be friends, Stefan. We can always be friends. Let's just give it some time before we start having dinner or drinks." They sit in silence, looking out on Lake Michigan until the waiter returns to ask if there is something wrong with the food.

"No, it's fine." River looks at the food and adds, "Can you just wrap it to go?" Three days later she puts her food down the garbage disposal.

Less than a year later, after River refuses Stefan's many invitations to dinner, he calls to tell her he is marrying Laurette, the woman he'd dated for five years before he met River, and that they will be moving to New York.

≈Another Problem≈

R uth Ann is working the evening shift at County General Hospital in Galveston and has just returned from her final rounds when she stops dead in her tracks. There at the nurses' station stands her father talking to the head nurse. Her heart starts beating faster, and she is scared. She hasn't seen or spoken to him since she moved out of the big house months ago. When he calls her at work, she hangs up the telephone as soon as she realizes it's him. The hospital is quiet, and at the sound of her footsteps, both he and the nurse turn and look in her direction.

"I need to talk to ya; it's about yo mama. She's sick, and I don't have yo new number." The head nurse turns and walks away from them. Ruth Ann doesn't trust him and wonders why Adam, or her other brothers, haven't called if their mother is sick.

"Thanks for coming by to tell me. I get off in a few minutes, and I'll call her." She walks behind the nurses' station, turns her back to him, and starts to finish charting patients' records.

"We need to talk, Angel."

"Please Daddy, not here, and please don't call me Angel, not ever again. My name is Ruth Ann." She doesn't turn to look at him when she speaks.

"I kin wait fa you. We kin talk outside, but we got ta talk. I ain't leaving till we talk."

The two nurses who work the midnight shift are walking toward the nurses' station. Ruth Ann knows she has to talk to him, otherwise who can tell what he will say or do? When the nurses are almost at the station she whispers, "Just wait for me outside, Daddy."

"I'll wait by the elevator." A grin spreads across his face as he leers at the younger of the two nurses he passes on his way to the elevator.

Ruth Ann wants to talk to Evaline and wonders if she should call her, but thinks maybe not, considering Evaline's hatred for her father and the many unpleasant things she's told her she'd like to do to him. She is scared, not that Harry will hurt her, not physically, but that he will confuse her and make her doubt herself as he always has. She thinks she is no match for her father. Her only hope is never to be alone with him. Otherwise he will win, just as he always has. "Not tonight," she whispers and decides she doesn't need to call Evaline, but that she will be strong tonight, not just for herself, but for her mother and Evaline. After work, she meets her father at the elevator and says, "Let's go."

The night is damp and cold, less than forty degrees, unusual for Galveston, and Ruth Ann pulls her leather coat around her, cinching the belt tighter. She stops at the end of the walkway, where the bright lights of the emergency room entrance give some safety from the dark night.

"My truck is right 'round the corner."

"Forget it Daddy. We can talk right here!"

Harry doesn't quite know how to deal with this new person. *So changed since she met that Evaline thing*, he thinks. "Don't

293

be silly, Angel. It's too cold ta stand out here freezing. Let's go ta yo car then if you scared to git in my truck."

"My name is *Ruth Ann*! We can talk here, or not at all. Mama's not sick, is she?"

Harry moves closer to his daughter and pulls at the belt of her coat. Ruth Ann snatches away her belt and raises her voice, "Mama's not sick, is she?"

A nasty-looking grin spreads on his face, and Ruth Ann steps away from him. "Naw, she ain't sick, not now, but I bet she'll be real sick, soon as I tell her how many times you tried to creep in my bed when she wasn't home. I bet she'll be mighty sick then."

Her courage begins to falter, but she thinks of her mother and wills herself to fight. "Do you know how much I hate you? How many times I've thought how much better my life, all of our lives, would have been if you were not a part of them? Maybe it's time I talk to Mama myself, maybe it's time we clear the air. I think she needs to know I forgive her for not protecting me from you."

Harry stares at his daughter, unable to believe that this is his Angel, and that she can talk to him in such a way. *That dyke Evaline*, he thinks, *has really messed up my baby*. He softens his voice and pleads, "I need you, Angel. You think all what happened wuz jes' for tha hell of it? Ain't nobody like you." His eyes glisten in the night. He easily calls up tears, and it won't be the first time he's used them to his benefit, crying to Ruth Ann in a last-ditch effort to convince her that he can't live without her, that there is something normal about them sleeping together. It worked every time before.

"Daddy, again, my name is Ruth Ann, and more than anything, except wanting to make peace with Mama, I want to stop hating you, but I don't know if that's possible." She hates him most for the times, late at night, when he slipped into her room, and she found it hard to understand why at times what happened hung between pleasure and guilt. She hates herself more than him for that hint of pleasure that tried to break through that came with him. "I want to be able to come by the house and see Mama without waiting until I see your truck leave. I want a normal life, as normal as I can ever hope to have." Ruth Ann ignores his tears.

Harry is losing his control over his Angel, and his grin slips away. "You call shacking up with a homo normal? Ain't nothing in the world no sicka than that shit."

Ruth Ann looks at her father and thinks there is nothing in him to love. "Does it matter to you that I'm happy, Daddy? Have you ever in your life cared about anybody but yourself?"

"Happy, my ass! This county ain't big enough for me and that dyke, not while she's shacking up with my daughter, making me a laughing stock. Git outta that shit, and I swear I'll never try 'n touch you agin."

"You can try all you want, but you'll never touch me again; I'll die or see you dead before that ever happens again. Do and say whatever you want, tell Mama anything you want, I'm living for me from now on. Me and Evaline." She reaches into her purse, pulls out her keys, and says with a smile, "I'm going home now. I have a woman I love and who loves me. Goodbye, Harry."

Her father, with his fists jammed into his pockets, watches his daughter walk away, wondering how he lost control of his world. Troubling thoughts ramble through his mind. *Mary has taken an uppity tone with me of late, maybe it's time I take her down a notch or two. Adam acts like he's lost all respect for me, maybe he does hate me. And now Ruth Ann is gone, my Angel is really gone*, he thinks. But what he hates most, is that his Angel is living with Evaline, and everybody knows it. Maybe, he decides, he needs to take a different approach with little Miss Evaline. Maybe, he thinks, she's never had a real man. He is still standing there, directly under the bright light of one of the lamps in the parking lot with his hands jammed in his pockets, deep in thought deciding on a plan, when Ruth Ann drives out of the parking lot.

He does not see Evaline, who is working the midnight shift. She stands outside the emergency room door and has heard every word.

≈Where's Alpha?≈

Adam looks in the bedside table and finds that the glass vial has very little of the white powder left, mostly dust. He wonders how long it's been since he talked to Alpha, then realizes he hasn't seen her since she had trouble with her car two days ago. He called her a day or so after that, at home and at work, and didn't get an answer. He grows a little concerned, it's not like her to stay away so long unless she's mad and trying to teach him a lesson. Maybe she is mad at him because he didn't stay around to get her car going. *That would be just like her*, he thinks. "Damned needy-assed bitch," he whispers.

It's almost ten o'clock, and he knows she should be home but is not answering her telephone. He takes the rolled dollar bill out of the night stand and snorts the last of the white powder directly from the glass vial. There isn't enough to make a line, so he runs his finger inside the empty vial and sucks it. He decides to skip the shower and pulls on a pair of tight, black jeans and a red sweatshirt. She likes him in red. After loading up on Gray Flannel cologne, Alpha's favorite, he slips on his leather motorcycle jacket and the Harley roars out of the yard.

It is close to midnight, and Alpha's car is parked in the driveway. The are no lights on inside, nor is there a porch light on. Adam knows Alpha always leaves a light on when she goes out or if she expects to get home late. She is afraid of the dark. He pulls in beside her car, and notices it is covered with pine needles from the large pine tree in the front yard. *Maybe it's still not running*, he thinks. Not wanting to hear her complaining, the only thing that keeps him from turning right around and backing his bike out of the driveway is his need to restock his blow. He has no stomach for dealing with whatever she is trying to pull. Instead, he kills the motor on the bike, leans it on its kickstand, and swaggers toward the house.

There is no answer to his constant ringing of the doorbell, his loud knocks, or his calling her name, but he knows she is inside. One hard jerk and the locked screened door gives way, and glad he kept the key she'd insisted on giving him, he lets himself into the dark house. It is cold inside. "Why hasn't she turned on the heat?" he grumbles.

"Alpha, you in here?" Not only is it cold and dark, but there is an odor he can't identify that leaves a metallic smell in his nostrils. He finds the light switch and clicks on the overhead light.

"Alpha, you here?" Adam passes through the room furnished with the expensive furniture from her apartment and makes his way to the bedroom. He flicks on the light and there she is, looking near death, in the large mahogany bed. She looks thin, almost lost in the bed, her blonde hair is dark and matted and her skin is dull, an ashen shade of gray. Adam is scared but walks closer to her and that unidentifiable odor becomes stronger.

Pale blue eyes ringed with purple shadows stare blankly at him from her bland face.

"Alpha, what the hell's going on? What's wrong with you?" He sits down on the very edge of the bed and runs his hand along her bare, cold arm. "Say something. What's wrong with you? Do I need to take you to the emergency room or something? You look like shit!"

She doesn't seem to know him and whispers, "He killed our baby." Her voice is watery, like it's stuck in her throat, and Adam can hardly understand her. He only heard "killed" and "baby" and wonders why she's acting this way about an abortion she had so long ago.

"Come on, Alpha. You need to get cleaned up and get something to eat." He pulls back the brown suede comforter and stares at the rusty, red-brown stain on the sheets. "Damn, Alpha, what's going on? You been bleeding?"

She follows his eyes to the soiled sheets and slowly runs her hand along the brown stain of dried blood. "He killed our baby, poor baby," she whispers as she caresses the stain, "poor baby." She's not making any sense, and Adam grows afraid, with no idea of what to do.

"Who in the fuck is *he*, and what damn baby? What the fuck...?" He grinds his teeth, and while making that dry, snorting noise tries to figure it out. He picks up the telephone and calls Ruth Ann. He feels better when, after she hears the panic in his voice, tells him she'll be right there.

"You coming by yourself? You need to be by yourself!"
"Yes. Evaline's no more anxious to see you than you are to see her, believe me. Besides, she's at work, doing the graveyard shift this week."

Adam believes it will take her about an hour to drive from

Galveston to Houston, and not knowing what else to do, covers Alpha and goes into the kitchen, wondering when she's last eaten. In the cupboard, he finds a can of Campbell's Chicken Noodle Soup. He watches the noodles dance about in the broth as it heats and thinks about his sister and Evaline. Ruth Ann seems happy, maybe, he thinks, being a homo's not all that bad. Then he thinks of his father and all he put Ruth Ann through. His hatred for him surges, adding to the headache that is already blooming, as he pours the boiling soup over saltines he's crumbled into a large bowl. He returns to the bedroom and that sickening smell and sits on the edge of the bed beside Alpha.

"Here, you need to eat this." She opens her mouth widely, looking bird-like, he thinks, each time the spoon comes near to her. Between spoons of soup she whispers, "He killed our baby."

"Stop saying that, Alpha. Just eat the damn soup and shut up!" He slams the bowl down on the marble top of the mahogany night stand and goes into the bathroom. He stares at the reddish-brown scum coating the bathtub, a filth he can't identify in the commode, and loses the urge to urinate. He flushes the commode and walks into the kitchen. He needs to get away from whatever has happened, and he wonders what is taking Ruth Ann so long and who "he" is. Adam doesn't want to be here with Alpha, finally understanding why she stopped snorting with him, and even stopped drinking and smoking. Then he thinks there just might be some people in this world who need killing, squashed without a thought, just like a filthy cockroach. When he goes back to the bedroom, Alpha has taken the bowl from the table and is pouring the soup into her mouth and onto her naked breasts. Not since

River left has Adam felt like crying, not until now, and then he hears his sister's car in the drive and rushes to the door.

Ruth Ann follows her brother to the bedroom and looks at Alpha, crumpled on the bed, who whispers to her, "He killed our baby, poor little baby."

"What's she talking about?" Confused, Ruth Ann looks to her brother for an answer. Adam is silent and stares beyond Alpha at the huge headboard. He doesn't answer.

≈Time to Talk≈

Mary Jones is sitting in one of the rocking chairs, the one without a seat cushion that causes some pain if she sits long enough, when Ruth Ann, after calling to make sure her father isn't home, walks into the living room of the big house. Immediately her eyes go to the family photographs that line the living room wall. They all are crooked. She's never seen them crooked before, and for the first time in her life, Ruth Ann sees that they are covered with dust. Her mother looks different, in what way she isn't sure, just different.

"Hey, Mama. How're you doing?"

"I'm fine, baby, just fine. What's wrong? What you need to talk about? It sounds serious." From the rocking chair where she sits, slowly rocking, Mary's eyes sweep around the room, as if she doesn't know it.

"Mama, I just want to ask you, I need to ask you, why you stayed with Daddy all these years? Seems to me our lives would've been a whole lot better without him." She doesn't want to make her mother feel bad, but it's something she's thought for as long as she can remember.

Mary, scared about where this is headed, lets her good eye rest on her daughter and answers, "Maybe. Maybe it would've been worse. Who can know?"

"I don't know how worse is possible, Mama. If only you knew." She doesn't have the heart to say any more. She'd expected to ask her if she knew what her father did to her all those years, but she can't. She can't destroy whatever her mother holds on to that keeps her living with him. Maybe, that just plain keeps her living.

"Know what, Ruth Ann? Has your daddy said something to you?"

Ruth Ann stares at the photographs behind her mother, her vision blurs, tears welling in her eyes. "Said? If only," she whispers, and hopes her mother didn't hear.

Mary stands, rubs her aching behind, and walks to her daughter, who is still standing in the door, so she can see her father's truck if it turns the corner. She wants to take her daughter into her arms, but it would feel awkward, she thinks, it's been so long since she's hugged her. They were never big on hugging or kissing in their family. She doesn't know what Ruth Ann meant by what she whispered. She doesn't ask her again, she doesn't want to know. She can't destroy all she's ever held on to that made life with the only man she's ever known worth living. Mary cannot accept what she thinks will destroy everything she's given her entire life to. She looks away from her daughter's falling tears and forces herself to ask, "What's happened, Ruth Ann, why're you crying? Gon' and tell me whatever it is you need to tell me if you have to."

Ruth Ann turns her back to her mother and looks out the screen door. "It's just that Alpha was pregnant again. I think something bad happened to make her lose the baby. And it wasn't an abortion, not one she did anyway. She's pretty torn up about it."

Mary doesn't say anything, just sits back down in the hard,

wooden rocking chair near the opened door. Relieved that her daughter changed the subject to one less painful, she asks, "Does Adam know?"

"That's how I found out. He called me over there last night after I got off from work. She looked awful. I told him to take her to the emergency room. He said he was gonna try and call her mother or somebody in her family. He's not here?"

"He didn't come back last night. I didn't know he knew anybody in her family, not good enough to talk to, the way they hate him. And her for being with a black man." Mary starts rocking slowly, back and forth, back and forth in rhythm. "What happened to her? To the baby? Did she say?"

Ruth Ann takes a deep breath while she dusts and straightens the crooked family pictures on the living room wall and answers, "She kept saying, 'He killed my baby.' Maybe somebody in her family found out and didn't want a half-breed, I don't know. Who knows what she meant? Made no sense to me. Adam neither, when I asked him what she meant. I kept asking her what she was talking about. She just kept repeating herself over and over. 'He killed my baby.' She never said who." Mary rocks faster.

≈Harry Jones is Dead≈

Harry sits at the bar at the Dew Drop Inn, and even though he knows he's had a few too many gin and tonics, he raises his empty glass to the bartender and orders one more. This is his favorite place. He can be found here almost every night; here, and sometimes in one of the twelve motel rooms behind the bar. The rooms are rented by the hour, and the garage attached to each room makes the Inn seem better than the few other motels in the area that offer the same hourly rates. Guests can simply pull right in, and with the press of a button your garage door comes down, and nobody is the wiser. That's never mattered at all to Harry, but some folks really like that feature. He glares at the group of four white men sitting at the corner table and wonders why they keep looking at him. "Black man can't have a place to call his own no more," he mutters. "They kin come in my place, in any black place at all, and feel right at home. Nobody thinks a thing."

That's the problem, Harry thinks. *Black people just too damned welcoming, too damned eager to have white folks be a part of whatever they do, thinking it gives it some importance.* He liked it better when things were separated. Everybody had their place. *White folks weren't so eager to come into black places, acting so high and mighty, like they belong. It doesn't work so fine when the tables are turned,* Harry thinks, knowing he won't be quite so welcome if he decides to drop in at the white biker bar on the other side of town. No, Harry reasons, if he walked in there it would be a whole lotta shit. *Somebody in there might call me a boy, or worse yet, some fool might call me a nigger, and expect me to answer, "yes sir."* Harry knows for sure, if he walked into their place, there would be a whole lotta trouble.

He's not so bothered by the two white women he notices sitting at the other end of the bar. He's pretty sure of what they're there for, probably eager to have some black guy take them to one of the rooms in the back, then he thinks of Alpha. It's been almost a week, he figures, since he gave her what she was so hot for, and he wonders if he's fixed that problem for good. She hasn't been back to the big house, and Harry is glad about that. Then he thinks of Adam and can't remember the last time he's seen him this week, either. Harry wonders if the gin is messing with his memory.

For sure, they haven't talked in a long time, of that Harry is certain. He remembers seeing Adam one morning. Was it last week? Or maybe it was a few days ago, and that Adam had glared at him, passing him in the driveway without so much as a word. That's his boy, he smiles, his favorite, the one he's been unable to break. Not like the two younger ones who pee their pants at the very sound of his voice. He asked Mary why Adam was acting so strange, but he can't remember what she said. He's confused. Did he really mention it to her? Maybe not. He doesn't think Mary's been in bed with him the last few nights, or did he go to sleep before she came to bed, he's not sure. *Damned gin, messing with my mind.* Then he thinks on how crazy Mary's been acting lately. *She's hardly ever saying a word, just sitting in the front room rocking in that damned chair. No matter to me, let her rock. She's not much use in bed anyway.*

Harry is mired in thoughts that continue to be muddled by too much gin and, at the bartender's call, looks up and realizes the bar is almost empty, just him, the bartender, and the guy putting chairs upholstered in red and yellow plastic on top of Formica tables and getting ready to sweep the littered floor.

"Hey," Harry yells to the bartender, "I got time for one mo?"

"No, Harry. You had enough. Gon' home, now. Probably don't need to be driving but seeing as your house is right 'round the corner, I guess it's okay. Gon' home!"

"Fuck you, man! I don't need you to tell me when I had enough. I know damned good and well how to hold my liquor!" Harry has a death grip on the bar rail to steady himself.

"Harry, you can gon' home, or I can drop a dime on your ass and let the police sober yo fat ass up. Now, gon' home like I said!"

"Fuck you, man," Harry says as he frees the bar rail from his grip and slides off the stool, almost falling. He fumbles in his pocket for his keys while he makes his way out the front door and, finding the parking lot empty, wonders where his truck can be. Then he remembers there had been no spaces left in front of the bar, and he'd parked behind the building. He leans against the building for support, as he makes his way in the dark, cursing when his foot is caught in the overgrown weeds. He trips and falls, cutting his hands on the shells covering the back parking area. Harry picks himself up, curses everything and everybody, makes his way to his truck, opens the door, and hoists himself inside. Then in a flash, someone is in the truck with him, shoving him hard toward the passenger seat.

"What the fuck...?" Before he can finish his sentence, the knife does its work, sliding easily between the fifth and sixth ribs, expertly hitting its mark. Harry's heart hesitates, missing one, then two beats. The killer sits next to Harry and watches him struggle to breathe until the struggling slows. Harry stares in disbelief and reaches for the killer, but muscles starving for oxygen spasm. Then his heart stops beating, and his arms drop slowly to his sides. The killer thinks about closing those staring eyes, but decides against it, leaving Harry Jones with disbelief frozen on his face.

≈A Phone Call from Texas≈

Before dawn Monday morning River's telephone rings, startling her. "Hello," she mumbles.

"Hey, girl!" Evaline sounds her usual chipper self, even at this hour.

"Evaline, do you know what time it is? What's wrong? Something better be wrong."

"I'm sorry, girl, but I just had to call you. Somebody killed Adam's daddy the other night. The man is dead! I would've called you yesterday, but the police've been all over everybody who ever knew him."

River pushes the covers back, sits up in bed, and through the partially open drapes looks out on the dark Chicago sky, wondering if she is awake or dreaming. "W-h-a-a-t? What did you say, Ev? Harry is dead? When? Killed, you mean murdered?"

"That's just what I mean. Three nights ago. Somebody stabbed him and left him in his truck, dead, behind the Dew Drop Inn. They say he'd been in the truck all day. People thought he was sleeping off a drunk, and then finally went over to wake him up."

"This is too much to believe." River shakes her head, hoping to clear away sleep, trying to grasp what Evaline said. "Stabbed?

Stabbed? Who could have done that?" Then she grows quiet thinking of all the possible answers. "Have they arrested anyone? I can't believe this, Harry is dead! How's Mary, and Ruth Ann? Have you seen Adam?"

"Yes, Ruth Ann is staying with their mother, but she said her mother is taking it better than she thought she would."

"That's good to hear," River mumbles. She thinks of the perfectly arranged family pictures on the living room wall of the big house and hopes Mary won't grieve too long. She told River once that Harry is the only man she has ever known.

"Have they questioned anybody?"

"Well, yeah, everybody. I hear they even want to ask me some questions. I'm not even going to act like I'm sorry, except for Ruth Ann's sake. I mean, he *was* her father. But just between you and me, she doesn't seem all that torn up about it either. I haven't seen her cry one time. And no, I haven't seen Adam, and don't know how he's taking it. I hear the police have questioned him more than once. I'm not sure Adam, or any of them, are ready to welcome me to the family, so I'm keeping my distance." "Yes, that's probably best." River sounds to Evaline as if she is speaking from a distance. "This is just too much, too hard to believe."

"Yeah, but there's more. Adam called Ruth Ann over to Alpha's house about a week ago. Alpha was pregnant again and lost it, was pretty messed up about that. Ruth Ann said the police asked about Alpha. Maybe they think she or somebody in her family had something to do with it."

"Hold on a minute, Ev." River puts down the telephone and goes into the bathroom, splashes her face with cold water, and thinks how glad she is to be in Chicago. Anywhere, but Houston.

"Pregnant again. I guess some women just won't learn, no

matter how hard the lesson," she says to the empty bathroom.

"Hey, I'm back, Ev. Well, I hope it all turns out okay for everybody. Thanks for letting me know."

Evaline knew she wouldn't but asks anyway. "You want me to let you know about the funeral?"

River sits on the bed and thinks about the play, *A Soldier's Play*, one of the last plays she and Stefan saw before they ended their engagement. In the play, Peterson is a black soldier who murders Waters, another black soldier who is consumed by self-hate and mistreats the black soldiers in his command. In the play when Peterson admits to the murder, he says that he hadn't killed much, adding that some things need killing. "I wonder," she whispers.

River thinks she will send flowers to Mary. While River thinks of Mary, Mary sits in Houston rocking back and forth, seated in front of the family photographs that are again collecting dust. Adam sits on the good sofa in the room with his mother and looks up at the family photographs and thinks, *I look just like him.*

"No, that's okay, but thanks for letting me know, Ev, and take care of yourself."

"You too. Hey, how's your social life?"

"I'm fine, Ev. I've had a few dates, nice guys. I guess I'm just not ready to get serious. Oh, I don't think I told you, Stefan and Laurette had a baby girl a few months ago."

River thinks Ev doesn't sound so chipper when she says, "Good for them," before saying goodbye.

Reaching a remote control on the night stand, River presses a button and heavy drapes slide open wider, revealing the Chicago skyline with the Crowning Glory building shining brightly. She sits there considering going for an early walk along the Point.

Instead, she pulls back the comforter and climbs into the comfort of her bed. Looking out at the skyline, she is surprised when she recalls her first promotion at Tony's Bistro came before she chemically straightened her hair. It came when she was wearing her afro. She smiles slightly and pulls the comforter over her shoulders. Daylight is breaking.

≈Back to the Present≈

If you don't count the birth announcement Stefan and Laurette sent on the arrival of their baby girl, Sierra, River has not heard from him in almost two years, not since he called to tell her Laurette was pregnant. So, the message he left on her answering machine saying he will call back surprised her, even though she was happy to hear his voice.

The ringing telephone disturbs River's thoughts. She gets up from the floor and the remains of the cold gardenia candle, and pulls her cashmere robe tighter. Hurriedly, she steps over Anna J. Cooper's writings on the floor, clicks on a lamp in the dark room, and walks over to answer the telephone.

Acknowledgments

It is the love I have for my daughters, Michelle and Lynn, my granddaughter, Sierra, as well as my need to write and my desire to create something important, that kept me writing this story. Thank you, my darlings, for inspiring me.

Thanks to my niece, Ollie Davis, my first beta reader. I realize it was a sacrifice as you had recently completed your doctorate and was teaching while reading. Many thanks to my amazing "Book Lovers" book club members for your encouragement: Betty Brown, Earlene Riser, Gaye Cummins, Gayle McAdoo, Ginger Nisbet, Jo Ann Williams, Leslye Mize, Mary Alice Trumble, Pam Barton, Patricia LaChance, Suzanne Milby, Vaness Hamilton, and Verva Densmore. The feedback from you wonderful women is responsible for many improved rewrites! Jane Ebone and Jennifer Callaway are two of the best beta readers ever!

David C. Hall, you read my manuscript when my protagonist was named Martha. Unsolicited, you sent me a letter asking me to keep my "…important story alive." Considering your long career as a child and family psychiatrist, your letter meant the world to me and my story.

You have inspired me without ever knowing it.

Thanks, Mark Meyer, for your kind words of encouragement and whose editing made this book better than it would have been.

Finally, thanks to my parents, for raising me to know my true worth, and to my siblings and family for challenging me to be my best.

About The Author

Taylor Thompson grew up in the suburbs of Houston, Texas. She is the mother of two daughters and has one granddaughter. She says they are her "guiding lights." Taylor's degrees are in Psychology and Medical Technology. While this is her first novel, she has published a book for children and a book of poetry. Taylor lives in Houston with her two dogs.

www.taylorthompson.us

Made in the
USA
Monee, IL